VIRTUE

THE BRIARCLIFF SOCIETY SERIES

KETLEY ALLISON

BRIARCLIFF ACADEMY STUDENT PLAYLIST

Hell to the Liars - London Grammar
The World We Made - Ruelle
The Almond Tree - Hannah Peel
Be Kind (with Halsey) - Marshmello, Halsey
death bed (coffee for your head) - Powfu, beabadoobee
Hide and Seek - Imogen Heap
Born Alone Die Alone - Madalen Duke
Say Your Prayers - Blithe
Hold On We're Going Home - ASTR
Breathe Into Me - Marian Hill

Find the rest of the playlist on Spotify:

http://bit.ly/briarcliffsociety

*T*he afternoon sun shimmers against the landscaped grass behind the academy and a cool, autumnal wind pulls at the loose strands of my kinky brown waves I'd attempted to tame into a ponytail this morning. The maroon ribbon I'd tied around it flaps against the side of my cheek before getting caught in my lip gloss, which I'm pretty sure is a sign I shouldn't be here.

Heck, if the wind so much as shifts, I'm taking that as solid proof that this is a terrible idea, and I'm turning right around and—

"Callie. Hey, you came."

Ivy separates herself from the crowd of students milling in the center of the quad where an elaborate stone fountain spurts water out of a rearing wolf's mouth, the rest of his pack keening beneath the curve of his majestic form.

"I didn't think it'd be right if I avoided it," I say to Ivy once she reaches me. Her pale blue eyes cloud with concern, but she hooks my elbow and drags me into the fray.

"Probably not," she agrees, and to my horror, ushers us to the front.

"Ivy, I'm not sure I—"

"Nonsense. If you're going to be here, you might as well put face-time in."

"Actually, I was hoping for the opposite."

"Why?" She spins to face me, her baby blues turning cold. "You didn't *do* anything. Not to Piper, not to anyone. Why shouldn't you be present for her birthday memorial?"

It's been twelve days since Dr. Luke was put in handcuffs, and the professors agreed that enough time has passed to lessen the trauma of violently losing a student and watching a beloved teacher be arrested for it. They decided the best way to honor Piper's life is to do it on her birthday. Because hers falls on a Saturday this year, the headmaster thought it would be better to hold the service on the Friday before, since on weekends, pupils are less likely to show up.

Oh, and did I not mention that today happens to be *my* birthday?

"Now that Piper's killer has been caught," Ivy continues, "any suspicion over your involvement should be long gone, don't you think? I mean, *you* didn't push her off Lover's Leap. Dr. Luke did."

Ivy's opinion seems to ricochet off the surrounding stone and into each nearby student's ears, and my cheeks burn as heads swivel to the source, then bounce over to the cause.

"Yep. Bad idea," I say as pinpricks of hate-glares pierce my body.

"Ridiculous," Ivy says, then spins us to face the front. "There. Now you don't have to look at them."

"Uh-huh. But now they all can look at me. With my back turned."

"Jeez." Ivy throws an arm over my shoulder and squeezes. "We need to give you some better memories here. After this shindig is over, let's head to my room and celebrate your birthday the classy way: with cake and cherry wine."

Last weekend, Ivy went home to visit her parents in Philadelphia, managing to smuggle her favorite Danish cherry wine in her luggage when her mom was busy baking her *hindbærsnitte,* the most delicious raspberry pastry squares Ivy also had the foresight to bring back with her and shove into my mouth.

Ivy means well, but I doubt the promise of sugar and alcohol will be enough to sweeten the taint left on me when Piper plunged off the nearby cliff just off school property. I was her roommate. I could've stopped it, or at the very least, seen it coming.

Murmurs sweep over the crowd, distracting me from my thoughts. I listen to the shoes scraping against the stone ground until a path forms through the middle of the gathering.

Ivy possesses the gift of being tall, and she sees whatever is making the students part like the Dead Sea before I do.

Her eyes widen, and her lips thin. "Incoming."

I don't look, because I know who I'll see. I'm happy to keep my gaze straight ahead, at the wolf barf fountain, as Chase and his friends saunter down the makeshift aisle.

That is, until I hear one word, whispered by a student behind me, that whips my head around.

Pregnant.

I force myself to look forward again. If caught, my devastation would only fuel Chase's crew. I can't react. I can never let them see.

Not if I want to discover the lies behind their motives and the secrets they've traded in return for their soul.

2

My stomach clenches as I feel heat start at the back of my neck and prickle down my arm. I glance to the side, catching the source, and I meet the soulless amber depths of Chase Stone's eyes.

We connect for a meager second, but to me, it's ages of time that tether us across the quad, an unblinking connection that shoots ice through my veins yet heats my blood to unbearable levels.

The last time I saw him, those eyes were lit with two candle flames burning their golden incredulity through the bronze. In that moment, he answered the question I posed, the truth that would define us with a simple, "Yes."

Chase's gaze flicks away the moment I flinch at the memory. His attention doesn't return.

His friends stalk behind him—Tempest, James, and Riordan. Piper's former best friends glide around them in beautiful, despondent repose—Falyn, Willow, and Violet. Piper's younger sister and doppelgänger, Addisyn, holds Falyn's hand as they keep close to the guys but force their chins up and eyes forward, while Chase and his buddies glare at the students daring to mumble their opinions nearby.

...pregnant...

Piper's...

...do you think...

Chase's...

Or Dr. Luke's?

Bile forms a waxy ball in my throat, and I swallow the lump as they make their way down a pathway sliced open by simpering student bodies and to the front. Voices ripple into choked whispers as they pass. To my relief, the elite crew takes position on the opposite side where Ivy and I stand. Students who waited early for a front row view scramble back to accommodate their chosen spot.

I'm suddenly desperate to meet Chase's eyes again, maybe find some sort of clue amid the cold bronze and pull out a reality different from what he told me the night I crawled into his arms, shivering from the night's air seeping through my dorm's windows.

"Mm." Chase stirs as I lift his upper arm while crawling back into bed, finding a warm nook under his chin to nestle under. "Who was that?"

I stare at my phone I'd placed on my nightstand, not yet locked and asleep. "Ahmar."

"Oh yeah?" Chase rolls to his back on a grunt, taking me with him until I'm sprawled across the carved muscles of his torso. "What'd he want so fucking late?"

"To tell me something."

Chase idly strokes the top of my head, the movement doing more to lull him into slumber than me. "What did he say?"

My lips part on the answer, but my throbbing heartbeat gets there first. Chase feels my racing pulse against his chest, because he stiffens and says, with careful resonance, "Callie, what's wrong?"

"Piper. She was pregnant. Before she..."

Chase's body, granite-smooth and impenetrable on a good day, turns cold beneath my touch.

I lick my lips, my fingers curling against his stomach. "Is it ... I mean, could it be...?"

"Mine?"

"Quiet, please!"

Headmaster Marron's booming voice, amplified by the surrounding structure of the academy, rips me from the reminiscence. He assumes his position behind the wooden podium centered by the fountain, brought outside for this specific occasion.

His silver eyes scan the crowd as smoothly as his combed back, graying hair.

"We're gathered here today for an important remembrance," he begins, "and what was a tragic ending to one of our brightest, most beloved students, Piper Harrington."

A few students snort their disagreement nearby, but I remain carefully mute.

"Many of you voiced your concern over a professor being responsible for such a heinous act, but while the investigation into Dr. Luke continues, I am here to assure you, and any parents or guardians who contact me, that you are safe on this campus. You are cared for, and your opinion is respected by every faculty member here."

Okay. Now I snort.

Marron cuts a look in my direction, and I cover up my derision with a cough. Ivy smirks beside me.

"We will do everything in our power to ensure your continued trust, including our full cooperation with the police while they valiantly pursue the closing of this matter." Marron clears his throat. "Now, onto the true reason we've assembled on these hallowed grounds. Miss Harrington, please."

Marron gestures to the front where Addisyn stands. She releases Falyn's hand and pulls out her prepared speech from the inside pocket of her blazer as she takes Marron's spot behind the podium.

With a trembling voice, she begins. "Piper was my older sister, my confidant, my best friend, my whole being." She rubs her palm down her nose in an attempt to collect herself, her fingers shaking with the effort. "We grew up as sisters, but we were more like twins. We did everything together, including ... including dreaming about going to the same college. Raising our future children together. Buying a house on the same, the same s-street..."

She breaks down. My heart pulls as I watch, feeling more like an unwelcome spectator to a violent car accident, one who doesn't have the right to be privy to such devastation.

I didn't have a strong connection to Piper, and while a good portion of the school moved on from her death, and the re-shuffling of social stature occurred with the ease of mixing a Vegas card deck, there *were* people affected. Piper's sister is now an only child. Her friends have lost their ride-or-die. Her parents have lost their oldest daughter.

None of it sits right with me. This gathering, Marron's thinly veiled speech to protect the school from liability during what should be a memorial, the fact that it's my eighteenth birthday ... and I'm turning an age that Piper never will.

And whether or not Piper wanted to be a mother, she'll never get to make that choice for herself.

"I need to leave," I murmur to Ivy.

She jolts at the way I grip her arm, much stronger than my voice. "Seriously? We're at the front. We'll make a scene."

"I—I have to," I say. My stomach isn't making any promises to settle. "I can't be here."

Ivy curses under her breath, but scans for a subtle exit-point.

I don't waste time and instead grab her hand and drag her into the space between the podium and the first row of students, bending low so we don't obscure anyone's view of Addisyn's sobs.

Ivy stumbles behind me but matches my speed, until a pair of non-school issued, knee-high boots block my escape.

"Leaving so soon, possum?"

I lift my gaze to Falyn's, her sterling eyes shimmering with well-placed tears.

She waits for my stare to land on hers. "By all means, stay. We haven't even gotten to the part where Addy mentions your home-wrecking, skanky ass."

Blood curdles within the broken chambers of my heart.

Ivy pulls on my sleeve. "Don't engage."

I ignore my friend, because it feels so much better to direct my unrest *somewhere*. "Careful, Falyn, your frown lines are showing."

Falyn's bleached blonde eyebrows pull together at my statement. The fact that she's already on a Botox regime is such easy fodder to use, and I'm a little disappointed in myself for not coming up with something better.

I add, "You're right about one thing. I'm not welcome here. So, let me leave."

Marron and the nearby professors lining the front of the makeshift stage eye our scuffle, but don't interrupt Addisyn. Not yet, considering our voices are low, and all they see is Falyn's stricken expression, like we're commiserating on Piper's loss, not testing the strength of our claws.

"No fucking way," Falyn says. "I want you to witness the hell you've caused. Piper's dead because of you."

I stifle the resigned sound wanting to escape from my throat. "And how's that?"

"Let her go."

The deep, leveled words, as dark as the soil beneath stone,

causes both our bodies to stiffen. Falyn tenses at the order, and I at the low purr in his tone, a permanent silk that always accompanies his voice.

Chase's gaze is molten against mine, burning into my core with such fierce heat, I can't look away in time.

"Go, Callie," he says.

We haven't spoken in weeks, and he's echoed the very last words I said to him the night he didn't deny that Piper's baby could be his.

My throat's too thick to voice sound, so I give a curt nod, aiming to skirt around Falyn, Ivy frantically pushing against my back. We're drawing too much attention.

Falyn's hand snaps out and wraps around my bicep when I try to pass. She hisses in my ear, "*Listen.*"

"... and while I can't bear to be without my sister, I'll fight for her," Addisyn continues into the microphone. "And bring some justice to her short life. Dr. Luke remains behind bars, but there are others out there who contributed to Piper's misery. A girl who made my sister so heartbroken, she ran into the arms of an older man for solace. A teacher."

Marron stands. "All right, Miss Harrington."

"*You*, Callie Ryan."

"That's enough," Marron says, striding to Addisyn's side and searching for the off switch on the mic.

"If it weren't for you, my sister would be here!" Addisyn screeches, pointing a trembling finger. Murmurs transform into loud voices as they follow Addisyn's direction to witness the center of the spectacle. Me.

I open my mouth. "That's not—"

"Not here," Ivy says, her hands clamping round my shoulders. "Let's go. Before this—"

"Chase was her soulmate!" Addisyn screams. "And you *took* him from her!"

I give in to Ivy's desperate shoves, but I can't tear my gaze away from the girl falling apart on stage. Yet, instead of watching her crumble, all eyes are waiting for me to break.

"Not her fault!" a male voice booms through the crowd.

A sense of relief washes over me at the thought that Chase would stand up for me—but it's not him. It's James, Chase's buddy with the shaggy, reddish-blond hair and hazel eyes sparkling with mirth, but not the happy kind. He gets off at making jokes out of people without giving a shit on where or how he does it, and he's zeroed in on his next target.

James's lips pull wide. "How could Chase resist those tits and that ass?"

I stop listening. The lewd words coming out of such a pretty face should be shocking, but here at the academy, it's not. There's no point in arguing that Chase and I were never together when Piper was alive, if I can even call us a pairing. There's especially no justice in pointing out that despite my "stealing," Chase still managed to possibly get Piper pregnant.

These people have their edicts and the prices they pay to stay at the top of the social chain. Chewing on the fragile bones of us lower mortals is part of their game.

Shoulders slumped more from the emotional weight of this school than Ivy's grip, I walk with her to the edge of the lawn, but not before glancing back, one more time, at James's gleeful maw, still spouting words like "tap that," and "dick her down," with Chase's glacial demeanor beside him.

My steps slow as I study Chase's walled-off features, too rigid and controlled to ever be confused with apathy. His eyes smolder through his visage as he stares straight ahead, a warning sign I notice too late.

Tempest has enough time to shoot his arm out before Chase launches and punches James in the face, toppling all three of them to the ground. Chase lands on James and doesn't stop pummeling his best friend.

"FIGHT!" someone bellows before a mass of prep-school-uniformed bodies jump into the brawl, arms and fists flying.

"*Students!*" Marron roars, and a few other professors join him in attempting to break up the fight. Addisyn hops back and nearly butt-plants into the fountain.

"Holy," Ivy breathes while scuttling me through the new gaps in the crowd. "You'd think it'd be blasphemous to do this at someone's memorial, but you know what? I think Piper's enjoying this, wherever she is."

"No kidding," I respond, my chest tight. "Her ghost must've possessed at least one of them. My bet's on James."

"Please, she had all three of them in her clutches well before her murder."

I squint in Ivy's direction but work to drown any other conflicting emotions threatening to surface. I'm not upset she's so cavalier about Piper's death—Piper wasn't exactly loved by anyone except her followers. I am, however, concerned over Ivy's tidbit that Piper had more influence over the boys than I gave her credit for.

Don't hope that the baby could've been one of theirs, not Chase's.

Ivy has no idea I've slept with Chase, and I'm not eager to confess.

We duck through the outdoor archway connecting the East and West wings, then burst through the doors of the academy, the natural hush of the heavy architecture descending upon us once the doors fold shut.

I take Ivy's hand and we cut through the foyer and to the front. I'm eager to finish this shitty day with some raspberry bars, Netflix, sweet wine, and a good friend.

Yet, Piper's ghost has broken off from the fight, trailing behind me in the cavernous Briarcliff halls, and she's relentless in her wails: *There's so much about this school you can't forget, not even for one night. Don't ignore me, Callie! Don't dismiss my death!*

Ugh. Happy birthday to me.

And happy birthday to you, too, Piper.

_____

3

*T*horne House is a modern addition to the otherwise Gothic ski lodge feel of Briarcliff Academy's 170-year-old structures. Automatic sliding doors allow us immediate entry, and the college student manning the front desk lets us through after a careful study of my student ID card. Ivy, she knows on sight.

You'd think I'd have an "in" with knowing one of the front desk staff of the dorms, allowing me ingress and egress well past curfew, but honestly, none of them cared enough to stop any of us.

Not until Piper died.

We take the elevator to the third floor, chatting softly as we hit the carpeted hallway and head to my room.

I swipe my keycard against the hotel-style lock, and when it flashes green, push in. Ivy's so involved in her discussion of how soothing British baking shows on Netflix are that she fails to notice my abrupt stall in the doorway, and *oomphs* into my back.

It's not enough to throw me off balance, but it does the job of jarring the reality of what I'm seeing into my brain.

My mouth falls open. "What the...?"

"Huh?" is all Ivy can come up with. "Is this your stuff?"

"Uh..." I scan the main room as my brows draw in. "No."

A gray leather sectional, so new, the scent of leather cleaner permeates the air, plops its fancy, tightly sewn ass where my pink suede secondhand piece I found on Main Street used to be. At least 45 inches of flat screen TV is bolted to a wall where I'd just installed floating shelves to hold photos of my remaining family, and a monstrosity of an espresso machine gurgles its presence beside us through its sleek nickel finishing, a spot I'd reserved for my Black & Decker drip.

Okay. Maybe I'm not mad at the last one.

But, seriously?

"I think you have a new roommate," Ivy states behind me.

I attempt an eye-roll over my shoulder. "You think?"

My sarcasm is fast overshadowed by a petrified thought when the door to Piper's old room swings open.

Oh God, don't let it be another Piper...

A figure steps through the doorframe. "Hey."

Ivy gasps so audibly that I turn to her with a frown.

"S-sorry," she says while a hand flutters against her mouth. "It's just ... I didn't think..."

The girl smiles with a wry tilt to her thin lips and finishes for Ivy, "...that the ghost of Emma Loughrey would come back to Briarcliff to claim all your souls for the Reaper?"

Well. That's enough of an introduction to leave my jaw hanging. "Holy shit, Emma?"

Deep lines form in Emma's cheeks. "Heard of me, have you?" Her steely bronze gaze, so like Chase's it's unsettling, lands on Ivy. "I see the town crier still has her horn."

I bristle at the connotation. "Ivy's been nothing but awesome, so if you don't have anything nice to say about her, then—"

Emma rolls her eyes. "Let me guess, don't say anything at all? Nice one, whatever-your-name-is."

She turns to her room and shuts the door with a firm click.

"It's Callie!" I call through the thick, mahogany wood. "And thanks for doing what I was *going* to say, which was to fuck off!"

"I don't think that's coming across as intimidating as you hoped it would," Ivy mutters into my ear. "Your voice is kind of high and wobbly—"

Clasping Ivy's hand, I lead us into my bedroom and shut the door. I splay my back against it, while Ivy whirls in the center of my room, her arms spread wide. "Holy moly, do you know who that is?"

I nod, suddenly antsy that some of my first words to Chase's twin sister were *fuck* and *off*.

Not exactly trying to fit into the family's good graces, are we, Callie?

"She wasn't exactly too friendly with her greeting, either," I say in a lame attempt to defend myself.

Ivy isn't listening. She continues a slow pirouette, her voice wandering and stupefied. "I haven't seen her in ... gosh, it has to be over two years. She's changed. Like, *really* changed. I barely recognized her, and oh my God, do you know what *happened* to her before she left?"

After a thick swallow, I nod. In a brief moment of weakness, Chase divulged a little about his sister's assault and the resulting fire while we lay in bed together, our hands intertwined.

A skitter of goosebumps pass over my flesh, at both the tragedy surrounding Emma and the remembrance of Chase's warm, naked body enveloping mine.

"Really?" Ivy asks, her high-pitched question refocusing my thoughts. "How'd you find out?"

"Oh, uh, during my research on the founders in the new library, I think I asked someone why it was called the 'new' library. They told me how the old one burned down and that Emma was trapped inside."

And she's the one who burned it down, but I don't mention that part.

"Yeah." Ivy nods sagely. "I didn't think people still talked about it. Chase put down a terrifying gag order on anyone who dared to mention his sister. Who'd you ask?"

"Can't recall," I say, then clear my throat and move from the door to perch on my bed. "But I was warned she was ... different."

"I knew about the burns," Ivy breathes as she sits next to me. "But I had *no* idea she'd, um, she'd..."

"Gained weight?"

"Yes! She used to be..."

"She's still beautiful," I whisper, recalling those bronze, goddess-colored eyes and streaming natural highlights of elbow-length, blonde hair.

It was greasier than Ivy probably remembered, matted and tangled. Emma's cheeks were dimpled and flushed with natural pink, but they were swollen, her jowls heavy with what I recognized not as weight gain, but a demanding, inner hunger yawning wide, constantly starving because it kept being fed the wrong emotions: anger, hate, resentment.

Only one form of sustenance could stop the clamoring and quell that gnawing ache forever. *Revenge.*

"She also came back mean," Ivy says. "But I can understand the why of it."

And there it is. I take a long study of Ivy, imputing her current expression onto every other student's face who Emma is about to cross paths with. It's an expression of pity. Relief it wasn't them. And while Ivy wasn't wearing it, I knew shock and revulsion would soon follow.

Emma chose to wear defensive armor to protect herself, but I wondered, with the wolves in this arena now led by Falyn Clemonte, how impervious Emma's sarcastic, angry armor will actually be.

More importantly...

"Does Chase know?" I ask.

Ivy shrugs. "You would think so, but, hell, I don't think

anybody knew Emma would finish her senior year here. I mean, what kind of therapist would send her back to Briarcliff?" Ivy leans closer, as if divulging a scandalous secret. "She wasn't just trapped in the old library, Callie. She was attacked there, first. Brutally beaten. I think both her eye sockets were fractured, and her back was broken—"

I hold up a hand, the imagery making me sick. "Let's not judge her new self immediately, okay? This is clearly going to be tough for her, and she's my new roommate. I'd like to maybe not become enemies with this one."

"Okay, sure, Miss *Fuck Off*."

"Yeah," I mumble, sliding my laptop onto my lap. "I'm gonna have to work on that."

Ivy and I finally settle on Netflix's new rom-com and *not* a baking show (Birthday Girl wins), but leaning back against the head-board and sharing a bottle of wine does nothing to calm my racing heart, nor does the sound on my computer obscure the noises coming from the other side of my door.

Emma must have started her move-in process when the entire school congregated in Briarcliff's quad. It makes sense; the campus was practically deserted. There was no one to notice the rental truck's tires bouncing across the academy's cobblestone driveway and to the western edge of the property's surrounding forest, where the Thorne and Rose Houses lie. It certainly escaped Ivy's and my notice when we wandered over here using the student paths.

The speed in which her furniture made it inside is also unsur-prising. The rich live as such, with white-gloved positioning, quiet alterations, and seamless decoration. With the gaps of quiet between wood dragging against floors and low-voiced instruction getting longer, I assume Emma is about done with her transition.

One question remains: Where the hell did my stuff go?

Visions of my furniture leaning against the dorm's dumpster causes a shudder, and I shift on my bedding to escape it.

"Meh. That was okay," Ivy says.

Credits roll on the movie I daydreamed through, and I move to close the laptop.

"That part where the monkeys came and devoured everyone's faces was cool, though," Ivy continues.

"Mm." I slide off the bed and place my computer on my desk.

"Dude!" Ivy shouts.

I jump, nearly toppling onto my desk chair. As I right myself, she adds, "You didn't watch a darned thing on the screen, did you?"

"Not really," I admit.

"I get it. You have a lot going on. I mean—more than your usual pile of a lot going on." After a light grunt, Ivy rises from my bed. "Do you want me to stay? I'm not sure how this will go with you and Emma." Ivy grins. "I kind of want to spectate."

"Nope." I give her a firm shove to my door. "I doubt she'll leave her room, anyway."

Ivy says over her shoulder, "She has to go to the bathroom sometime."

"Then I'll be in *my* room. Thanks for the support, but I'll be fine."

"If you say so. But text me for anything, okay? If you need an escape route, I'm pretty sure I can be the Ivy to your ivy."

I raise a curious brow.

"You know, out your window." Ivy gestures behind me. "It's unclear if all that clinging ivy will hold your weight, but I can wait down below to catch you during your grand escape if need be."

I can't help but smile at the image she's conjured. For sure my ass under this skirt would be on full display.

"There we go." Ivy nudges my side. "I was hoping to get a smile from you on your birthday."

My chest warms at her words, but before I can reciprocate, she gets there first and envelopes me in a long hug.

"Love you," she says. "Now you can vote and own a firearm. Happy friggin' eighteenth, my friend."

I laugh into her perfumed shoulder, notes of wildflowers playing against my nostrils. "You're the best."

"Later," she says once she releases me, and when she opens my door, carefully peers around it. "Coast is clear. I'm out."

Shaking my head on a laugh, I pull the door wider as Ivy beelines to the front door, making a U-turn only once when she notices a line of Emma's shoes she's yet to put away. Ivy flutters a longing hand through the air above the Louboutins, Jimmy Choos, and Manolo Blahniks before she shuts the apartment door behind her.

I'm also distracted by the gorgeous array of prestigious color and design, blown away that Emma's brought such expensive footwear to school. One: where will she wear it, and two: what about her self-imposed hermit status?

So what? I chastise myself. *One can be a hermit while donning fabulous heels.*

A shuffling in my periphery draws my eye up. Emma hovers in her doorway, staring at me as warily as I was studying her shoes.

In the fading golden hour of the setting sun through the bay windows, Emma's features are softened, but only skin-deep. One eyelid stretches slightly more crooked than the other. Her hair, as wavy and tousled as a beached mermaid's, is cut short around her face to obscure the pink-tinged scar trailing across her forehead. She's chosen an oversized hoodie to hide her upper body, with a faded Briarcliff crest and two oars crossed behind it, *Briarcliff Crew* written underneath.

I'm so busy wondering if that's Chase's sweatshirt that I

almost miss the crooked, re-healed knobs of her fingers pulling at the hem to cover herself better.

My heart swells with the need to explain my staring, but experience has taught me it's no use when a person already sees herself as a target.

Instead, I'm the first of us to experiment with a quiet, "Hey."

She nods, her lips pursed, then scuttles to pick up her shoes lining the wall of our small entryway.

It's a new side of Emma I'm seeing now that Ivy's gone, and I don't think Emma's hesitant, uneven gait is solely due to her injuries.

"I'm not like the rest of them," I try saying. When her metallic stare pings against mine again, so steady compared to the way she moves, I have to force my breaths even. "I mean—I won't bother you. If you don't want me to. You're here for senior year, right? We can always study together, or—"

"Are you as vacant as you look?" Emma spits. My heels knock backward against the floorboards at her vitriol. "If so, let me sum up my newly fucked-up status for you. I've missed two years of classes due to nearly having my skull turned to mush by assholes who probably still attend this school. I'm starting twelfth grade late while finishing up the last of my tenth and eleventh grade papers, because my dad paid the crooked headmaster double a normal student's tuition to allow me back in, and also had the gracious thought to put me in my *murdered* friend's old bedroom, along with the empty-headed roommate that comes with it. Or, maybe you're not such a dumbass. You were a suspect in Piper's death for a hot second, weren't you?"

So was your brother, I want to retort, but bite my tongue.

Emma sneers. "Don't do that. Don't stop yourself from saying what you really think because you're *sad* for me, like the very thought of what I look like—"

I storm forward.

"If you're trying to satisfy your hatred for this school by being cruel to me," I say, "Consider your aim a misfire."

After a beat of hesitation, she lifts a scarred brow. "Putting you down does nothing to lessen how much I despise Briarcliff. Maybe I'm just doing it because I want to."

Ugh. She is *so* like her brother. "I'm not exactly a fan of this place, either, but here we are. Attending anyway, for our own reasons."

"And why would a girl like you hate a school like this?" She laughs dully. "This is the fast-track to the best colleges in the world. The cafeteria menu is designed by a Michelin starred chef. You're practically guaranteed an engagement to the son of some corporate empire if you play your connections right. Or daughter, if that's where your preference lies." She hums in thought. "I don't recognize you from before, and you're not staying on Scholarship Row so ... who did you sleep with to get a spot here? Someone's dad? Headmaster Marron?"

I ignore her goading. "Perhaps I've witnessed the price a soul has to pay for that kind of unlimited access."

Emma narrows her eyes, hopefully stumped by my honesty.

"Can we agree to co-exist?" I ask on a sigh. "Because I have to tell you, living with a person who despises you is exhausting."

A whisper of a smile flirts at one corner of her mouth, but she squelches it with a glower. "I'll get back to you on that." Arms laden with shoes, she turns back to her room, but tosses over her shoulder, "Don't fucking touch my coffee."

Emma heels her door shut.

I let out a singular laugh, shaking my head as I run my hand through my hair.

If there was ever a thought that Emma and I would be bonding over our mutual misfit status at Briarcliff Academy, *holy hell*, was I so utterly misguided.

4

'm outside.

I rise up on one elbow, squinting at my phone, my tongue thick and fuzzy from breathing through my mouth while I slept. Three dancing dots appear as I'm trying to decipher the meaning behind the text, and the messenger.

Meet me.

At last, my vision clears of sleep, and I sit up, sliding my heavy nest of hair to one shoulder.

"Chase?" I whisper to myself.

He hasn't said a word, sent a text, or exhaled in my direction since our last conversation involving Piper's secret pregnancy. To believe what I'm reading would mean Chase is standing outside the dorms, waiting for me to come out and see him.

This afternoon's events flash into my mind, its dreamlike quality becoming clearer the harder I blink. Chase punched James's lights out because he was saying vile things … about me.

Chase, the boy who prefers to ignore me when he's not horny, chose to beat up his friend for daring to insult me.

I stare up in thought. Does that deserve a secret, nightly meet-up?

Me: Go away. I was sleeping.

Blacking out my phone's screen, I move to toss it on my nightstand and nestle into my bedcovers, still warm from when I was snoozing comfortably.

It buzzes while leaving my palm, and on a huff of annoyed, yet curious, breath, I glance at the text's preview.

Chase: If you don't come down, I'm coming up.

Fack. Chase doesn't bluff. And knowing him, he'd probably be noisy as all hell, waking up his sister and—

Oh, God. His *sister* lives with me now. Does he know that?

Besides that, what time is it? My phone says four in the morning, and I groan. I was hoping to use this Saturday to sleep in and get used to my new dorm environment, or failing that, going into town and studying at the public library, far away from the other students here. Why does Chase have to ruin the tentative peace I've established while trying to finish out this semester?

Chase: 5…

Chase: 4...

Damn it. I slide out of bed, fumbling for a hoodie to throw over my sleep tank and shorts, then slip into my white sneakers.

Chase: 3...

The bastard is probably already through the sliding doors. I have zero faith in the "heightened" security of this place, especially considering the last month when my nocturnal, cloaked visitor left me rose petals. I *swear* the Cloak is real, even if no one believes me. Even if Chase has made me question whether my convictions are fact or remnants of my previous hysterical break-down...

Chase: TWO

I text two words on a growl, my thumbs slamming against my screen. **COMING ASSHOLE.**

Slipping the hood over my head and tucking my phone into the front pocket, I tip-toe out of the apartment, noting the dim, golden light shining out from under Emma's door with vague curiosity.

My dorm room neighbors the stairwell, and I choose to pad down the steps rather than risk the *ding* of the elevator. Once on the ground floor, I take the second exit out the side of the building so as not to enter the lobby and possibly be spotted by night security.

They were brought in for extra safety, but would I trust their

nightly flashlight sweeps with my life? Absolutely not. I have
more faith in the kitten a girl on my floor smuggled in under
their noses.

I round the corner of the red, brick building, the grass tips
wet and speared with a cold dew that brushes against my ankles
like tiny skeletal fingers. Once the coast is clear, and I swing
around the blind corner, I see Chase leaning against a luxurious,
midnight blue BMW, headlights on and engine growling low. It's
not the type of BMW I associate with middle-aged businessmen
like my stepdad. This is sleeker, lower to the ground, with a lot of
black detailing and strange, red, under-wheel lights illuminating
the tires.

No security guard comes out to scold him. He probably paid
them triple their hourly salary to keep quiet.

"Like what you see?" Chase purrs as I walk toward him.

His voice tightens my chest with tangled nerves, and I hope I
cover up the falter in my steps before he notices.

I've always seen Chase in school uniform or athletic gear,
never in a T-shirt and jeans. Yet, here he stands, in all his mouth-
watering glory, his strong, muscular legs hidden in dark denim
that hugs his butt as he leans casually against his car. Chase's
shirt is tight against his pecs and tailored to his wide shoulders
and narrow hips. The muscles of his crossed forearms ripple with
devious intent as I step closer.

"What are you doing here?" I ask, then point at Thorne
House. "Oh yeah, and your *sister* is living with me."

He pops off the passenger side, opening the door before he
steps back. "I know. Get in."

"You can explain yourself right here, Chase Stone."

Chase rounds the front of the car. He reaches the driver's side
and says to me over the hood, "There's coffee in your cupholder."

No five words have ever sounded so sexy.

Chase pounces on my hesitation. "Lots of cream, no sugar.
How you like it."

I shuffle my feet, digging my clenched fists into my hoodie's pocket. "Is it from the bakery in town?"

Chase's mouth lifts. "Marta has a soft spot for me."

I bet she does. Not a lot of women would open their doors at three in the morning, unless it holds the promise of Chase Stone on the other end.

But she makes *really* good coffee.

And it would be the freshest pot of them all—the first of the day while the morning employees prepped dough before opening their doors.

"And monkey bread," Chase adds. "First batch."

"Damn it," I mutter, and slide in at the same time he does.

The car's dashboard emits a subtle, blue hue against our silhouettes. Chase's profile takes on a devilish tone, shadows layering with the flowing indigo lights of the interior.

This, right here, is physical proof that demons prefer blue over red.

I study his sharp jawline with unintentional awe before I snap my mouth shut and stare straight ahead.

He's not your personal playground anymore. You're not allowed to keep picturing him naked.

The tug in my belly, tied in his direction, tells me otherwise.

Chase's long fingers grip the wheel as he steers us out of Thorne House and onto Briarcliff's private road.

My gaze flicks back to him, not just for appreciation. I'm searching for signs of the fight, bruises or cuts or fractures. "Are you hurt?"

His lips tilt. "For someone who refused to come talk to me, you sure have a lot of questions."

I busy myself with his promised cup of coffee, lifting it and sipping at the perfection. The scent of cinnamon and caramel tickles my nostrils, and like a hound sensing a fox, my head whips to the backseat.

Chase chuckles. "Had I known all it would take to lure you

into my ride was some sugar and caffeine, I would've left a trail of it into the forest long ago."

The relaxed, semi-threat drives my attention away from the white bag spotted with melted butter and to the front. "So, instead of leading me into the woods, you're what, taking me prisoner in your cursed castle?"

"Save the food for when we arrive," is all he says.

"Fine." I settle into my seat, cupping the coffee close. "But I'm not going to leave the question of why you woke me up until we reach our mysterious destination."

"I never thought you would."

The car's wheels turn gracefully under Chase's hands when we exit Briarcliff Academy's gates and merge onto the deserted main road, rimmed with tall, untended trees. For a moment, departing the manmade, landscaped, and carefully chosen flora and fauna of the academy and driving into the natural wildness of the protected forest is jarring, but I stifle the feeling, preferring not to ponder why I'm more comfortable within the school's gates than out.

Especially considering the chauffeur I've chosen.

"Why am I here?" I ask him.

"I thought that'd be obvious. Because I want to talk to you."

Sighing, I rephrase the question to something more specific, since I really should know by now Chase doesn't deal in generalities. "Why didn't you tell me your sister was coming back to school?"

A muscle tenses in Chase's cheek. "You and me, we haven't spoken much."

"A few weeks," I agree. After a beat of silence, I risk adding, "If you want the truth, I knew bringing up Piper's pregnancy would drive a wedge between us, but I never thought you'd—"

"Emma isn't here with my approval," Chase says. We make another turn into the darkness. The speed of his driving sets my teeth on edge. There aren't any streetlights to help us along. I'm relying solely on Chase's fancy headlights to keep me from becoming a crushed soda can against an errant tree.

"I told her it wasn't a good idea," he continues. "But Emma isn't known for listening."

Sounds familiar, I add silently.

"She has this ... strange vendetta," Chase says. "I'm happy she wants to get out of our dad's house, but I was hoping she'd transfer to Dover Shores or hell, some school in California. Anywhere but here."

I nod in full agreement. Briarcliff isn't known to spit out well-heeled, sweet individuals. "So, she refused to listen to you, but what about her therapist? Or doctors?"

"They all had the same opinion as me. It was our father who poisoned Emma against us. He encouraged her reentry into this school. Said it might be healing for her to face her demons."

"But she..." I shake my head while my thoughts realign. "When she moved in, she said that the people responsible for her assault might still be here. She thinks her *attacker* is at this school, be it a teacher or a student or..."

"I know." The whites of Chase's knuckles poke through his grip, notable even in the low lighting. "My dad thinks it's her paranoia talking."

For the barest of seconds, his eyes flick to me.

I tense, but don't add kindling to that fire, since I'm supposedly reformed and no longer victim to the delusion that my stepdad is responsible for my mother's death.

"She could be right," I say softly.

Chase cedes my point by dipping his chin, but says, "Dad's convinced it was a rogue event. A townie breaking into Briarcliff grounds. Marron thinks so, too. And the Briarcliff police force."

"And you?"

"I..." Chase works his jaw but doesn't tear his eyes from the road. Probably because he's afraid of the questions reflecting in my eyes, the ones threatening to unleash the instant he gives me an opening.

"It wasn't your Cloaks," he says.

"Call them what they are," I say. "The Nobles. The Virtues."

"Callie," he warns.

"Hey, I'll even accept Briarcliff Academy's secret society. I *know* they exist, Chase."

"Don't do this."

"You're the one who called *me*. You had your escape hatch all mapped out when you dipped on me that night, and I'd even come to accept you weren't going to talk to me for the rest of the year. I'd made my peace with it." *Not.* "Yet here I am, in your car, on your invitation, because you want something from me. Well, it goes both ways, buddy."

Chase makes an impatient sound in his throat, but his next turn is sharper, and I'm thrown against his side before I can brace. I latch onto the hard length of his arm, so stiff with muscle my fingers don't dimple the skin, as he finishes the turn and we coast up another private road.

I twist my face away from his intoxicating scent, seemingly crafted just for my pheromones, a mix of salted sweat, freshwater, and pine, and focus on where we are.

The forest is heavier here, tree branches and their falling leaves yawning over the roadway, creating a natural, curving archway we drive under. Chase's tinted sunroof is so large, it takes up the entire top of the car, and it's like I'm given wings, taking flight through fantastical woodland under the twinkle of stars.

"Wow," I breathe, the stars' silver specks poking through like sparkling jewels worn by the black, skeletal hands of the branches above.

"You can let go now."

Chase's voice draws my chin down, and I unfurl from his arm. We've slowed to a stop in view of a massive glass structure, a building spanning the size of a New York City block that I'm coming to understand is the length of people's homes around here.

"Come on," he says, exiting the car with slick, effortless grace.

I'm less tranquil, my knees hitting my chest as I swing them to the ground after elbowing open the door. I make sure to swipe the tantalizing bakery bag and balance my coffee before I let myself out.

Chase is already striding down the small walkway, swinging a keyring in his hand. I'm slow to catch up, because I'm too busy clocking the scope of this house, a looming shadow clawing out of its spot in the forest and dominating the sky.

"Is this your place?" I ask his retreating back.

He responds over his shoulder, "It's our lake house."

I swallow the forgotten saliva building in my mouth.

Turns out I was wrong. Chase didn't ferry me to his cursed castle.

The dark prince of Briarcliff Academy took me to his vacation home instead.

I hurry to catch up with Chase, reluctant to continue hanging out in the darkness. We're still in the middle of the wilderness, and the idea of neighbors other than bears being nearby is laughable.

Wolves, too. The real ones.

"Wait up!" I call, and Chase pauses once he unlocks the large iron doors.

He steps back to let me in first, and I pause for half a second on the door knocker in the vivid shape of a sleeping bat before stepping over the threshold.

"So, your lake house, huh?" I say as Chase steps in behind me. He heads to one side of the foyer, turning on lights. "It's ... quaint."

Chase has illuminated a vast, open area, with a gray brick fireplace built in the *middle* of the room and stacked to the vaulted ceiling, the exposed wooden beams creating a cabin-like feel only the wealthy would consider essential. Thin, white leather couches are placed on one side of the fireplace, and a formal dining table on the other. A throw rug in the shape of a wolf is spread out between the couches, and while I'm hoping it's fake, I'm pretty sure it's not.

The floor-to-ceiling windows on the opposite side probably provide an amazing view of the Stone's private property, but nothing can be seen through the black of the night but our own pale reflections.

Chase laughs under his breath. "Follow me. We'll eat and talk in the kitchen."

"I didn't know you had a place so close to the school," I say, trailing behind Chase down a single step and into the main room until we reach the open, luxury kitchen.

Chase spins to take the bakery bag from my hands, and I settle onto a stool while he opens cupboards.

"Probably because I consider it more of a prison," he says while placing two plates between us. "This is where I'll be riding out next week."

I put my finger to my lips and *pretend contemplation*. "Don't tell me, your decision to club another Neanderthal upside the head for insulting me has resulted in your suspension."

"What'd you expect?" Chase responds, as if *I* was the one who asked him to be such an idiot.

"You shouldn't have hit James."

He slides a plate of still-steaming monkey bread closer, and I stare at it for a minute before giving in.

"He deserved it." Chase licks the drippings of my portion off his thumb while keeping his eyes on mine. An internal shiver wraps its way around my chest. Never have I wanted to be icing sugar more.

Chase bites the pad of his thumb in thought, then says, "James was being an ass."

"He's *always* an ass."

"When it comes to you, my buddies and I have an agreement. You and I may not be currently fucking, but my moratorium on anyone saying anything negative about you or doing anything to you still stands."

I lift another piece of bread to my mouth. The hot caramel and the spicy notes of cinnamon hit my taste buds under pillowy vanilla dough, and I moan.

Chase freezes while plating his piece, his jawline going rigid. Pieces of fine blond hair fall into his eyes, and while I can only see his profile, I sense the solar flare within him, his irises going black with expanded pupils.

My breath hitches as I set the bread down carefully. The raw, tingling pressure against my nipples is almost unbearable. "I don't need your protection."

"No?" His question is soft. Dangerous.

"Piper's killer is behind bars. There's no more risk of a murderer strolling through Briarcliff halls," I say. "And according to you, my discovery of a secret society poses no danger because they don't exist." I add an eye roll as final punctuation.

"There's still Falyn to consider," Chase says as he rests on the stool next to mine. His presence is too close, too warm. "And Addisyn. Without my protection, they'll make it their mission for you to regret ever enrolling at this school."

I grit my teeth. "I can handle a few mean girls." I side-eye Chase. "And mean boys, if it comes to that."

His mouth quirks.

I stare at him for a moment, worrying my lips.

Because, without a doubt, if I stay any longer, I'll jump him.

And I can't let that happen. He ditched me a few weeks ago without a word, and I'm not giving him the satisfaction of coming back for more.

Or perhaps my reluctance stems from him dropping me before *I* could leave him, this high school alpha who will give me his body, but wraps his soul in impenetrable, ancient armor I have no hope of piercing.

Why put my heart through it again?

"Unless you brought me here to appreciate how your virtual learning experience will go this week," I say, picking at my bread, "I'd like to get back to the dorms."

Chase swallows his bite. He stares at the kitchen cabinetry. "I'd like you to do something for me."

I lean back as much as I can in a stool and reach for my coffee, more for comfort than thirst. "What's so important you couldn't text me, or, I don't know, talk to me between classes?"

"This cop connection you have, the guy you talk to in the city," Chase says.

"Ahmar?"

"Yeah, him."

The fact that Chase is bringing up my pseudo-uncle causes my stomach to plummet. I stepped into Chase's car with full knowledge that he needed me for something, but the smallest whisper inside my head wished for it to be unrelated to Piper. For her to be buried to rest so we could all move on.

It's a cold, selfish thought I'd never voice out loud, but that part of me molded to Chase, the piece of me he kept for himself, will always wish to fit against him without the jagged edge of Piper in between.

Chase cups his coffee, his forearms resting against the granite counter, the trail of veins running under his skin matching the threads of gold woven in the marble. "I need you to find out if it was mine."

I inhale, a silent swish of breath that freezes my entire form.

"It's the only way I can know for sure," Chase continues. "The local cops aren't saying a word. More motive evidence they're keeping to themselves, I guess."

"Or they're still waiting on the results," I say, impressed at how steady I sound. Nothing like scientific facts to ease emotional turmoil inside one's head.

Chase shifts his focus, and his copper-toned eyes meet mine. "Is that your honest opinion?"

I shrug as offhandedly as I can. "It can take a while. And think about it. If the results come back to match you, that unravels the entire case against Dr. Luke. If it were yours, they ... they'd pull you in for more questioning."

Chase's head jerks in a nod. "Exactly. I'd like to know before they take me by surprise."

I mull this over. "You're asking me and Ahmar to meddle with an open investigation and interfere with Briarcliff PD's potential plan to interrogate you."

Chase's Adam's apple bobs, the only motion in his perfect form as he stares me down.

This is the moment where I say no. Where I stand up, demand to be taken to back to the dorms, or call myself an Uber.

What I shouldn't be doing is sitting here, contemplating the ins and outs of obtaining such information and the effects that would ripple out because of it.

Worse, I *want* to do it. For him.

"Ahmar may not be successful. It's not his jurisdiction," I say. "He could outright refuse, too."

Chase nods. "I get it. But it's a way to try."

"And if it's yours?" I whisper. "You just punched your airtight alibi in the face. Friends fight. Friends lie for each other."

"I know that, too." His burnished gaze finds the inner heat it needs to flicker with golden flames. "You gotta believe me, Callie. I didn't hurt her. The baby could be Dr. Luke's just as much as it could be mine."

The gears of my mind shift, rubbing together all wrong because of their blatant misuse. I should be planning how to live out the rest of my senior year without Chase and all the problems clinging to the Briarcliff blazers of his entire group. Instead, I'm busy drumming up a solution as to how *I* can benefit.

When the riskiest answer clicks into place, I say, "I'll do it."

Chase's shoulders ease away from his neck. "Thank you."

"On a condition."

Chase stills. Then, once he processes what I've said, his mouth kicks into a saddened grin. "You're learning survival skills pretty quick."

I ignore his statement. "You're suspended for a week, right?"

His brows draw together. "Yeah. Why?"

I sit straighter. "I'll do my best to get the information for you, but in return, you'll let me ask you three questions per day for an entire week, which you have to answer honestly and with the *full* truth."

Chase's nostrils flare. His stare doesn't waver, and I tell myself to be strong against the heat of his microscope. He takes the next few seconds for himself, the mechanics of his mind possessing more expertise on the subject of trickery and traps than mine.

He says, "One."

I shake my head. "Two questions."

"Fine. But the questions have limitations. No asking about your Cloaks. And only one personal question per day."

My heart flutters with disappointment, but I'd factored in that possibility and figured out a few workarounds.

That he's playing into my hands should feel good, but it really, really doesn't. "Deal."

One flawless cheek of his tics with his clenched jaw. "Should we shake on it?"

Dear Lord, if I touch him now, I'll have no hope of leaving this place with my clothes on. I've developed shivers in places that aren't supposed to be sentient, but they're going off on their own anyway, demanding orgasmic release.

"No need." I stand, brushing invisible crumbs off my legs. "Can you take me home?"

After a pause, Chase moves from his eerily still position. "Sure."

Dregs of coffee remain in my cup, but I take it anyway, needing something to do with my hands as Chase guides me out of his lake house and opens the passenger door of his car, an oil-slicked beast waiting silently within the shadows of the forest.

We're silent under the ultraviolet hue of the interior, me taking pretend sips of my coffee. Chase doesn't blast any music on our way back to Briarcliff, and I don't ask him to, preferring the low hum of the vehicle to regulate and calm my thoughts.

At 5 AM, Chase pulls up to Thorne House. I unbuckle my seatbelt, and he leans back from the wheel. I feel his study like the fine pinpricks of sewing needles as I move but pretend I don't.

"Thanks for the..." I pause to think of what this was between us. "Visit."

Chase responds with a closed-mouthed smile, resting one wrist on the top of the steering wheel. "I appreciate what you're doing for me."

After a careful nod, I step out.

"And Callie?"

I bend down to catch his eye.

"Happy birthday," he says.

Chase leans over to pull the passenger door shut, and I stumble back as his vehicle purrs across the driveway before disappearing around a corner.

With my hands on my hips, I watch his departure, a hesitant smile playing at the corners of my lips.

6

*A*fter my shower the next morning, I send Ahmar a text, asking him to call me when he gets the chance, preferring to get this chapter over with so I can tell Chase I held up my end of the deal.

I scrape my hair into a top knot using the small vanity mirror in my room, some strands still damp at the ends, since I didn't have the patience to blow-dry it all the way.

Before leaving my room, I recheck my bag to make sure I have the supplies I need to go into town.

Emma's bedroom is open and deserted when I slip through the main room, but the smell of fresh coffee is sharp in the air. My stomach gurgles. The few hours' sleep I caught after being dropped off by Chase has reinvigorated my digestion, and I make a mental note to raid the Wolf's Den pastry bar before calling a car.

Outside my apartment, a few of my neighbors mingle, Saturday morning bringing with it a happy need to socialize, make plans, or stay in pajamas all day. A few girls glance in my direction when my door shuts behind me, and with the stares being more curious than feral, I figure news must've hit that I have a new roommate.

Or, for most of these girls, news of the return of an old, traumatized friend.

Relief should settle upon my shoulders at the idea I'm no longer the fresh meat of the week, but Emma's loss of her formal social status doesn't sit well, regardless of her crisp, pissy attitude. Someone experiencing tragedy like that should have friends surround them and be supported by their environment, not smuggled into the cobwebbed corners of a lonely mansion and forgotten about, only to come back to derisive bitches.

I lift my chin in defense of the stares and murmurs, then take a hard left into the stairwell, preferring to chew off my all fingers to the first knuckle than wait for an elevator while these girls mingle over caffeinated mugs of gossip.

A burst of fresh air hits me when I push through the ground floor's side exit, the same one I took to meet Chase. This time, I hop onto the pathway leading to the school rather than hedge around the bushes and soak my sneakers.

I spot Ivy walking with her roommate, Eden, and run to catch up to them.

"Hey," I say once I'm close enough.

Both turn their heads. Ivy smiles. Eden scowls through her curtain of long black hair.

"You guys headed to breakfast?" I ask, sidling up to Ivy.

"Definitely," Ivy says. "I need a load of eggs and bacon to help digest what I just heard."

I frown, hooking my fingers around the backpack's straps at my shoulders while I match their pace, sun dappling their shoulders, and the wind carrying the scent of cut grass and damp wood. "I get why everyone else is whispering, but why are you surprised? You were with me when Emma first moved in."

Eden's brows hitch up. "Emma's back?"

"Is that not what we're talking about?" I ask.

"Nope." Eden snorts, but the delicate skin around her eyes remains tight. "I guess the return of someone. beat up and nearly killed in a fire while the school did nothing is yesterday's news."

"I thought the same thing," I say to Eden.

Eden glances my way but doesn't return the sympathy.

"I'm talking about Dr. Luke," Ivy says, her ice-blonde hair bouncing as she strolls. I swear, rumors provide her more energy than espresso. "I spoke to Lisa who knew Carl who heard from Sebastian whose dad is on some sort of state council that Dr. Luke's been released."

I grind to a halt. "*What?*"

Eden stares at the ground and keeps walking, but Ivy whirls to face me. "It's all over school this morning. Apparently, Dr. Luke had an alibi, but she was reluctant to come forward and corroborate because, well, it would ruin her life."

I blink at Ivy, who leans in and lowers her voice to a conspiratorial whisper. "Dr. Luke was having an affair with Sebastian's *mom*. She was with him that night."

"But..." I think back to Piper's diary entries while Dr. Luke's last words to me play in my ear.

I was there to dump her!

"...he saw Piper that night," I finish. "He admitted he was the *last* to see her."

Ivy nods, then shrugs. "He also insisted he left her alive. And if Mrs. Dorian is to be believed, he was with her during Piper's time of death. In her *convertible* on Briarcliff's private driveway. Ew, right?"

"That can't be true." I shake my head and start walking again, with Ivy prancing beside me. "He all but admitted he killed her."

"Did he, though?"

"*Yes.*" I grab Ivy's arm. "He's the one. Dr. Luke did it. He *has* to be Piper's killer."

"Ow. You're kinda hurting me."

"This is—there has to be a hole in this alibi somewhere. He's lying. She's lying. The police've made a mistake."

"Callie, I don't think so. Mrs. Dorian has a time-stamped video of it."

My grip tightens on Ivy's arm. She yelps, and I shake myself out of it, releasing her. "Sorry."

"What's going on with you?" Ivy asks, rubbing her arm. "Mrs. Dorian filmed them having sex. I guess to masturbate with later? Whatever the reason, it's proof, Callie. Think about it."

"No, I..." I dig a hand into my hair, pulling out strands from my hair-tie. "It can't be. Dr. Luke *did* it. No one ... no one else..."

My vision blurs with the possibilities I'd hidden in the recesses of my mind once I'd heard the *chink* of handcuffs locking around the beloved professor at Briarcliff.

The Cloaks.

The roses.

Rose Briar's secret letter.

The lost pages of Piper's diary.

None of it was supposed to matter anymore. I'd stifled the deep-seated, obsessive need to investigate...

"Listen, I don't know why Mrs. Dorian waited so long." Ivy's voice breaks through the shimmering fog of my mind. "She must've found her morals where she originally stashed them to sleep with her son's professor, deciding *not* to let Dr. Luke rot in prison for the sake of her reputation." Ivy wrinkles her nose. "What a decent thing to do."

In a surge of contorted memory, my stepdad's face replaces Dr. Luke's stricken expression when handcuffs snapped across his wrists.

Dad's shock when his arms were wrenched behind him. The desperate words he uttered when police escorted him past me and out the door.

Cal, what is this? Why do they think it's me?

I'm innocent, Callie!

...Don't do this, please...

Honey, you have to believe me. I loved your mother. I love her.

His pleading didn't stop until Ahmar's arm folded over my shoulder, and he turned me away from the doorway, my cheeks soaked in tears.

"Oh, God..." I moan, then stumble off the pathway and fall to my knees in the grass.

"Callie!" Ivy rushes over, her hands on my back as she bends down.

Why did you do this? You were like a daughter to me...

"It can't be," I say, licking the sudden salt from my lips. I'm crying.

"Here. C'mere." Ivy gently pulls on my shoulders until she envelopes me into a hug, oblivious to the small crowd gathering around us, asking if I'm all right.

"It may not be Dr. Luke," Ivy murmurs into my ear, "but it's someone. And they'll catch him. You're safe. You'll be safe."

"That's not..." My face crumples into the line of her neck and shoulder. "I'm not afraid for my life. I'm..."

Afraid of being wrong again.

More students pause in the walkway, some for concern, most to spectate. Ivy pulls me to a stand and puts a protective arm around my shoulders as she guides me through the collecting crowd and toward the school.

"If you want to go back to your room, I can bring you some breakfast," Ivy says.

While it's tempting to shut out the world and pull covers over my head, I say, "No. I'll be all right. It's a shock, is all."

"No kidding. You and Chase were the ones who got Dr. Luke to say enough to confess, right?"

I wince. *It wasn't exactly a confession.*

Ivy notices and adds, "Not that you're responsible. You're *not*, Callie. Dr. Luke still slept with Piper. And Mrs. Dorian. And God knows who else. He's still a dirty sleezeball who ruined his own life. You know that, right?"

I nod, but don't necessarily believe it. It's one thing to be a jerk-off. Another to be a murderer.

"Piper's parents are still pressing charges, too. Statutory rape..." Ivy continues the morbid pep talk meant to make me feel better, and I appreciate her efforts to reduce my involvement in this clusterfuck, but I never told her how deep I went into Piper's investigation.

How I tend to obsess over these things.

I gnaw on my lower lip, desperate to tell her, but too embarrassed to admit it.

How is one supposed to explain to their only friend their growing habit of implicating the wrong man?

"I'm glad you caught me on the way to the dining hall," Ivy says. "It's all anyone will be talking about over their breakfast. It sure would've been awkward if you puked on their pancakes."

Ivy elbows me after the joke. I smile wanly in response. "I'm not headed there, anyway."

"No?"

"I'm going into town to study at the public library for a while."

"Can't say I blame you. Gossip is so distracting, isn't it?"

This time, my laugh is genuine. "I'll catch you later. You'll text me if you hear anything else, right?"

"One hundred percent. And text me when you're back."

We separate at the academy's front pavilion, Ivy hopping up the steps and into the school with a few other students dressed in their weekend casual.

I pull out my phone and tap on the Briarcliff app to call the personal chauffeur service. After receiving an alert that the wait will be 10 minutes, my thumb hovers over my text list, instinctually tempted to message Chase.

I have to believe he already knows. He has his finger on the pulse of Briarcliff better than most faculty members, and his sources would've told him about Dr. Luke.

So, why didn't he text me? Did he know all this last night?

The realization pisses me off, and I shove my phone back in my bag without bothering to contact him. I'm better off anxiously awaiting a call from Ahmar, not Chase Stone. Ahmar could help me clear up some confusion and possibly shed light on what is now a crucial piece of the puzzle.

The DNA of Piper's secret pregnancy.

Evidence that could mean everything, and not just to Chase.

7

*B*riarcliff's town car pulls up to the center of the circular driveway, and I greet my favorite driver of the three, Yael, when I slide in.

"Sorry I was late," he says as he completes the half-circle to exit school grounds. "It's a popular morning."

"Really?"

Students tend to avoid the town and the chauffeur service, preferring to use their own cars to get to their nearby vacation homes and mansions on weekends.

Yael chuckles. "You and me both, Miss."

"By all means, Yael, don't ever refer to me as *miss*." I smile at him in the rearview mirror. "Callie's fine."

Yael shows a line of bright white teeth in response. "Sure thing, Callie."

The rest of the drive is quiet, the sun-soaked trees and moss-covered rocks blurring past as I take out my phone but hold it up with an unfocused stare.

The pages of Piper's diary aren't there anymore, but I'd come close to memorizing each and every sheet of paper she scrawled across, full of her thoughts but barren of clues, before the pictures were stolen, then deleted. She never mentioned a surprise pregnancy. But her sexual encounters with Mr. S took up most of the pages, a man I'd convinced myself was Dr. Luke.

It's still him. I know it deep in my soul.

Is he a murderer? Or did Dr. Luke actually dump her, like he insisted he did, which made her so devastated, she didn't think before she plunged into the black sea below Lover's Leap?

Yet, the day she died is the same day Rose Briar is assumed to have jumped off the same cliff, the tortured wife of Briarcliff Academy's founder.

And Cloaks haunt the school at night, a society of students, or faculty, or *both*, whose motives are more sinister than sacrificial.

"*Argh.*" I massage my temples with both hands, the phone dropping to my lap.

I can't do this again. I can't fall down the rabbit hole with the full confidence I'll climb out.

"Are you all right, Mi—Callie?"

I open my eyes and force a smile. "Project jitters. I'm still getting used to the demands of this school."

Yael murmurs in agreement, pulling on to Main Street and parallel parking by the town's library/post office. "Don't put too much stress on yourself. You have the right idea, coming here instead of using the school library. I hope you find what you're looking for."

"Me too," I say, with a lot more meaning than Yael could understand, and climb from the car.

I fix my backpack on my shoulders, wishing I'd thought to pack my jacket, now that I'm closer to the ocean shore and there's a bitter, salty chill to the air that the academy seems to have walled off. As I'm adjusting the heavy load, I naturally glance down the street, noting how deserted the seaside town is, despite the tourist attractions of a lobster shack, bakery, and candy shop.

It's said the town's income comes mostly from the academy, without much effort going into keeping the small economy going.

Almost like the pastel, clapboard shops and fluttering, colorful flags touting the incoming Halloween Festival are window dressing, rather than failing decorations that folks passing through don't bother to look at as they aim for more desirable locations, like Newport or Providence.

My attention lands on the lobster shack, saddened it's not more populated, because they make a mean lobster omelet for brunch, and I pause on the two people out front.

They're about two blocks away on the other side of the street, but it's easy to make out the smooth brown hair and the headband that keeps it out of Addisyn's face. The boy she's gesturing to, Jack, is her boyfriend and works at the restaurant—the gasp-worthy relationship of a prep school darling and a local townie out in the open for anyone to see. And by anyone, I mean ... only me.

I don't judge, or care. What keeps my stare on the couple is the way Addisyn moves, her motions stuttered and sharp. Jack responds with wild gesticulations of his own, both their expressions dark and storm-fueled.

In the middle of a sharp explanation, Jack's head tilts, and he catches my eye. The conversation halts.

Addisyn follows Jack's focus, and when she lands on me, she's not nearly as ominous and glowering.

"The hell are you looking at, possum?" she calls across the street. "Are you so tired of creeping around campus that you've come into town to jerk off instead?"

Aaaaand she's picked up right where her sister left off. How magical.

I shouldn't, but... "If I open a door to a room where you're expecting privacy, *then* you can be mad."

Addisyn hisses, and Jack throws me the finger.

I'm not in the mood to joust, so I turn my back on them and trudge up the library's steps, inwardly eager to get away before Addisyn launches into full attack mode.

Which, she may have a right to, now that Dr. Luke's been released.

Crap. Now I feel bad. Maybe her anger at the world is warranted. Funneling it into me is a sad byproduct, but unavoidable when such a vast amount of torrential hate exists inside you, there's nowhere to unleash it except for on the ones stupid enough to prod and goad at the edges.

I did it, too, and my stepdad was the sorry victim.

"Why, hello! You're back!"

I blink, realizing I've stepped through Briarcliff Library's doors and hover at the reception desk, where Darla sits, her fifties-style glasses perched on her nose while her eyes, enlarged by thick prescription lenses, regard me.

"It's quieter here," I say as a lame explanation. Aren't all libraries naturally quiet?

"I can imagine," Darla agrees, then motions to the middle of the rectangular room, bordered on all sides with stacks of books and topped off with a low, corkboard ceiling. "The place is yours. Well—yours and another young go-getter. Seems your secret's out."

I stiffen at her last sentence, but instinctually search the designated study tables. When I find the person Darla's referring to, my shoulders slump and I mutter, "No wonder Yael was so busy this morning."

First Addisyn, and now Emma.

"What's that, dear?"

"Nothing," I say to Darla.

She smiles, then flicks her fingers. "Go on, now. Studying ain't built in a day."

I shuffle forward, but no matter where I place my butt to do my work, I'll be in Emma's scope. The public library is so small. There are three study tables in total, and all in the center of the room.

As silently as I can, I pad over to the farthest table away from

Emma. She's chosen to be nearer to the stacks of books, and mine is closer to Darla.

Emma had the better idea. There's a great risk that Darla will get so bored with her Harlequin paperback, she'll try for idle chit-chat.

My bag thumps on the bleached wooden table. Emma glances up at the sound. When her eyes connect with mine, she sags.

I scrunch up half my face in response. *Sorry. I was hoping to get some space from Briarcliff, too.*

She glares but says nothing as she gets back to her laptop. I exhale in relief, and work on setting up my station.

I toss my phone on top of my spiral notebooks. All signs point to me needing to work on my English Lit paper due in a week. My phone's black screen shouldn't be so distracting, but it is.

Dr. Luke's out.

Someone ripped important pages from Piper's diary that I never saw.

That person could be her killer.

I splay my hands on my closed laptop, mentally prepping for actual schoolwork once I sit, but my eye is continuously drawn to my phone.

Lips curled in frustration, I grab it and open the photos, swiping until the beginnings of Rose Briar's nineteenth century letter scroll across the screen. The original is hidden away in one of my textbooks, but it's so delicate, it's better to reference the copy.

"Damn it," I mutter, and place the screen face down on the table, but it's too late.

I'm not going to get anything done until I explore more of this library and see if it has more gifts to impart.

I ask Darla in a low whisper, "Where is that section on the founders of Briarcliff Academy again?"

"Don't you remember, dear?" Darla responds in a regular

voice. Emma's head lifts. "Stack eight is where you'll find information on the Briars."

I briefly glance at Emma in apology for the noise, but instead of facing annoyance, I read a cautious alertness in her expression.

"Thanks," I say to Darla, then slide out from my seat and search for the stack, which, if I recall, is closer to the back of the building.

"That reminds me!" Darla says, *still* in an outside voice. "Briarcliff's mayor has just donated Thorne Briar's original office supplies for our educational pleasure for one whole month. It's on the back wall, honey, in a glass display, along with a few other artifacts from the Briar's time that we like to showcase during holidays. For the tourists, you know."

"Yes. The tourists," I say, my sarcasm at its lowest setting. I doubt the meager out-of-towners who come by want to know the historical progression of a ridiculously pompous preparatory school for the spawn of the nation's 1%, but what do I know?

It doesn't escape me that *I'm* an out-of-towner who is extremely curious about Briarcliff's origins.

"That is," Darla continues, "what remains after the f—"

She stops herself by clamping a hand to her mouth. Her gaze skitters over to Emma with such dismay, my cheeks flush for her.

To Emma's credit, she raises her eyes skyward and shakes her head in disdain.

"Thank you," I say quickly, then beeline through the stacks and to the back, where a map of the Briarcliff township, including the academy's grounds, is drawn to scale and takes up the entire wall.

"Whoa," I murmur, my eyes tracing the detailed forest terrain and hand-drawn buildings interspersed throughout. Gray roads cut through the greenery, dividing into smaller roadways like tentacles brushing against buildings, cliffs and oceanic shores.

An invisible string pulls taut against my vision, halting my scan with anchoring precision. The jagged end of Lover's Leap emerges from the northeast corner, as ominous in acrylic as it is in real life.

"Why are you here?"

The voice smacks between my shoulders and jolts down my spine. I spin, my heart pattering harder than expected.

Emma stands in between two stacks, her hulking form casting her in the light of a fabled hunchback escaping from one of the books lining either side of her.

"Research," I manage to say.

Emma's frown lines grow deeper. "On what?"

"The—the founders." I gesture behind me, where a bench-length glass display showcases the Briar artifacts I haven't gotten a chance to study yet.

"Nobody comes to the public library."

"Exactly." I arch a brow. "I assume that's why you're here, too."

"I have reason to be." Emma takes a step forward, her focus wavering on mine. She ends up losing whatever inner battle she's waging, and stares at the line of Briar-owned items.

"Such crap," she mumbles.

I follow her movements by turning until we're both facing the display. "Why do you say that?"

"They make it seem like he was such a good man. That he did this world a favor by creating this town and building a school for boys."

Emma studies the glass case with dangerous wonder, her upper lip frozen mid-sneer. Standing this close to her, I notice the faint, puckered scar tissue running along the side of her face and cauliflowering around her ear.

Emma's body stills, but her eyes snap to mine with the speed and haunting eeriness of a ventriloquist's doll. "Problem?"

The after-effects of Emma's attack are well-known, but the details kept strictly mute. I never read up on what happened to her, because it was none of my business and—if I'm to be honest —irrelevant to my investigation into Piper's death.

Or so I thought.

I'm disappointed in my reaction, though. This is the type of violence my mother faced as a full-time job when she was alive, and sometimes, she couldn't help but bring it home. I've been exposed to this kind of brutality, in vicious, high definition.

"No," I say, covering my faux pas by focusing on the display. "It takes a lot of hatred to despise not only a school, but the entire town that comes with it."

"It sure does." I feel Emma's stare against my profile burning holes into my pores. "But I've had a lot of time to nurture it."

"Is that why you're back? To get some answers?"

Emma cocks her head in my periphery. "Answers have many different interpretations." She pauses. "Perhaps I'm here to let them know they haven't won."

I turn to her. "Who's 'they'?"

Emma notches up her chin. Something tells me she rarely makes a mistake with what she says ... not anymore.

"You tell me," she says. "Have you discovered anything while doing your *research*?"

"Not much. Just a hidden society within the academy," I deadpan.

Emma sucks in a breath, but her stare remains level, and dare I say, a flicker of respect shines within. "You shouldn't be spouting off about that."

I motion to where we are. "I'm not exactly screaming it from the rooftops."

"But you're certain they exist."

I cling to this brief spurt of bravery. Emma's testing me, and I have the sense that out of everyone, she may be the one to actually speak the truth. "I even have names for them. The Nobles. The V—"

"Don't say it," Emma says in a wet whisper. My side presses harder into the display when her face transforms from assessing to deadly. "Don't you dare repeat that name, not if you don't want them to come for you."

My breath becomes smaller in my chest. Tighter. "Did they attack you? Is that why you set the fire?"

Now, oh, *now*, I wish I'd grown Emma's ability to carefully craft a sentence before giving it the mistake of a voice.

Emma bares her teeth, her eyes like fossilized amber, except hers melts to reveal the creature encased within. "*Who told you that?*"

"N-no one. It was a mistake. I didn't mean for it to come out like that." Fuck, I'm a terrible liar. "I meant did *they* set the fire and trap you?"

Emma steps into my space, so close, her nose nearly brushes mine. Her breath heats my lips to a terrible level, but I can't retreat. Not if I want her to believe me.

"You knew Piper," I say, despite her flaring nostrils. "Do you think she killed herself, or was she attacked by the same person who hurt you?"

"How *dare* you?"

Exactly. How dare I. I'm putting my theories into dangerous existence, threading a needle so deadly, two women have been brutalized from it—one killed.

"If I don't ask the questions," I say, clenching my trembling fingers into fists, "no one else will. Piper deserves justice. You deserve justice."

"Piper was a twat, and you don't know me from shit," Emma says, but she backs off, the stale air of the library reclaiming its place between us. "This is because of my brother, isn't it? Don't tell me, the new girl falls for the perfect, popular guy, but he doesn't return the favor. So, in order to gain his everlasting gratitude, she tries to solve his twin sister's assault and his ex-girlfriend's death. Do I have that right? *God.*" Emma lets out a cruel laugh. "So pathetic."

My lips part on a snarl. "You have it completely twisted. It's this place." I spread my arms. "This school. There's a poison here, and terrible truths are covered up." I point to Thorne Briar's business log, open to some random page of handwritten profits and losses. "I've discovered enough to know that it doesn't start with Chase. It doesn't begin with Piper. Nor did it first strike with *you*. It begins with Rose Briar."

I let out a whoosh of breath, unused to such emotion crossing over my tongue, not since it was capped and bottled in an involuntary psychiatric hold. I vowed never to put myself in a position where dry pills were forced down my throat again.

Yet ... here I've landed.

Double fuck.

Emma stumbles back, her face, stiffened with old scars, spasming with long forgotten muscles. Fear. Apprehension. Denial.

Her skin takes on a ghostly cast, and her hand screeches against the glass display where she drags it, her palms soaked in sweat. "Do you like the way my face looks? Because I'm pretty sure yours will end up this way, too."

"So far," I say quietly, ignoring the spasm of panic in my chest, "not one person has truly acknowledged the possibility that these societies exist. Until you."

Emma regains enough composure to snap, "Both Piper's and my *tragedies*, as you idiots call them, circle around Chase. Why don't you be as unoriginal as everyone else and consider him to be the problem?"

"Is he?"

Emma flinches.

"Because in the rare times he's talked about you, it's been with nothing but love and defense," I say. "And he punishes himself. I hear it whenever he utters your name—he thinks he's responsible for what happened, not because he wielded the weapon, but because he wasn't there to protect you."

I'm stunned by my statement, and I press my fingers to my

lips at the continued passion, draining my spirit faster than I can contain it.

Emma eyes grow small with suspicion. "Chase doesn't talk about me. With anyone."

I swallow, take one last look at the glass case, then come back to Emma. "My mistake, then."

I'm brushing past her before Emma can think up a proper, scathing response, and hurry to collect my things.

But I can never escape. The Briars will follow me, and so will the Harringtons and Stones.

I've introduced myself to their demons, and they will continue their dark suffocation until I unearth the hidden details that can one day set them free.

That is ... if I can do it before they bury me, too.

8

*T*here's no wait to take the Briarcliff chauffeur service back home. And thankfully, no forced Briarcliff carpool either.

Addisyn must still be off with her boyfriend, and I left Emma within the shadowed recesses of the library, so I'm safe from them, for now.

My feet hit the asphalt of the school driveway along with a deep urge to see a friendly face and immerse myself in banal activities, like painting my nails or watching garbage TV. Anything to get my mind off the spindly critters circling the back of my brain, spinning their web of names.

Piper. Emma. Rose.

Is their trauma related? *How*?

Leave it alone, a voice whispers from within. *This is not for your wounded heart.*

Nor is sitting on my ass, doing nothing while the person responsible for hurting these girls goes on with their life, merry and free.

They are not your mother.

"Shut up, Voice," I seethe, ignoring the startled looks cast in my direction as I pass them by on the student pathway to the dorms.

I end up bypassing my own, lonely dorm and head to Richardson Place. It's where Ivy and Eden live, and I hope at least one of them is there when I knock on their door.

It pulls wide to reveal Ivy. At the sight of her, I pause with my fist still held up to knock. "What's with the face?"

"Oh, this old thang?" Ivy circles her freshly powdered, foundationed, and glammed-up face with a finger. "It's Saturday, girl. Let's play dress up, and make-up, and drink up, then we're going out. Didn't you get my text?"

I picture my phone, crammed at the bottom of my bag under my books and computer in the hope that it'd stay there. "Nope."

"Chase is holding a huge party at his lake house." Ivy yanks me inside. "We're going."

"A party for what? His near expulsion?"

Ivy laughs. "He's too precious to Marron's bottom line to be expelled. Do you have stuff to get ready or do you just want to borrow some of mine?"

Ivy, here on full scholarship, barely has a chest of drawers to call her own. Her and Eden's room is much smaller than mine, with bolted, standard, grayish-blue furniture and a twin bed that might as well fold-out Murphy-style for each.

Meanwhile, my stepdad's new wife sends me seasonal outfit changes on the regular, my self-conscious rebuffs largely ignored.

"I have a better idea," I say. "Let's go back to my place and you can raid my closet for a dress for me *and* for you."

Ivy's eyes light up brighter than holiday fireworks, and a laugh escapes my throat as she half-pulls, half-drags me out of her room, and we scamper over to mine.

This is precisely what I needed, a friend and a fun time—things I haven't had the beauty of basking in for a while. Chase might be the gatekeeper to my Briarcliff experience, but after the morning I've had, I'm willing to pay his price.

Plus, *everyone* is going, and his lake house is huge. I figure there will be plenty of chances to avoid him until I'm ready.

Emma hasn't returned to the dorms, and after Ivy's tentative questions on how the first night went and what Emma's like, to which I answered noncommittally, we blast music from my computer and sift through the curated outfits Lynda thought would suit me.

When Ivy pulls out a short, black mini dress with a plunging V where boobs should be, I'm positive my stepdad did *not* approve this "seasonal pick" for fall and winter.

Where the frick are my snow pants?

"This says you all over it." Ivy flips the dress back and forth on the hanger, humming and hawing in ways that are newly foreign to me. My ex-friend back in New York, Sylvie and I, often got ready like this, but we added lines of coke to our outfit changes and snorts between eye-liner applications.

The flashback fogs my vision, and for a minute I see Sylvie bending close to my closet mirror, dabbing at the corner of her eyes and sniffling, *"Make a few more lines for us, will you? We'll be so badass at the club tonight."*

"Callie?"

Ivy's face sharpens as she holds up the dress, an unsure smile plastered across her face.

In so many ways, Ivy is the complete opposite of Sylvie. There will be no drugs tonight. No stranger's hard-ons rubbing against the small of my back as I whirl and stumble under strobe lights.

"No freaking way am I wearing that," I say. "That's more Falyn's taste."

"Mm." Ivy's expression is morphing in a way I don't like. She's appearing more as a reality TV fashion judge than my friend, and ... I'm fairly confident I'll be freezing my nipples off tonight. "You're trying it on."

"No, I'm—"

The dress whacks me in the face.

"And this one."

Another whack.

"This, too."

I predict Ivy's next toss and hold my dress-laden hands out to catch it, but Ivy fakes me out and pauses mid-throw. "On the other hand, this purple would totally complement my eyes and hair..."

Laughing, I perch on my bed. "Wear whatever you want."

"And you, my dear, will wear what I tell you to," Ivy says, then spreads her fingers and descends on me.

※

Ivy won.

A few hours of primping and sipping later, I'm in the risqué black number, my knees knocking together as we wait for a car at the front of the academy. Ivy chose the off-the-shoulder, deep purple dress, its sequins catching the nectarine glow of the setting sun whenever she turns.

Other seniors have taken their own cars to the lake house, and those juniors, sophomores, and freshmen who aren't allowed off-campus on weekends but have figured a way to smuggle themselves out, have long departed.

"Isn't it only cool to attend parties at, like, eleven at night?" I ask Ivy as we wait.

"Usually," she answers through the flat-ironed curtain of her silvery blond hair. Ivy's head is bent as she scrolls through her phone. "But, you and me, we don't have the hook-ups to give us anything more to pregame with at the dorms. Hence..." She lifts her head as she tucks her phone into her clutch. "Why we, and every other invitee, are going to Chase's place early. Free booze."

After the scandal between Piper and Dr. Luke broke, the spine of Briarcliff's student manual cracked open, too. Professors referred to the rules constantly, be it for our curfew or what we could keep in our dorms. Random searches were reinforced, and the first time they were implemented, Thorne and Rose Houses had a *lot* of plumbing issues.

One thing the faculty couldn't revoke was the seniors' privilege to leave campus on weekends. Not if they didn't want a riot on their hands. They did, however, forbid any access to Lover's Leap and put up a new gate with barbed wire curling its metal thorns at the top.

I've only seen the cliff once, soon after Piper died. It starts with a natural clearing in the thicket of trees where students gathered, well away from the dropping off point. For Piper to have stepped so close to the edge, someone would've had to corner her and cause her to back up, her heels scraping against the forest ground until it turned to stone, then ... air.

I shiver at the thought.

"Cold?" Ivy asks.

"I'm good," I say, unfolding my denim jacket from my arm and sliding it on. "Though it's getting frosty."

"Yeah." Ivy glances up at the sky, where burnt orange tendrils are giving way to gray dusk. "It gets bitterly cold here, and soon. October's our last month of pretty."

Yael pulls up, and we both slide in, my dress hiking scarily high when I sit. I mutter a curse, but Ivy laughs, telling me I should showcase my jay-walker legs more often.

"Just because I'm a city girl," I say while elbowing her, "doesn't mean I can't be athletic."

"Oh, yeah? Join crew then."

"No way in hell."

"Figures." Ivy laughs.

Ivy's the only one who knows I can't swim. In a school surrounded by water, where the most popular sport is rowing, vacation homes are lake houses, and cliff faces jutting out into the ocean are the hot hookup spots, my lack of ability to tread water seems like a glaring weakness.

Do you like the way my face looks? a tiny voice whispers. Emma's. *Don't say their name, not if you don't want them to come after you...*

I pull my jacket tighter across my chest.

Ivy's my best friend. She may love to gossip, but when it comes to me, she's reliably mute. She doesn't talk about my mother's murder, despite having an unwanted first-row seat to the crime scene photos, and she's never brought up my inability to swim with anyone.

Relief lightens my chest when Ivy doesn't push the issue.

We arrive at Chase's lake house fifteen minutes later than when I was in his car. Yael slows at the beginning of the thin private drive, the paved roadway clogged with a line of luxury vehicles, most lazily parked without giving much thought to leaving space for other cars to nudge through.

I lean forward to the middle console. "It's okay, Yael. We can walk the rest of the way up."

"You sure?" he asks.

Ivy scoffs. "Speak for yourself."

She lifts a freshly shaved leg shining with moisturizer. A three-inch black heel caps off her outfit.

"It's a short walk," I say as I push the door open. "Come on."

"How do you know how far it is?" she asks but steps out on her side. Our doors slam at the same time.

Shit. I love how I was just thinking what good a friend Ivy is to me, and meanwhile, I'm hiding my meet-up with Chase like he's my dirty little secret.

At least it's a meet-up this time and not pornographic sex that made you blow your load the minute his tongue found your—

"Stupid voice," I mutter again.

"What's that?"

"Nothing." I grab Ivy's hand and we toddle up the drive.

I glance at Ivy, hobbling beside me but maintaining her good spirit as we toddle through cars and people, heading to the front.

My phone rings in my purse as the drive levels out and the lake house comes into view. At dusk, it's easier to appreciate the one-way planes of glass used for walls and the multiple levels of pointed roofs. The home is cabin chic meets million-dollar view, and Ivy unfurls her arm from mine, gaping at the structure.

"Go on in," I say to her, popping open my purse. "I'll find you."

"Don't have to tell me twice. Why did I avoid off-campus parties again?" Ivy asks, then flashes me a bright smile and joins another group heading inside, where music blasts and bottles clink.

AHMAR flashes on my screen when I pull my phone out.

"Hey," I say, tucking the phone between my shoulder and ear while wandering closer to the edge of trees. Someone turns the music up.

"Sounds like you're somewhere you shouldn't be," Ahmar says, but I hear the smile accompanying his words.

"My first weekend party experience. Wish me luck."

"You're the smartest kid I know. You don't need it." Ahmar pauses. "You know never to accept a drink you didn't make yourself, right?"

I huff out a laugh, but I don't miss the hesitation in his voice. He saw me at my worst. He held back my hair when I stumbled to his apartment at 4 AM, because I couldn't go home and face my stepdad, and coughed up vomit for hours. "Yes, Dad. I'm being good. Promise."

The name sounds more heartfelt than I intended, but if Ahmar senses it, he keeps it to himself. "I trust you, Calla. You paid your dues. So, what do you need from me?"

"Well…"

"Uh-oh. I sense hedging."

I pull my lips in, pressing down hard with my teeth, then decide to get it over with as fast as possible. "Could you find out if they've matched the DNA of the baby to anyone?"

Static pops on the other end of the line as I picture Ahmar shifting, wherever he is, clearly uncomfortable. "Calla..."

"I know. *I know*. It's a lot to ask, but it would clear up a lot. Did you hear about Dr. Luke?"

"Yeah, kid, I did, just this morning. I'm sorry. I wanted to call you to see how you're holding up, but—"

"You're on the job. I get it." And I do. "But that means you agree, right? Finding out the DNA of the baby would answer some serious questions."

"Sure, but you have to remember, the paternity of the fetus doesn't necessarily mean it's the perp's. And the vic—sorry, Piper —was only ten weeks along."

I press the phone harder to my ear. "You've been told how far along she was?"

A growl curse into my ear, then nothing.

"Ahmar?"

"Yes," he admits. "Calla, you're like a daughter to me. Even if you hadn't asked me to, I would've kept updated on this case. I've got to make sure you're not in danger by staying at that school."

Warmth encompasses my soul, a comforting blanket I haven't felt since leaving NYC over a month ago. "Thank you for keeping me safe. Now tell me what you know."

Ahmar gives a low, appreciative laugh, but his tone is serious. "The DNA results came back about a week ago."

I breathe in sharp, evergreen air, its pine needles spearing my lungs. I chance a look at the lake house, as if Chase would be standing near one of the massive windows, watching me.

"You ... you know who the father is?"

"It's partially why this teacher guy was let go. Where did you hear the news of his release, anyway?"

"Gossip. Friends. I don't know. Ahmar, *tell me*."

"Easy, kid. There was a match. It's no one you associate with."

While this should come as a comfort, Ahmar has no idea who I associate with at Briarcliff. He's ignorant to the boys, societies, and mean girls frequenting these grounds, and I'd like to keep it that way. I'd rather he think of me as reformed. An enterprising young student ready to take on the world with a world-class diploma, whose roommate happened to be killed in an accident.

Not as a girl deliberately immersing herself in the elite underworld to solve a murder.

"Can you give me a name?" I ask.

"That's confidential. You know how it works."

"But it's me you're talking to. My roommate was killed. Ahmar..."

He exhales, and I refuse to wince at the pang of guilt that hits when I know I've won.

"I'm already aware of the possibilities," I argue. "Dr. Luke or Chase. And if you're saying it's not Dr. Luke's..."

I realize my mistake too late.

"Chase, huh? Since when are you so familiar with that dude?"

"I ... he's well-known. By everybody. And he's Piper's ex. I'm only repeating what I hear, but maybe if a *reliable* source gave me information, I'd stop listening to gossip."

Ahmar chuckles. "I see what you did there."

"I'm begging you. Is it—"

"This Chase guy? No, it's not."

My chest cracks from the released pressure. I hold a hand to my heart, ensuring it's still beating.

"He's just well-known, huh?"

The dangerous edge to Ahmar's tone makes me grimace. "He's just a guy, Ahmar."

"A guy I gotta meet?"

"No. Definitely not."

"Mm."

It's easy to change the subject. "I don't understand. You said the DNA result was partially why Dr. Luke was released. So, it's not his, either?"

"Nope."

My hand stills in the middle of tucking my hair behind my ear. I frown into the copse of trees, noting the growing, cold shadows creeping onto the asphalt and over my feet.

"The DNA's been tied to a kid in the system. A boy named Joaquín del Pozo. Heard of him?"

My brows pull down, hard and low. "Not even a little bit."

"Exactly. That's the end of that. You don't know the dude. I did you a favor by giving you that name, and in return, do one for me."

Ahmar's talking, but his voice seems so far way, tinned and faint compared to the rush in my ears.

Who the *hell* is Joaquín del Pozo?

"Calla?"

"Yeah." I finish tucking my hair back. "I'm still here."

"This roommate of yours, Piper, it looks like she was involved with a few guys. Her death could be related to this boy, but it might not be. Because of that, I need you to stay back, okay? Let the police do their jobs, and run through their witness and suspect lists, as they've been doing. Are you listening?"

"Yeah," I say, my voice a whispery trace of its usual sound. "There's a process. I know that."

"I'm doing what I can behind the scenes, but I have my ear on this. Leave me in charge. Can you agree to that?"

His question is not a simple request. He remembers, as much as I do, how the weeks after my mother's death went. How I fell apart and screamed for him to arrest my stepdad, then, when that didn't work, turned to artificial mind-altering.

I respond quietly. "This isn't that, Ahmar."

"Not saying it is. But I'll never stop looking out for you."

I smile through the welling thickness in my throat. "I love you."

"I love you, too, kiddo. Now, go try to have some safe, wholesome high school fun. I got this."

We hang up, and I wiggle my phone back into a clutch chosen by Lynda that seems to only fit lip gloss, wrestling it shut.

An adult taking the reins—and a competent one at that—would usually have me feeling buoyant, secure, and hopeful. But ... there's so much Ahmar doesn't know.

I'm not sure how much I can tell him, because my confession would have to begin right here, with the boy I made a deal with. And if I divulge the DNA results to Chase, I have no doubt he'll stage a reaping until Joaquín is found. Then destroyed.

$\mathcal{T}$he lake house's front doorway—twice the size of normal entryways—is packed with bodies, shifting, drinking, hooting, hollering, all of it.

I'm amazed at the transformation of the Briarcliff elite, though it shouldn't come as a surprise that as soon as the uniform's stripped off and the weekend's pulled on, revelry ensues.

And ... a lot of belly buttons enjoy their freedom.

I duck under errant elbows and arms, alcohol-tinged droplets escaping from red Solo cups and landing on my shoulders and forehead, but I forge on. The music pushes through my soles and into my chest, a deep, rhythmic bass turning my heart into an 8-count thump.

First, I search for Ivy, but don't see her in the expansive main room. A ring of people surround the fireplace that crackles and spurts, nearby blunts and cigarettes finding the flame.

I look into the kitchen, but can't see Ivy through the throng, and I don't spot Chase, either.

Chase.

Smokey trails of relief float alongside the thought of his name.

The baby isn't his. He won't be pulled in for more questioning ... hopefully. And maybe, his anxiety can be eased over the unexpected loss of something so precious and fleeting in its existence.

Ahmar's warning battles for recognition, his urging to keep the revelation to myself and go on with my schooling like none of this ever happened.

If only, Ahmar, I think dully. *Except, I don't think I've been forged that way.*

An ice-cold rivulet presses into my arm, and I realize that during my musings, I've wandered to the back of the house and against the windows, so black during my first visit, now midnight blue with nightfall.

Branches frame the glass, most barren of leaves, and stretch to some point past my view. A lake glitters beneath a thin, vertical dock, and I picture Chase's silhouette seated at the end, dangling his feet into the fractured blue, his face tipped to the sky.

A *boom* of thunder has me jumping back from the window and staring up, wondering when storm clouds decided they wanted to join the party.

A guttural laugh warns me of an incoming clobbering before the guffawing guy slams into me, and I duck as he stumbles against the glass.

"Fuck, whoops!" he says, the features on his face more diagonal than is probably usual. He thrusts an arm in my direction, his cup sloshing. "Drink?"

"No, thank you."

"Ha! The possum's polite!" the buffoon hollers, then stumbles to his group of friends.

From this vantage point, I can see the packed room in its entirety. People mill, dance, and stumble, the music cranked to its highest level, and there's more spilled liquor than wood showing on the parquet floors.

Is this really Chase's kind of thing?

This doesn't resemble the sleek, deliberate boy I see in the halls of Briarcliff, nor does it describe the naked Adonis curved in my bed, murmuring dark promises in my ear.

Uncomfortable memories float within the drunken haze of my writhing classmates, sharpening the flashback of when I used to be this, free and drug-fueled and forgotten, preferring pills melting on my tongue and powder up my nose to the reality of my murdered mother.

Six months into it, there was an overdose scare involving Sylvie, and I haven't been up to no good since. I wish I could say it was my stepdad being written off as a suspect that made me change my ways and sober up once I realized the power my words could have over someone's life. But, with his innocence came a reckoning of a different sort: I was deemed unhinged. A liar. My voice became an intangible, cloudy mist dissipated with the swipe of a medical practitioner's hand.

Shuddering, I peel away from the windows in search of another room. I could wait out Ivy's fun and collect my thoughts. It'll give me time to sort through the revelation of Piper's third lover.

A darkened hall peeks out from the writhing, dancing bodies, and I carve a forward path, careful to avoid more spill-over. From my dress or people's drinks, I'm not sure, but I keep a forearm pressed to my boobs just in case.

Once I break from the weed-cloud, the empty space of the hallway fills me with oxygen. I breathe, glancing around, and walk farther in, my eyes trailing across professional portraits of Chase and his family.

When I come to a photo of the four of them, Emma seated beside Chase and their parents behind them, I stop.

"My God..." I murmur, my hand going to the picture before I can stop it. My fingers trail across one side of Emma's face—the former one, her cheekbones slim and sharp, exactly like her brother's.

Her eyes seem to shine through the photo and light up the hallway, her hair, a gorgeous cascade of copper-blonde waves, hiding her shoulders but putting her beauty on full display.

All their postures are stiff, the smiles composed and perfected for the photographer behind the lens. Even the navy blue and white of their outfits is deliberate, chosen to match the backdrop of the lake behind them. But Emma's smile lines are deeper than the rest. Her eyes are crinkled with private mirth, and she looks .... the happiest.

My attention moves to Chase, as gorgeous staged in a photo as he is in real life, but a *thump* behind the picture distracts me, my hand falling from the frame.

The music and shouts are quieter here, the party softer around the edges. I've drifted well into the hallway and a descending staircase is near my feet.

Another *thump*.

There's no door I can make out, so after a final glance behind my shoulder, I take the stairs leading down.

They descend deeper than I thought, considering the sprawling, two-story architecture of the lake house, and once I hit the last step, I move to the doorway beside it.

Another hallway forms within darkness—two actually. They're so black with shadow that I shy away from treading deeper, preferring the doorway I can see to the ones I don't.

Besides, I heard the thumps at the top of the staircase. Movement has to be coming from somewhere nearby.

I hesitantly push on the lever.

It briefly occurs to me that I could be interrupting a hook-up, but I can't find Ivy anywhere, or Chase, so I push the lever all the way down.

Hinges in this kind of house don't creak. The door swings open silently, and I step into the haunting blue glow of an office.

Indigo-purple light ripples over a wall of books, shelved all the way to the ceiling and guarded by a heavy, wooden desk. A plush, black leather chair sits empty, but swiveled to the side, as if someone just left it.

Curious, I walk over and press my palm into the seat, the warmth of a recent body seeping into my skin.

Another *thump* draws me straight, but I can't locate the sound. It's coming from in here, but it's ... not.

A large fish tank, nestled against the wall closest to the hall-way, draws my attention, and I pass behind the chair and lean forward, instinctually searching for the fish.

I don't see anything but white specks, floating within the water enhanced by blacklight.

"Don't you—"

"But I've tried—"

Thump.

"Try harder!"

My spine goes rigid, and I search the room, positive I hear voices. Both obscured and muffled, but one is easier to hear because of its lighter, feminine tones.

"Are you sure?"

A third voice, a female, joins the conversation.

"...last chance. Otherwise, I'm taking..."

"Tell her."

"No. Lie to her before she discovers the truth."

I force a single blink, long and hard, because I swear these voices are coming from behind the bookshelf, but there was no entry I could tell during my descent that would indicate a room beside this office.

I cock my ear, tucking my hair behind my ears and leaning closer to the books.

"Too close."

"She's uncovering—"

"—we have to go on the defense, not bring in an outsider—"

"She's NOT an outsider!"

"Shh! Look. There's someone..."

I reel back, scanning the ceiling for a vent or something that's allowing me to hear voices that have to be coming from the opposite side.

I splay my fingers across the books, the amateur sleuth inside me determined to find the source. I run my finger along the middle row, then the next, one below, then the ground-level shelving, the tomb raider in me now confident I'm about to uncover a secret room, unlocked by the hidden lever inside a book...

My breath hisses when my finger stalls on a leather-bound spine, creased and crumbling with age. It has no title, no author, but an insignia is stamped at the center in gold.

A perfect circle with raven's wings as its Eastern and Western points.

I pull it out, handling it carefully with both hands. The leather is aged and worn, the gold embossing faded, but I'm able to read the title.

Correction. I can read the name. *Daniel Abraham Stone.*

"You puking down there?"

My knees lock.

I recognize the relaxed cadence, equivalent to a lion licking his fangs before he strikes.

Footsteps round the desk, and I hurry to push the book back in its spot before large, calloused palms move under my arms to lift me.

"Easy, Callie." Chase says near my ear, goosebumps tingling across my neck. "My father vows ruin on anyone who messes up his office."

"I'm—I'm not sick," I say, once my voice fights through the rush of tingles. Man, I wish Chase would stop affecting me like I'm some giddy freshman about to screw the class senior president.

Chase turns me to face him. In the UV blacklight, his skin is lavender-blue and ethereal, like I've been captured by a Faerie Prince.

Ugh. Stop relating him to dark fairy tales. Chase is a guy. A regular dude.

With abs and a pert butt I could bounce a coin off.

Chase searches my face, his stare heating my cheeks. "Then why are you here?"

"Looking for you."

"You found me." His lips close and curve with a smile, but my brows grow tight. I'm certain of the sadness within his grin.

The same expression when he left a few weeks ago, seconds after I told him that Piper was pregnant.

Chase's eyes slide away from mine, and his gaze moves past my shoulder and to the fish tank. "You know what those are?"

"I heard voices," I blurt out instead of answering. "But there's no room they could be coming from."

Chase ignores me, stepping around, but stays close, my nose following the drift of his cologne as he moves. "These are some of the smallest, most venomous jellyfish in the world. Irunkandji, they're called. Their sting is one hundred times worse than a cobra's. They can cause instant brain hemorrhages in humans."

I hedge backwards. "Cool pet."

Chase grunts, his attention on the aquarium. "They're rare, illegal to own, and incredibly fragile, yet my father has them flown in and replaced. Constantly. "

"All that fuss, and they're not even that pretty to look at."

This time, a genuine smile crosses Chase's profile. "So, did you sneak down here so you could learn about the Irunkandji?"

"I told you. I heard thumps and voices, and following them brought me down here." I point to the bookshelf. "Do you have a Chamber of Secrets back there?"

"Is that one of your two questions?"

I jolt, then suck in my lower lip. It's amazing how a little news like Piper having a third secret lover derailed me from my initial goal of pumping Chase for information.

I stare at him hard. I *want* to know where those voices were coming from. "Yes."

He turns away from the tank and angles his head toward the shelving, murmuring, "There's a room. Yes."

My answering expression must amuse him, because he adds, "I promised you the truth. Did you think I'd lie outright?"

"Um. Yep."

He chuckles, leaning a hip against his father's desk, which probably weighs more than an elephant. "I don't make deals for kicks."

"Can you—?"

"Think carefully about how willing you are to waste your next question," he says. "Because, no, I won't show you how to get in, or tell you what kind of room it is."

I grumble, but my mind's already recalibrating. *He won't tell me because it has to do with the Cloaks. And our deal prevents me from getting any information about them.*

I flit my gaze back to Chase and see a reluctant admiration there. He knows where my mind has gone, and that his lack of an explanation equals an answer.

"Fine. Then tell me why a prep school would have a secret society."

Chase sighs and lifts off the desk. "We agreed none of your questions would involve your Cloaks."

"And this one doesn't," I say. "I'm merely asking for your theory on *why* a high school might have a secret society, since most of those cults start in college."

He grunts and crosses his arms. "Cults."

"Prove me wrong." I mirror his posture. "And explain it to me in hypothetical terms."

Chase's eyes glimmer in the shadows.

He exhales, his focus moving to the bookshelves behind me.

My concentration becomes a hawk's, anticipating that his attention will go to the leather-bound book with the raven's insignia.

Any tell, however small, will lead me closer to unlocking this mystery. I just *know* it.

"Perhaps," Chase begins, and I snap to attention, shocked he might actually answer me, "the founder of that school created it as a way to both fund and propel certain qualifying students to prestigious colleges, with the intention of placing them into certain careers."

"Like politics, government, top corporations," I say. "Economic influencers."

After a long exhale, Chase casts his gaze to the ceiling. "What a shocking Secret Society rumor you've uncovered. I keep telling you, there's nothing here. Just benign, old-century tradition."

"Yes, but unlike the Illuminati or ... I don't know ... the Knights Templar, Briarcliff didn't start with adults. They wanted their influence to sink into *children*."

Chase vaults off the desk, framing either side of my head with his arms as he presses his palms into the bookshelf behind me.

The backs of my shoulders press into the books, the scent of stale pages wafting over our bodies. I gasp, furious at how loud it is, but I don't cower.

Chase lowers his head, his eyes coming dangerously close to a glittering explosion. "You're in high school. Do you consider yourself young and impressionable?" He angles his head. "How about me?"

Chase presses a thumb to my lips, the hardened, rower's blisters cutting into the soft tissue, but I let him drag my lower lip down. I allow him to watch when his thumb hits my chin and my lower lip bounces back into place.

He shifts, the front of his pants skimming across my stomach, the hard length of him proving how much this stare-down is costing him.

Costing me.

A guttural moan builds in my throat, almost reaching my lips, but I swallow it down.

Sadly, my hips aren't nearly as compliant, and they push against him in a half-circle of lust.

I've missed him.

I've dreamed about the moment when I could have him again, physically and virulently, without thought of recourse.

But these have to be my hormones. The unquenchable sex drive Chase awoke inside me. It's not real life. It definitely doesn't resolve the endless questions, circling in my head like an unkindness of ravens.

I want to get out of here with my heart intact.

"You know who's responsible," I dare to whisper near his lips. "Who's hiding behind these books? What don't they want discovered?"

"I believe," he responds, low and under his breath, "you've exhausted your questions for the day."

Chase doesn't step back. The space between us grows smaller and hotter the longer our eyes duel, and I'm about to crumble, licking my lips at the remembered taste of him, my thighs trembling at the thought of his fingers, then his tongue, inside me.

Chase ducks down, my chin tilts up, and damn me to hell, I'm ready for him to kiss me.

10

*C*hase's hands move from the shelf to my hips, his face so close to mine, I feel the curl of his lips as he unleashes a hopeless snarl—

"Am I interrupting something?"

The feminine voice might as well be buckshot. Chase and I dive apart, but my muscles are too puddly with untapped passion. I fall back against the bookshelf on a heavy exhale.

Chase spins, slamming his palms on the desk and tipping his head to the person who caused the interruption.

Addisyn.

She stands at the doorway, a languid hand resting on her hip, but the rest of her is stiff with judgment.

"Get out."

Chase's demand is practically a whisper, but it's succinct.

Addisyn's jaw locks at the same time her eyes flash, but she stews for only a moment. "Moving on so fast, Chase?" Her gaze flicks to me. "You can do better than this."

"It's none of your business what I do. I said get out."

Addisyn shifts her weight. "I came down here because everyone's looking for you. There's a party going on without a host."

"Like you give a damn," he mutters.

"I give a lot of damns about appearances." Again, Addisyn cuts her eyes to me. "And you should, too, Chase. My mom just texted. Remember how we were told Piper was pregnant before she died?" Addisyn's eyes shine with tears, pronounced by the purple-blue light encasing this office. "Or have you already forgotten?"

Chase bows his head, the rigidity of his shoulders loosening with grief. "No. I haven't."

"Mom just texted," Addisyn repeats. "The baby wasn't Dr. Luke's."

My vision sharpens on Addisyn. I glance between the two of them, bracing for the knowledge Addisyn's about to impart.

Chase looks back at me, those seconds silently communicating our agreement and what I had promised him.

What I failed to deliver the very moment I saw him.

I frown. Why do I feel bad for him?

As if with a nudge, the book with the raven engraving spears against my calf. I imagine heat emanating from it, steamy tendrils of illicit knowledge circling my ankle.

This is Chase Stone. The guy who hides everything, has everything, and shares his secrets only through deals befitting his needs.

He knows about the Nobles and deliberately cuts me out of it. I'm certain he's aware of the sign of the raven and what it means.

It's how we were first introduced, after all.

Yet, I feel sorry for him when his expression crumbles upon hearing Addisyn's news, before he sets it into his famous Stone scowl. "I didn't get the update."

"Well, there you have it," Addisyn says, her voice growing thick. "It's not his, so it has to be yours."

Chase rubs a hand down his face. "This isn't the place. We can talk about this tomorrow."

"We'd better." Addisyn lowers her chin, shadows creating

deeper indents in the purple crescents under her eyes. "Because you have a lot to atone for. You know you do."

"Yes." Chase doesn't hesitate in his agreement.

It's not yours, I want to blurt. I have the impulsive, desperate urge to smooth the bulging tendons in his neck, to take his face in my hands and whisper the truth, lightening his shoulders and his mind.

I peel off the yearning, but its sour onion peels stick to my skin. No matter what I say, Chase will always have darkness inside him. By refusing to tell me about the Cloaks, he protects them, and if Rose Briar's secret letter is anything to go by—a letter Piper was the first to find—these people don't deserve protection.

Addisyn flicks her attention to me, but only long enough to ensure I note how much she despises my presence, then turns on her heel, the sounds of her shoes hitting the stairs fading as she ascends.

I'm so focused on the empty doorway, gnawing my lip at the thought that Ahmar provided me with information the police hadn't even released to the family yet, that I don't sense Chase's whirl until he's inches away, burying his fist in the row of books by my head.

"God*damnit!*" he shouts, then pounds again.

I flinch, but don't retreat.

"Fuck fuck *fuck!*" He beats the shelving again and again, turning to ripping the books from the shelves and scattering them across the floor.

One flies against the fish tank, and I yelp, terrified that those angry things will flow out from shattering glass and search for one last sting before they die.

"Chase." I grab his arm, so hot, hardened, and rough, I have to convince myself I'm clasping skin and not the scales of a dragon. "Chase, stop."

He spins on me with a roar, his teeth bared. "She had my *baby* inside her, Callie."

"You don't—"

"She was at Lover's Leap that night, drinking, smoking, snorting. Did I tell you that? She was at our party and didn't give a fuck if she was pregnant."

"There's still so much unanswered," I say, aiming for calm. "She wasn't that far along. At ten weeks, she might not have known she was pregnant."

Chase lunges for the wall, heaving books, punching wood, and I dance back but can't avoid everything. The corner of one hits my thigh, and I cry out.

Chase's arms drop to his sides. "Shit. Callie." He comes up beside me, leading me to the office chair.

"It's fine," I grit out. "I've never been Charlie-horsed by a law book before, but turns out, those fuckers *hurt*."

He lowers enough for his hands to grip the chair's arms as he watches me massage my thigh. "I wasn't thinking. I'm so s..." He looks down at the floor. "Wait. Ten weeks?"

Shit.

I bite my lip, but don't meet his eyes, instead focusing on rubbing the pain out of my leg.

"Callie."

My name, used as a warning many times before by many different voices, has never sounded so ominous.

"Ahmar got back to you, didn't he?"

"Kind of," I admit, but barely. "I spoke to him maybe an hour ago. They've narrowed down the weeks she was pregnant, yes."

Chase does the math, then bows his head, his silky strands brushing the tip of my nose. "Then it really is mine."

My hand comes up to cup his cheek, the stubble clinging to my palm. "No."

The word is out before I want it to be. I couldn't have stopped it if I tried. He's suffering, and I can't, in good conscience, use the DNA as a weapon for more information about the Cloaks.

It's too cold a maneuver. Too calculating. And the deeper I get into this mess, the more I'm certain that I'm not like these people.

I can expose their games, but I can't play them.

His hand covers mine, squeezing before he lifts his head and meets my eye. "What do you mean, 'no'?"

I swallow. "It belongs to someone named Joaquín del Pozo."

Chase's eyes harden into opaque marbles. He says, with the roughest edge to his voice, "Who. The fuck. Is that."

"I have no idea."

"And why didn't you tell me as soon as you saw me?" His composure cracks, and I don't know whether to embrace him or run. "Callie, do you know what this has *done* to me?"

I nod, lifting from the chair. Chase falls back to give me space, a surprising move on his part. "I'm telling you now, Chase. I've only found out myself. It wasn't like I was hiding it from you—"

"But you wanted to know about your Cloaks, first," he sneers. "Asking me some bullshit about recruitment in high school, and hidden rooms, because they're more important than me knocking up a girl who's now dead, right?"

His tone strikes like a whip, its spiked tail searing my chest. "Don't do that—don't say I'm trying to toy with you, because I gave you the name *knowing* that I can't play your games. I could've held onto the name, tried to see if I could get more information from you—"

"So, you thought about it." Chase's mouth twists. "Using my fear as some kind of weapon to make me do as you please."

"That's precisely what I *didn't* do."

"What would you have done if Addy hadn't come in here? Would you have kept that powerful little nugget to yourself? Become one of my family's many enemies and exploit me?" Chase corners me, backing me up against the emptied-out bookcase, a few missed texts lying flat against the shelves. They tremble when my back slams into the wood.

Chase exhales, brushing his nose against mine, coaxing my chin up. Invisible strings of lust tilt my head, my lips automatically angling to meet his.

Energy, both pissed-off and hot, sparks between us, blanketing my mind from the dangerous consequences and urging me toward satisfaction. Passion blinds me, just as rage blackens him to soot. We can do what we're known for—screw our angst out of our systems and fuck our worries away.

Oh, how I want to.

"You look so fucking hot in that dress."

He dips his hand between my thighs, my legs spreading of their own accord. My breaths turn heavy, his tongue playing along the center of my lower lip, but when I dart to catch him, he jerks away, yet his fingers circle closer.

Chase nudges the tip of my nose, his lips brushing against my skin when he says, "You're right, sweet possum. I'm better than you at getting what I want."

Cold air blasts over my front when Chase retreats on a snarl, and I'm treated to a terrible apathy that crosses his expression as he backs away.

"How does it feel to be played?" he asks me.

I pull my lips in and clamp down hard in an attempt not to cry.

I'm not cut out for this. For him.

Digging my fingers in my hair at the base of my neck, hot and damp from adrenaline and desire, I say, "You're hurt, Chase. And I'm sorry. But can't you, for one second, believe that my digging into the Cloaks is for you and Piper?"

Chase growls and strikes. I dodge to the side, terrified of the cold mask he's slipped on his face, but his movement isn't to charge or trap me. He bends down, pulling the raven engraved book from its spot and tossing it at me.

I fumble to catch it against my chest, blurting out—

"You want more on your fucking Nobles? There," Chase snarls, but he's not done.

He pulls a handful of hardcovers from the middle shelf and throws them over his shoulder, the tombs thumping against the desk and carpeted floor with a heavy, accelerated charge. Delicate spines crack. Hardbound leather dents.

I look from the mess back to Chase in time to see his palm slam against a button that was hidden behind the books, and the wall of shelving sinks in before sliding back.

I gasp, the leather-bound book held in my clutches, as a heavy, metal door is revealed, a security panel at its center.

Chase pushes past me, enters a code, and that door *beeps* and slides open, too.

A single room, cold and sterile, comes into view, a simple couch, a metal kitchenette, and a row of small TVs of cameras lighting up under the automatic floodlights in the ceiling.

"There," Chase spits so close to my ear, I flinch. "A panic room. In case my family is robbed and some of us are inside the home. This is where we're supposed to go." He gestures toward it sharply. "By all means, look around, Callie. Search for ancient textbooks or cloaks in the closet, or hell, fucking underwear Piper left behind. Do all the detective work you want. I'm done."

"But I ... I heard voices," I say.

"This house is brimming with people." Chase scoffs. "You heard nothing but your own paranoia."

The hurt, when it comes, hits my heart with a *splat*. Only Chase is aware of my wrongful accusation and what my misguided convictions did to my stepdad's and my relationship. How I questioned my own sanity afterward.

And it's only Chase who would use it to effectively shut me up.

But pain claws through his composure. It's in the stiffness of his pose and way he curls his fingers at his sides. It builds against the tension in his clenched jaw. Most of all, his eyes shine with barely contained injustice, and he pins it on me before turning away.

I spring forward and try to catch him before he leaves. "Chase, wait."

He pauses at the door, his profile still in shadow. "You can have all the conspiracy theories you want. But this is my *life* being dicked around with. That baby was mine until you told me it wasn't."

I wince.

He adds, with the softness of a snake moving through the grass, "Piper's manipulations beyond the grave are enough of a mess to clean up. I don't need you taking her place."

"Chase—"

But he's gone, and I'm left in the rubble of my own creation.

11

J collect myself enough to exit the office. Music reaches in and pulses inside my skull the higher I ascend, the party more raucous and disjointed than when I left.

Limbs fly in drunken dance interpretations, some choosing smaller crowds along the edges to laugh and chug with. I pass by a keg stand, where someone is being held upside down and told to *drink, drink, drink!* and I wish, so much, to take part in the senior life, to get drunk and do drugs and have sex in an unfamiliar bedroom ... acts the old Callie would've been happy to oblige in.

I'm not her anymore. I'm a broken semblance of myself who seeks out mystery as a healing savior, when all it really does is chip more pieces off, adding to the crumble of ashes on the floor.

A flash of sequined purple draws my attention, and I cross the designated dance floor and find Ivy leaning against the fireplace, laughing as Riordan whispers something in her ear.

"Ivy!" I call over the music. "Hey."

She giggles while she trails her hand up Riordan's bare forearm, and I think: *Well, this is new.*

Ivy catches sight of me when I'm practically on top of her. "Callie! You came!"

"Yeah, I came with you, remember?"

My reasoning is pointless, because Ivy, the sweet girl, is drunk off her ass.

She fixes her eyes on mine for a millisecond before they drift off. "This is so fun, isn't it? Why don't I come to more of these?"

I laugh, shifting the black leathered book to one arm while reaching for her with the other. "Because you can't handle your liquor."

Riordan's expression grows mischievous as he chucks under her chin. "She's handling it just fine."

Riordan is the one friend of Chase's I can't get a proper read on. James is easy. He's the guy with all the jokes, using the comedic relief to probably hide a lonely childhood as the sole kid of two power-hungry parents who are more loyal to their international obligations than what they've left behind in their blood.

Tempest is as his name defines—a gray, brooding storm bearing down on those who dare to show joy around him. He's quiet, assessing, and when he speaks, it's with cruel purpose. And Chase is ... Chase. Mysterious. Hardened. Experienced and, when pushed, brimming with embers of anger he works hard to temper.

I'm guessing Riordan falls somewhere in the middle. Not funny, not sociopathic, but likely the weakest of the four, because I've never seen him participate in the follies of his friends that cement their rule over Briarcliff. Only film them.

Riordan tucks Ivy under his arm, laughing at something she's said and staring at her with a strange sincerity that's missing from the rest of these boys.

Am I confusing weakness with kindness? Is that what I've come to?

I reach for Ivy. "C'mon, let's go home."

Riordan angles himself to block my view as he tightens his arm around Ivy's waist. "I'll watch over her."

"Uh, thanks, but there's something called girl code."

"Callie, it's cool. Rio and I, we're ... hanging out," Ivy says, working hard to blink me into focus.

"That's great, but I don't trust him for shit," I say.

Rather than be insulted, Riordan's dark eyes dart to what I have in my hands. He asks, with a buttery purr and hardened eyes, "What's that?"

I hold the book snug to my chest. "I'm borrowing it from Chase."

His stare narrows. "With his permission?"

Too late, I realize my fingers haven't properly covered the insignia.

"Yes, not that I need yours on top of it," I reply.

Riordan's hand drops from Ivy's waist. She mewls in protest, stroking his chest to retain his attention, but he shakes her off, his attention never straying from the book.

"Hey." I bristle on behalf of my friend. He steps closer. "Back off."

The sharp stones of the fireplace dig into my back, but instead of serving as a warning, it pisses me off. This is the *second* time I've been backed into a corner tonight, and I'm not here for it anymore.

I grit out, as Riordan's shadow passes over my body, "Unless you want a knee to the balls, step *back*."

"Rio, come on." Ivy giggles in an attempt to lighten the growing storm cloud above us. "It's just a stupid old book." She hooks his elbow and pulls, but Riordan doesn't so much as twitch. "What's the big deal?"

Riordan's glare won't stray from mine. "I think you know how important that is, and how much you shouldn't have it."

"Chase gave it to me." I notch my chin up. He may have thrown it at me in a rage after tearing up his dad's office to prove his point that my meddling is fucking up his life, but Chase *did* give it to me. "I'm not lying."

Riordan cocks his head. "Give. It. To. Me."

Why did I ever think this guy was the weakest of the bunch? He's stronger than I am.

Gripping the book, I move to step around him, but Riordan's hand flashes out, tearing the hardback from my grip before I can so much as gasp out, "Hey—!"

He tosses it into the fireplace, red and gold sparks spiraling up the chute as hungry flames eat away the dried, leathery flesh.

"No!" I cry at the same time Ivy yells out something to Riordan.

My answers are in there!

The key to the secret societies that Chase literally lobbed at my head as a finality to our deal is burning to ash.

I'll never know.

I'll never understand.

I'll never discover what the raven means.

In the span of a second, such dreaded certainty shrouds my shoulders that my stomach clenches with the sudden rush of acidic bile.

If I don't do something, any connection to Piper's uncovering of secret Briarcliff writings and her death will turn to unreadable ash.

I'll be labeled unreliable again. A liar. A fool. Chase's last expression before he stormed out of his father's office will forever be etched on his face whenever he looks in my direction.

Don't let it be for nothing.

I leap toward the hissing flames.

In my periphery, I register Ivy grappling with Riordan, her lips peeled back as she tries to get to me first, to stop—

But my hand has already plunged into the fire.

12

A lightning bolt sears up my arm, fraying nerves and singeing skin, but I bat the book out of the flames, a crumbling skeleton of its former self skidding across the parquet floor and leaving streaks of black soot in its wake.

Someone cuts the music.

"Are you *fucking insane*?" Riordan roars, but I rush over to the book, holding its delicate pages to my chest and pushing into the crowd rather than respond.

The growing half-circle of witnesses eagerly step aside, unsure what to make of a chick who dives into fire as a party trick.

Falyn separates herself from the crowd. "Was it worth it?" she hisses in my ear as I shove forward.

Willow steps out to block my path, palming my shoulders and sending me stumbling back.

"To look so mentally disturbed in front of the entire school?" Falyn continues. She searches the crowd with overdramatic flair. "Uh-oh. Looks like your knight in shining armor is nowhere around to save you this time. What was so important you had to rake yourself over coals to get to it? I would've happily lit your ass on fire for you."

I twist in a protective maneuver. The movement makes the tightening, blistering skin on my hand burn to an almost unbearable level. "It's not like there was a fire poker lying around." I take a moment to look her up and down. "Chase must've thought to put all safety hazards away before allowing his dumb bitches off the leash."

Falyn's mouth falls open in an *O* of shocked fury.

Well. If I wanted to leave unobstructed, I've pretty much screwed up that goal. But *ugh*, Falyn gets to me in ways Piper never did.

Piper at least had reason to hate me, petty as it was. I took her room and unknowingly prevented her from meeting Dr. Luke without any prying eyes.

Falyn inherited Piper's hate, but it's like she's not quite sure where to source it from. Maybe, at first, it was because she thought I killed her best friend. But that's all over now, despite Dr. Luke walking free. I've never been near Lover's Leap, and a part of her knows it.

Not that it matters. All Falyn understands is, she needs to be mean in Piper's place.

"Stop, before you make a bigger fool of yourself," Riordan says as he steps into view, Ivy tottering after him. He hungrily eyes the book's remnants in my arms but pulls out his phone and starts tapping.

"Aw," I say, but my voice shakes with both pain and humiliation. "Are you telling Daddy on me?"

"Someone has to get you under control," he mumbles. "Might as well be your keeper."

My jaw drops in outrage. I'm nobody's *problem*. Indignation stings the back of my eyes.

"How dare you," I seethe. "All I want is to escape you bastards—"

Before I can finish, Willow shoves me again. This time, I spear her with my elbow, clipping her boob. She stumbles away with a cry.

Falyn settles a disdainful glance on her friend, but easily dismisses her, preferring the easier mark that everyone's staring at. She says, with saccharine venom between her teeth, "Oh, honey, it makes sense that you'd want to earn sympathy points by becoming a burn victim, but sadly, that role is already taken in Chase's life. Now you're just a waste of skin that poor Emma could be using."

Shock jolts through me faster than singeing my flesh against flame. Emma was Falyn's friend before the accident. How *could* she?

"Say that one more time."

The whispered warning stalks through the crowd before I breathe a word.

"But louder."

The crowd parts, revealing Chase.

He knifes through, stopping just short of me, but his vision is centered on Falyn. He stares at her with brown eyes so bright, he must be calling upon the forest around him to emit such vicious energy.

"By all means, expand upon my sister's pain." Chase offers a predatory grin, licking the top row of his teeth at the expectant bite. "Then, we'll see how well you'll fare after that."

Falyn blanches under his stare, but unfortunately, doesn't stay quiet. She points at me. "Did you see what the crazy bitch did? If you want to fuck someone over for insulting Emma's name, look to her. She's the one playing in the flames, thinking she won't get burned."

"I thought I told you, what Callie does is none of your business," Chase says.

Riordan joins the conversation, and points. "Did you really give her that?"

"Guys," Ivy says, holding out her hands. She waits a beat while all eyes turn to her, giving a single, slow bat of her eyelids while centering her balance. She lifts her finger at me. "I'm pretty sure my bestie needs a hospital."

So many fingers. Pointing at me. I scan the faces behind them, and the faces behind *them*, all staring, a mixture of awe, mirth, and horror. A few phones pop up above heads, camera light on.

I'm barren. Adrift. Exposed.

"If you're taking such responsibility for her," Falyn sneers, but her voice sounds muffled and far away. "Then explain to your sister why you've decided to fuck a pyro while her burns are still healing—"

"Screw you, Falyn—"

"Fuck, Chase, why have you given Callie access—"

A keening tremble spreads inside my chest until my entire body silently quakes.

"Burn harder, next time, possum..."

"—the bitch dives in after it like she's the fucking Dragon Queen—"

"I'm trying to save you from the biggest mistake of your life—"

"We're elite for a reason. We don't defend pathetic school transfers..."

"You have your orders. Your obligation is over. Let her stake herself in a burning woodpile for all I care..."

Possum. Bitch. Pathetic. Mistake. Obligation.

"Callie, is what they're saying true? Are you sleeping with Chase?"

The last voice, light and sweet, has me blinking out of my fugue, and I lock onto Ivy.

She teeters toward me, yet her expression exudes sobriety after asking the question.

But her perfume's too strong, the colors of her dress suddenly too loud, and burning pain, so hot it's turning my fingers into nubs of blue fire, won't stop pulsing its distress within my skull.

There are so many watching. So few of them care.

Riordan has the time to spit out, "Just fuck her and leave her, the way you were supposed to," before a savage, piercing wail splits through the room.

The small part of my mind that's removed itself from the situation realizes it's coming from me.

My lips are stretched wide on a scream, so loud, so brutal and rough, that I've silenced both the argument and the room.

Hush weaves around me like a blanketing mist, and I glance from face to face, backing up, skittering forward in the meager circle of space they've allowed.

Chase blinks at me, the first show of surprise I've ever seen in him, while the rest gape.

Ivy takes a hesitant step. "Callie…"

"*Let me leave!*" My voice is shredded paper, a nest of hornet stings, eroded rocks rubbed raw from saltwater.

Falyn clutches Willow in stunned horror, and they both dance to the side when I dart toward them. I use those few seconds of their dumbfounded shock to sweep past.

Riordan attempts to say, "Don't let her—"

"Shut the fuck up." Chase's tone is deadly. Final.

I stumble out the door, turning my back on them before the moonlight can illuminate my tear-streaked cheeks.

13

*U*sing my good hand, I call the Briarcliff chauffeur service, enduring the extended wait by crossing my arms around the book—holding my burned hand closest to my chest—and jumping from foot to foot to keep warm. Ivy doesn't come after me. Chase doesn't track me down. I'm left alone to stew or recover. I've yet to decide which one.

My cheeks are sticky with the half-frozen saltwater of my tears, but I've stopped crying, choosing to quell my upset into an inner trembling instead. Sobs will get me nowhere. Breaking down will make me fall. If my goal is to uncover Briarcliff's trove of secrets, I can't keep losing it around Chase, or his friends, or the school.

I swipe a hand across my eyes and find the positive. If anything, my freak-out will serve as a handy distraction while I continue to get to the bottom of things.

After twenty minutes pass, Yael rolls up, and I dive into the back seat without a word.

He takes stock of me through the rearview but remains professionally silent as he drives me to the dorms.

Charred leather scrapes against my fingers as I carefully lay the book on my lap, resisting the urge to begin reading it under pale moonlight and Yael's mixture of scrutiny and concern.

The knowledge between these pages is both the source of my misery and the match lighting my power. I gave up a lot to keep this in my clutches. Trust. Pride. Skin.

Please, mysterious raven book, be worth it.

When Yael pulls up to Thorne House, I murmur a thank you and step out.

"Promise me you'll get that looked at?" Yael asks softly from the front seat.

I glance down at my hand, my fingers curled against my cleavage, the wounded flesh desperate for both the warmth of my chest and the frigid coolness of the October night.

"It's not that bad," I reply.

Yael snorts. "You don't have to put on an act with me. I know how it goes around here. When that wound really starts screaming, at least go to the nurse in the morning, okay? My wife won't forgive me if I don't make sure you're all right. If my daughter left a party all disheveled and hurt, without her parents nearby..."

The heartfelt concern in Yael's tone causes a tortuous lump in my throat. I'm caving at his concern—the first show of in-person, grown-up worry I've received since coming here—and dying at the thought that I *have* no parents at the same time. Any daughter-like relationship with my stepdad, I ruined with two, self-destructing words: *It's him.*

"Thank you, Yael," I manage to croak out before shutting the passenger door. I lean down into his window that he's since rolled open. I manage a shaky smile. "Tell your wife not to worry. I'll see the nurse in the morning."

Yael nods, the lines around his mouth smoothing. "You need to go anywhere tomorrow, you know who to ask."

"I do," I say, and to his shock, reach out to squeeze his hand resting on the steering wheel. "Your concern means a lot."

"Ah, kiddo," he sighs, and my heart *twangs* at his use of

Ahmar's affectionate term. "Not everybody gets out of this place unscathed."

He rolls up his window as I retreat, and I give one last wave before entering Thorne House, fumbling one-handed with my clutch for my student ID.

Our shared area is dark when I step into Emma's and my dorm room, not that I expect her to be awake and cracking open beer cans while holding a party on Saturday night.

The question of why she wasn't at the lake house pops into my head, but I dismiss it just as quickly. No way Emma would want to immerse herself in that kind of crowd, with every room at a party-goer's mercy the drunker and hornier they got.

Well. Not *every* room.

I blink from the vision of the Stone panic room, so sure it was a hidden entry into ... what? Secret Society headquarters?

Jesus, I really need to think before I spew my theories into the universe—no, into *Chase's* universe.

I've really fucked it up with him, but I can't linger too long on that thought, either.

Laying the book on the kitchen countertop, I think of how much I've ruined by keeping it in my possession. All those questions I'd bartered for Chase to answer this week? There's no chance in hell he'll be willing to give me information now.

I set that thought aside, too. At this rate, my mind will become such a blank slate, even robots will envy it, and *oh*, how I wish that could be true.

The inner light of the freezer casts its glare directly into my eyes, and I wince as I claw around for a handful of ice to put in a hand towel.

"Do you mind?" Emma snaps behind me. "A starving cat makes less noise at this time of night."

Still halfway into the freezer, I peer over my shoulder. She stands just outside her doorway, her glowering silhouette illuminated by the soft lamplight behind her.

I straighten, moving fast to drop the ice into the towel before my good hand becomes my frostbitten hand.

"Sorry," I say. "This is all I needed. I'll be in my room."

I press the hastily made icepack to the burn starting at the outer edges of my pinky finger and moving down to my wrist. When the cloth contacts my skin, I wince and curse.

Emma hisses in a breath. "What is that?"

Her stare bores into my hand.

"Nothing. Just..." *shoved my hand into an active fireplace to save an unknown text...* "an accident."

She comes closer, her eyes carving a path for her strides, and grasps my wrist.

"Hey—ow!" I whine, but it only makes Emma inspect it closer.

She whispers, "You've burned yourself."

"Yeah, I got too close to the fireplace at the lake house. Don't know what I was thinking, sitting by the hearth."

Emma's gaze flicks up, her familiar, coppery brown eyes searching my hazel ones. She utters two words, and they stick to the base of her throat. "Don't lie."

I stiffen. Against my better judgment, the professional photo I saw of her interposes onto her face, my vision combining the two, the darkness of the kitchen making it easier to pretend to see the old Emma. She still has the same cheekbones, though now they harbor the twisting vines of pinkish scars. She has the same straight, pert nose, the same Cupid's bow lips. Her hair has kept its burnished gold, but it's dulled by lack of care.

For the first time, I wonder if the scars left on her body are but a glimpse of the mutilation she suffered inside her mind.

Without releasing my wrist, she flips the light switch by the door, bathing us in halogen light. I blink at the sudden brightness, but Emma's unaffected. She jerks her chin at the book I've left on the counter. "Do you have a lie for that, too?"

"No, I ... well, I didn't steal it. I can tell you that much."

She spends a few seconds studying the book's jacket—or what's left of it—but I cannot, for the life of me, read her expression. Daniel Stone's name is obscured and melted to ash, but does she know it's her father's? That it was in his study? Is she mad I have it?

Her attention snaps to my wrist with such predatory precision, I have to resist the urge to yank my hand away.

"You shouldn't put ice on a second-degree burn," she says, twisting my hand until I expose my inner wrist. "It could cause tissue damage."

A rush of guilt flows into my stomach. What am I doing, showcasing my minor burn to a girl who was trapped in a fire? "Really, you don't have to—"

"Tap water or cool compresses only," she interrupts. "No sprays, no Vaseline, because that will cause the skin to burn hotter. And don't pop any blisters, either, even though you'll want to. You'll cause an infection."

"Emma..."

"Put your hand under running water." Emma pulls me to the sink and turns on the faucet. She doesn't look at me when she says, "Wait here. I have stuff."

"Thank you."

I don't know what else to say, but Emma doesn't give me an opportunity to expand, anyway. She scurries into her room, and I spin to face the sink, listening to the opening and shutting of drawers as she moves around.

Emma returns, sits me at one of our—new—stools by the counter, and wordlessly cleans and dresses my wound.

We must spend at least fifteen minutes together in silence, but I don't feel the need to cut it with sound. Her movements are soothing, her touches delicate and light, her hands moving with grace and confidence, her full focus on my hand.

I stare at the crown of her head for a while, then watch her wrap my hand with sterile gauze, and I wonder, with a surprising ache, whether the nurses and doctors handled her with the same care that she's showing me.

Don't feel sorry for her, that deep, inner voice of mine reminds. *She set the fire. Chase told you, remember?*

Yes, but she was attacked, first. Her scars aren't solely from burns.

As if sensing my deeper study, Emma sits back, propping my arm at the elbow and raising my hand. "Keep this elevated for an hour or so. It'll help with swelling."

"I ... I don't know how to thank you," I say, my voice sounding strangely weak after not using it for a while. Then I remember— oh yeah, I screamed it to shreds about an hour ago.

"Then don't." Emma stands, cleaning up her first aid kit and washing her hands. She turns as she's drying them, her gaze straying to the book.

I'd known it was sitting there. I felt its proximity like licking flames, though it emits no heat. I'm desperate to dive in, to carefully turn each page and figure out the sign of the raven.

I gather the courage to say, "Emma, about the library earlier—"

"If information on the Nobles is what you're after, you'll find it in that. It's my father's rule book."

My brows jump in surprise.

Amusement glitters in Emma's stare, but it's gone too soon. "Don't tell me you dove into fire for something you knew nothing about?"

I frown at my bandaged hand. "That obvious, am I?"

"Doesn't take a genius to see a burned book—that wasn't barbecued when I last saw it—with a burned hand, and put the two together."

"Yeah." I chew on the inside of my cheek. "Your brother's pretty pissed at me."

"Oh. Of that I have no doubt." Emma tosses the towel she was using to dry her hands on the counter. "But it's not because of what you'll find in there."

I lift my head. "No?"

Emma's lips turn down in an agreeing *no*, and as she passes me on the way to her bedroom, she tosses over her shoulder, "Those answers you're wanting? You're looking at the wrong side of the coin, Callie."

I spin in my stool right as Emma's door shuts.

And if I go and smack my hand on the door, begging for her to elaborate, I know what I'll get in response.

Silence.

If I'm wanting to expose the society and potentially involve them in Piper's murder, it's clear I'm on my own.

Piper.

Her name sears into my brain, and I scramble for my clutch, amazed I've been so distracted, I didn't think to look up her third lover. Her unborn child's *father*.

In my defense, a *lot* happened between Ahmar's admitting of the name and parking my ass on this stool.

But now, under the kitchen lights of a quiet, undisturbed dorm room, I have the time to try and figure him out. Yes, the police are two steps ahead, but perhaps it'll soothe the rush of urgency in my mind if I could put a name to a face.

Is he a student at Briarcliff? Part of the Nobles? The reason Piper fell off a cliff?

Spurred by a new burst of energy, I set the phone on the counter and tap with one finger while my other hand stays raised, starting with the online Briarcliff Student Directory.

Sadly, it's not that easy. No one named Joaquín del Pozo is enrolled at this school.

Deciding on a more generalized approach, I open my internet

browser to search his name, narrowing down the geography to Briarcliff and its neighboring towns. If nothing of use comes up, I'll have to figure out a way to cajole Ahmar into either letting me see this guy's rap sheet, since he was in the system already, or at the very least, get Ahmar to admit where this dude comes from.

Now, there's an idea. I switch from the search engine and go to the free criminal background check database and type in Joaquín's full name. If he's a minor, nothing will show, but if, by chance, he's an adult, and considering Piper's proclivity for older men...

BINGO.

Two results pop up, one guy with a DUI rap in Westerly, and I dismiss him at first, moving onto the second result. Both mug shots have yet to load.

My finger hovers over the second name to expand the results, but right before I do, the first picture loads, and...

Oh.

Oh, my God.

I'm staring at Jack.

Jack, Addisyn's boyfriend.

14

*S*unday morning passes by in a frenzied blur.

First off, my hand was *fire*. It literally took on all the components of a flame and turned my delicate hand-bones to dust. I caved and ran to the nurse's office, waiting impatiently with the few students in front with pounding, alcohol and drug induced migraines.

After having it checked out and being administered Tylenol, I gritted my teeth against the continued gnarled heartbeat my wound created and strode to the new library.

I spend my time there not catching up on history, calculus, or English lit like I should be after the disaster that was my quarter-term grades, but instead researched how to safely read old, falling apart, burned books.

When I attempted to lift the flap of Daniel Stone's mysterious "rule book" last night, it nearly disintegrated in my hands. Unwilling to let such important material be destroyed, I set it aside, though it killed me not to absorb the knowledge instantly. But a steadier hand had to prevail.

After reading a few articles off my laptop, I start to hash out ways to use the science room when a *whoosh* of air puffs out beside me.

My spine goes rigid when the accompanying scent tickles my nose.

Citrus. Wood. Crisp weed.

It's similar, but not quite perfect, to Chase's cologne.

"Can I help you?" I ask without glancing over, pretending to be busy typing on my keyboard.

"Not unless you're willing to do a repeat of last night."

Ever so slowly, I pivot to face Tempest.

The green of his eyes pop against the thick rim of his lashes, the same color as his ebony hair. The high cut of his cheekbones, matte rose color of his lips, and lean lines of his body give him a vampiric aura, yet his skin is sun-browned from hours spent on the water as second-in-command in Chase's crew.

He elaborates, without me asking, "Sadly, I only received the video version. Didn't get to see your breakdown live."

"It wasn't a breakdown," I say stiffly.

Tempest angles his head. "Sure looked like one."

"People were crowding in on all sides. No one was moving. So, I figured"—I attempt to keep my voice light—"screaming the walls down would get them to move the hell back. Guess what? It worked."

"Really?" Tempest frowns. "I thought small spaces was Chase's schtick, but maybe you two have more in common than I thought."

My brows pull in, but I work hard not to show Tempest just how interested I am in Chase trivia.

A slow, lupine grin spreads across Tempest's face as he watches me battle for indifference. "The guy never takes elevators. Go ahead, try and make him." Tempest leans toward me, stretching his eyes wide. "I dare you."

A tingle of ... something ... rushes up the center of my back, and I quickly glance away from Tempest and his weird allure.

I face my computer, subtly minimizing the articles I had up. "Is there a reason you've come to chat with Briarcliff's social pariah?" I risk another glance. "Or is that why you've sat down next to me? To let me know exactly how my behavior at the party went over with the school? Spoiler alert: I'm aware."

Tempest doesn't answer. Instead, his fingers drift over my bandaged hand, and my instant, tense reaction causes me to wheeze against the pain of stretching raw skin.

"That must've hurt," he muses, but doesn't draw his hand back. "Was it worth it?"

I lick my lips. "I don't know."

Tempest makes a murmuring sound of agreement, and thankfully, withdraws. My shoulders sag in relief at the distance he puts between us, however small.

Tempest reaches down and sets his bag on the table, languidly searching through, then pulling out his computer and schoolbooks.

I watch all this in horror as the rest of the students using Sunday for studying stare at us and whisper to their friends.

"Um, what are you doing?" I ask.

"What does it look like?"

I resist an annoyed scoff. "You're at the wrong table. Isn't the trust fund seating section over there?"

Tempest runs his tongue along his top teeth. "All my trust fund baby friends have gotten themselves sent into time-out." He bats his lashes at me. "I'm lonely."

"Last I checked, Riordan isn't suspended. Go bother him."

"Rio's otherwise engaged." Tempest's smile is directed at his laptop as he flips it open, but it grates against my nerves nonetheless.

A ripple of guilt follows. I should check up on Ivy. I pull out my phone to do just that, but Tempest covers it with his large hand before I can so much as unlock it.

"Hey!"

"I wouldn't do that, possum. Take a few days before you face the consequences of your actions. Trust me, it's a lot better to judge your foibles at a distance."

I yank the phone—and my hand—from under his. "I don't care what everyone here has to say. I care about my friend."

"And so do I. Which is why I'm sitting here instead of getting my dick sucked off like Rio probably is." He pauses. "Hmm. Now I'm jealous."

"*Ugh.* Stop pretending like you care about me and buzz off."

Tempest's red-carved lips split wide, genuine laughter leaving his throat. "Have I brought out the worst in you by *buzzing* into your proximity?"

"Okay, *fuck* off."

Tempest flicks a brow in response before his expression turns rigid. "Apologies, but I can't."

"Why not? I didn't ask you—"

"Your opinion of my presence means shit-all, but unfortunately—for both of us—the opinion of someone else is written in stone."

I fake gag at his pun, but I stiffen at his insinuation. "Chase told you to sit with me? Why?"

"Haven't you heard? Chase got himself suspended for defending your honor."

I unleash another sigh, this one with a long, drawn out exhale. "Chase wouldn't help me even if I was stuck under the wheels of his car."

"That's where you're wrong, possum." Tempest shifts in his seat to get more comfortable. "He's sacrificed quite a lot for you."

"Oh, come *on.*"

Tempest shrugs. "Believe what you want, but I'm your Siamese twin for the better part of the week. Get used to me."

I groan. "Why? I don't need protection when Chase is here, never mind when his ass is kicked off school grounds for a week."

Tempest responds in a cold, flat tone, "I beg to differ."

My jaw clenches at the ice he's directed my way. Tempest has always been calm and undeterred, but I've never heard him summon so much winter in his voice.

I part my mouth, but Tempest prevents any defense by resting his gaze on my browser displaying the preservation tactics for damaged books, making sure I see him do it, then going back to his work.

Dang. I forgot to close the last tab.

"You're pissed about the rule book, too?" I ask. "Riordan already had me sacrifice skin. What is it you now want?"

Tempest chuckles, but his attention is on his calculus text he's propped on his lap while he leans back, balancing his chair on the two back legs. "What I want doesn't matter. Accept our buddy system and move on. Maybe do some homework instead of becoming Briarcliff's latest Ghostbuster."

I latch on to his unintended meaning. "So, you're saying there was someone before me who tried to figure out the Nobles, too, huh?"

Tempest groans. "You're worse than the paparazzi surrounding my parents' compound."

My eyes cut to his. "Only you would call—"

But I'm cut off by a sudden, shattering scream ricocheting around the room.

15

*T*his time, it's not me.

    Tempest vaults from his chair, shoving his textbook against my chest, but I shake off the obstruction and sprint after him, toward the sound.

The cry came from the rear, behind the stacks and nearer to the back wall. Tempest streaks into one of the aisles, and I follow suit, both impressed and frustrated at his speed, since he'll get there first.

I swing around the corner in time to see Tempest hunched over a figure puddled on the floor, her bare knees drawn to her chest, and her arms folding around her head as she sobs.

Falyn stands nearby, fingers tapping against her lips, with Willow at her side, murmuring something as she types into her phone. Their third musketeer, Violet, stands behind Falyn, watching the scene unfold with wide, too-bright blue eyes.

Violet notices me first, her shocked gaze holding mine. She mouths what I think is *run*, but I can't be sure.

"Addy," Tempest says, rubbing the hunched girl's back. "What is it? What happened?"

She lifts her head and wails, "The-the police!"

Her face is blotchy and streaked with tears, the pale, robin's egg color of her irises made stark against the bloodshot whites of her eyes.

Chase, I think. Unreasonably. Stupidly. *Something's wrong.*

I step into their aisle, and I know the instant Addisyn notices me, because blood floods her cheeks and she clutches Tempest's arm.

"What's *she* doing here with you?" she shrieks. "She's the reason—"

Tempest shushes her, then raises his chin to her friends. "Anyone want to tell me what the fuck this is, or am I supposed to read the room?"

Falyn shakes her head, her fingers drifting to her neck. "I ... I've got nothing, other than this must be the Harrington way..."

"BITCH!" Addisyn snarls, rearing from the ground with her nails drawn, but Tempest pushes her down by the shoulders.

"Jack," I whisper. When I inadvertently get Addisyn's attention, I say, clearer, "Jack is the reason you're upset, isn't he?"

"And just *what* in the good Lord's name is going on back here?"

The librarian, Mrs. Jenkins, comes up behind me, patting my shoulder as she passes by. "Have you lot never heard of the sanctity of a library?"

Tempest rises smoothly out of his crouch. "A simple misunderstanding, ma'am. We'll be quiet."

"I sure hope so. You had me running in heels all the way back here. Everyone okay?"

We all nod, everyone except for Addisyn, her expression hewn with trembling, spasming muscles.

"Any peeps out of either one of you, you're cleaning litter off the grounds for one week. Am I clear?"

We nod like good little soldiers, Falyn adding extra *oomph* in her good-girl facade, and wait for Mrs. Jenkins to depart.

She doesn't.

With the type of glare mastered solely by over-worked and underpaid teachers, she stares down her nose at us, her glasses perched on the end. "If I were you," she says, "I'd scatter."

I spin on my heel, unwilling to garner any more attention *or* detention, and head back to my table. I'm almost through the aisle of books before a hand claws into my elbow and whips me around.

"What the hell do you know about Jack, possum?" Falyn whisper-yells, her usually beautiful, storm gray eyes tightened into beady little balls.

"Lucky guess," I say, trying to pull my arm from her hold. She doesn't give an inch.

Falyn glances down at the bandage around my wrist and palm. In one vicious maneuver, she clasps the gauze, digging her nails in deep.

I choke on my yowl, my knees buckling.

Falyn bends with me, dipping her head close. "Tell me how you know that name, since we, as Addisyn's support system, have only just heard of it."

"Callie has connections," a voice says quietly. I unscrunch one eye enough to see that it's Violet. "She knows a detective. Now let her go."

"I say extend the pain," another voice, Willow, says at my back. She must've gone down a separate aisle, then U-turned into this one to watch the encore to Addisyn's show. "She clearly gets off on it, if last night is any indication. Who knew fire play was a thing? Is Chase into it?" Willow smiles as she enters my view. "Can I ask him? Maybe I'll add hot candle wax to our role play. Aren't those little freckles around his dick just the cutest?"

I flinch at Willow's accuracy, but there's nothing I can do about it, not when Falyn twists me at an unnatural angle and Willow's strangling my heart.

It's not like Chase was a choir boy when I met him. He played, he lured, and I experienced firsthand how well he knew his way around a woman's—

Willow dips forward just enough to whisper in my ear, "He asked for me, just last night. Turns out he was frustrated as all hell and needed to ... vent. God, I'm sore."

She giggles, and Falyn smiles along with her, snide and domineering.

"Stop," Violet says, and puts a hand on Falyn's arm. "Hasn't there been enough violence to last us the year?"

"Not even close." Falyn exposes her teeth. "I'm about done entertaining this bitch's Nancy Drew fetish. Why aren't we allowed to off her already?"

The succinct way Falyn asks about my death should have me worried, but mean girls are at a whole new level in this school. I have no doubt she wants to punt me over the nearest cliff, uncaring of the fact that her supposed best friend recently died from falling off one.

"Jack is Addisyn's boyfriend. He works at the lobster shack in town," I say, pushing against Falyn's hold. We're in a weird sort of arm war, and my burn screams to be released. "And the reason Piper got pregnant. He's been brought in for questioning. Right? That's what has Addisyn so upset. Her boyfriend cheated on her, impregnated her sister, and probably murdered Piper. I'd scream in a library, too, if I heard that news."

Abruptly, Falyn releases her hold, and I clutch my pulsing forearm to my chest, backing away from this half-circle of vultures.

"Maybe Chase was right," Violet whispers to Falyn.

The statement causes Falyn's brows to shadow her eyes as she stares at me. "Unless you decide to use the limited space in that brain of yours for actual study subjects," she says to me, "Your time at this school is ending. Make the right choice, Callie."

Commotion at the end of the aisle draws all our gazes, and

Willow steps aside enough to reveal Addisyn and Tempest, Addisyn gripping Tempest's waist like she has trouble even taking one step.

"Have you guys had your fun?" she asks through a quaking lip. "Talking about me? My family? Jack?"

"Ding ding ding." Falyn flips her hair, her lips twisted with disdain. "You're the talk of the school, Addy. Callie should thank you. And what you wanted?" Falyn scoffs. "You're never going to get. Now that your *boyfriend* murdered our best friend."

Addisyn leans out to swipe, but Tempest keeps a hold on her.

My shoulder brushes against a row of books as I attempt to sneak away from the conversation, but no one's looking in my direction, anyway.

I complete a one-eighty by spinning on my heel, and power-walk to my table, collecting my books and laptop as silently as possible.

It's amazing, how not two days ago, Falyn and Addisyn were attached at the hip. I was convinced Addisyn was being groomed as the next Piper, both in looks and poise, Falyn replacing their fallen member as easily as slipping on the Briarcliff uniform.

Now, though ... a rift has cracked open between them, and is it really all because Addisyn failed to tell them about a townie boyfriend?

Secret boyfriend.

Secret lover.

Secret society.

It's all secrets and lies with these people.

Hiking my bag on my shoulders, I mull over Falyn's not-so-subtle warning to fall in line like most students here. Ignore the strangeness and do my time in order to graduate from Briarcliff intact.

But can I do it? Can I let these puzzle pieces I'm collecting scatter and swirl in the salt-tinged air?

Nope. I can't.

And so, I switch my mind on how to best break into the chem lab after hours and not get caught.

16

*E*asier said than done.

For the rest of the week, I'm unable to find any time to bust open Daniel Stone's half-destroyed rule book, Falyn's warning becoming all too real with surprise quizzes, an oral Spanish test, and English Lit paper round-ups.

To add to the fuss, our new History professor, Miss Carroll, isn't nearly as amicable and endearing as Dr. Luke was—err, save for his preference of sex with minors—and she sends all our spines rigid, her voice crackling throughout the classroom, the loose skin around her smoker's throat trembling like a turkey's gullet.

I find myself fascinated by it and can never look away.

Tempest, as he promised, stays close to my side from Monday to Friday, taking Chase's vacant seat if it happens to be closer to mine. And it is, in almost every period.

The electricity dancing across the outlines of my body are missing without Chase nearby, but besides Miss Carroll's unnaturally old appearance, I've developed an advantageous tunnel vision where I'm focused and determined, paying attention in class and finishing my homework a few hours after dinner.

News of my freak-out at Chase's party came as a big wave on Monday but was low tide by Tuesday morning, considering the irresistible ripeness of Jack's arrest, Piper's betrayal against Addisyn, and Emma's sudden appearance in their classrooms were juicy, low-hanging fruit.

Emma and I have two classes together, and each time she came in, whether she was seated there before everyone else or coming in after, the room always stilled, and the students unleashed everlasting stares. She handled it for a few days by glaring and snarling at anyone who got too close, but eventually, I noticed how the attention kept chipping away at her, her snarls becoming sneers, then nothing at all.

Emma isn't around our dorm much. I have no idea where she goes, but when she is around, she doesn't initiate any sort of talk between us. Our schedules are practically opposite—she showers in the mornings while I take one at night, she wakes up at eight, with barely any time to get ready, while I'm up just before dawn.

But our one conversation, held while she bandaged my burn, seems to have made her docile, and my theory turns out to be correct when Emma offers me an espresso before scurrying off to whatever mysterious errands she runs. Despite that one moment, though, she doesn't search me out, and I don't try to find her.

I spend most of my evenings hanging out with Ivy, anyway, catching glimpses of her roommate, but never getting enough alone time with Eden to expand on her knowledge of Piper being a Virtue.

I admit, I'm split between finding out more about the Nobles or the Virtues, and my stagnant week has propelled my unfounded theories to the front of my mind. So much so, it's almost impossible to try to balance a routine of schoolwork while carving out time for detective work.

I stare at my phone, sitting silently beside my laptop as I finish off my calc homework, my legs cramped under the thick wooden desk in my room.

I haven't asked Chase any questions this week. I assumed our deal was off the table as soon as he destroyed, then stormed out of his dad's study. I'm not so brazen as to expect his answers when I've so utterly pushed him beyond patience.

But I miss him. I miss *us*, whatever there was of us. Piper's pregnancy shook him badly, and I have a new understanding on why he cleaved such distance between us after I told him what Ahmar knew. Then, I fucked it up worse by pretending to help him figure out if he was the father, when really, all I wanted was details on Briarcliff's underworld.

I pick up my phone, and after unlocking it, my thumb hovers over the message chain with Chase.

It's Friday evening, and he's expected to be back at school on Monday. It'd be nice to try and smooth things over with him before then, right? It wouldn't be desperate to text and make sure we're on neutral ground.

Besides, he asked Tempest to stay close to me while he couldn't this week.

He punched James in the face for insulting me.

The guy has veins of ice, eyes the color of a frozen forest ground, and the frostiest demeanor, even toward his friends. But he did all that. For me.

I type out a sentence and press SEND before I lose my nerve.

Me: Do my daily questions still apply?

I slam my phone face-down on my desk, then swivel back to calculus. I won't wait for his response. I will not.

A few minutes later, my phone vibrates, and I whip it face-up.

Chase: You don't have much time left.

. . .

Smiling, I pick up the phone. I'll take that as a yes.

Me: Did you

I delete the message, my head falling back on a sigh. *Sack up. You can do this.* Schoolwork and Ivy have made my imagination easier to handle, but it's never truly gone away. Not when all I can picture is Willow's auburn hair mixing with his golden locks, a blend of shimmering metals I could never emulate.

Me: Willow tells me she slept with you at your party.
    Chase: Where's the question.

Does he *have* to be so obtuse? I huff out a breath, daring myself to do as he says and ask, instead of assume.

Me: Did you?

...

Three dots appear, and I watch them with way too much intensity. I'm desperate to see his answer, and I'm not sure how proud I am to feel that way. Nor do I have any idea how he'll react. On Saturday night, he'd said he was done with my investigation, and therefore, with me.

A guy has never made me *this* before. Turned me into a girl who can put all her insecurities, concerns, and the bigger picture aside, just to read his words.

Chase: No. I haven't been with anyone since you.

I fall back against the chair, pressing the phone to my chest. *Okay. He doesn't seem mad.* Maybe I can salvage the wreckage of Saturday night with one simple question, unrelated to Cloaks, or Briarcliff, or Piper's murder.

And entirely centered on us.

Me: Do you miss what we had?

I'm nervous.

Holy shit, I'm so beside myself with nerves. I push to my feet, pacing my room while biting down on one corner of the phone.

Nothing.

Oh, Callie. You may have screwed the pooch with this one.

I busy myself with homework and an unnecessary cleaning of my bedroom until an hour passes, my phone annoyingly quiet and black on my nightstand. I check it twice to make sure there's a signal, and still, Chase doesn't respond.

With my stomach settling somewhere near my feet, I go about my nightly routine of a snack, a shower, and then bed, all the while trying to put a positive spin on Chase's no-answer answer.

It's for the best.

You won't be distracted by your crush on a boy anymore and can lessen the pressure of dividing your time.

The hours of hurt can be better utilized by focusing on the

Nobles. Use the last gift Chase gave you and read Daniel Stone's rule book.

This weekend, bust into the chem lab, use its tools to open the book, and satisfy your curiosity, once and for all.

Forget. Him.

My eyelids grow heavy. The ceiling I'm staring at grows darker, and soon, I give in to a dreamless sleep.

Well into the night, my phone goes off with a loud, buzzing sound.

I snap awake, rubbing the grit from my eyes, and squint at the screen, swiping open the message.

Chase: Yes. I miss it.

17

*B*efore dawn on Sunday morning, I decide to do it.

I tossed and turned ever since receiving Chase's answer, both delighted and afraid of our lasting connection. My mind kept firing off instead of spiraling down to sleep, and until I used that time wisely, I wasn't going to get any semblance of rest.

With the sky still indigo with waning moonlight, I slide out of bed and change, choosing warmer clothing for my trek to the academy in the dark. I toss a jean jacket over a crimson sweater and gray leggings, then slip on knee socks and my white sneakers before heading out.

I have my own granola stash these days, so I throw a handful in a snack bag and grab an empty thermos in hopes the kitchen staff has already started the coffee brewing process.

As I'm bending into the cabinet, I hear, "Jesus, I thought you were a raccoon."

I jump up on a yelp, then scowl at Emma as she stands near the kitchen counter, her hair flattened on one side and her night-shirt askew.

"They call me a possum, not a raccoon," I say, stuffing the thermos in my bag. "Or a cat."

"Neither one is very creative," Emma muses, and I harrumph in agreement. "Or amusing."

"Tell me about it."

"In my defense," she says, "I thought an *actual* rodent had made its way up here, but it turns out, it's just you, before sunrise, banging through our kitchen. Again."

After one second of hesitation—because Emma never keeps conversations going, *ever*—I hold up my granola bag as evidence.

Emma grumbles, then gestures to her espresso machine. "Take one for the road, then."

I smile. "Aw. Are you warming up to my sweet, morning charm?"

"No. I'm giving you something productive to do rather than use our cupboards for target practice. Make me one, too."

I keep a straight face, despite the giddiness going on inside me at the thought of a freshly brewed mocha. "Coming right up."

As I'm fiddling with the milk steamer, Emma asks, with a begrudging tone, "What are you doing up so early on a Sunday?"

I doubt she truly cares, so I answer with my back to her, "Getting an early start on the chemistry assignment."

"Okay." Emma doesn't sound convinced. "But we have bio this semester, not chem."

After pouring the espresso into my thermos and sliding her mug over to her side of the counter, I turn. "I'll tell you mine if you tell me yours. Why don't you elaborate on what you're up to during your evening disappearances?"

Emma crosses her arms and glares through her lashes.

"That's what I thought," I say.

I cap the thermos and exit our dorm on a cheery wave.

The soft, golden glow of the school's windows guides me up the hill on the quiet pathway, my footsteps the only sound breaking through the rousing bird chirps and light rustle of wind through the trees.

Not even the enterprising rowing team has left their dorms yet. From what Ivy says, they don't get on the water until about 5:30, and I've beat them outside by an hour.

Usually, being the lone pedestrian on a walkway is a gift, especially coming from New York City, but after being accosted by Cloaks in the forest last month, and Piper's demise, nature hasn't been as calming to me lately.

I pick up the pace, suddenly thankful that Tempest had my back all week while Chase was absent. The mockery I'd expected after Chase's lake house party never manifested, but I still had to manage the usual vermin insults and Falyn's bitter gaze, her expression more than indicating her plans for my removal from this school.

More importantly, no Cloaks have accosted me. Barely a whisper of the Nobles crossed my ears, and since nobody knew or cared what I reached into the fire for (the act itself was enough ammo against me to last an entire semester), there wasn't any reason to. And, by keeping my mouth shut, Tempest didn't ask me about it again. Perhaps he believed I'd grown tired of the hunt.

Not exactly.

I keep my eye on the tree line the entire way to the school, anxious of a Cloak appearing, memories of my previous encounter near Lover's Leap filming over my vision. Clouds of my breath come in shorter bursts, the sounds of my footsteps pound harder and faster, and the bird chirps fade away into silence.

The side-door into the school comes into view, and I scamper the rest of the way, pushing in and leaving the quiet, darkened forest far behind. My cheeks are cold and stiff from both the outside and my concentrated anxiety, but the minute the door thumps shut behind me, my shoulders relax.

The hushed clinking of plates and tinned sounds of pots

floats down the hallway, the kitchen staff getting ready for break-fast, but the lights remain dimmed, and won't go on full blast for another hour.

I tip-toe past the dining hall, the low lamplight casting shadows against the stone walls, changing the stained glass motifs into stark, gloomy figures.

Don't look at shadows too long, my old friend Sylvie always said during our childhood sleepovers. *At some point, they're going to start moving.*

Shuddering at the memory, I fly past classroom doors until I find the one I want, thankful it's unlocked when I twist the knob.

I'm conscious of being caught, so I don't turn on the overhead lights as I pick a lab table and toss my pack on the metal counter. I'd carefully placed Daniel Stone's manual in a gallon-sized Ziplock, and after turning on the specialized table lamp and twisting it to illuminate the metal countertop, I pull it from top section of my bag.

A row of beakers and chemistry supplies stand in a row by the personal sink, cleaned and ready for the next class. I slip on disposable gloves and choose a pair of large, lab-grade tweezers, adjust the microscope, and, instead of using my fingers, I painstakingly crack the book open and slip it under the lens.

The pages are charred and brittle, but the magnification helps decipher the writing through the ash. It says, in part:

Those who choose to turn these pages accept thee into thy mind.

Oh, boy.

My conscience flickers to life enough to question why Chase gave me his father's rule book, but my appetite's too whetted to listen to it. I carefully slip the book from under the microscope and turn the page, repositioning it under and adjusting the clarity of the lens:

Upon the second week and the seventh night, meet in the Vault, where your blood will be tested.
    Choose your paper, where your mind will be guided.
    Wear your robe, where your identity will be shielded.
    Wait for the key of your master, so you may be commanded.

What the *what*?

Leaning over so far, I've nearly crawled onto the table, I tweeze my way to the next page. The handwriting's changed, no longer the thick, black ink professional cursive. Thin, blue-inked swipes of hastily written notes take over:

March 16, 1971

I, Howard Mason, class of '74, broke into the Nobles' hidden tomb long enough to steal one illuminating page, and have documented, from memory, what I else I discovered.

The stolen poem above is, in part, the initiate ritual of the Nobles, creating its own chapter, and thus utilizing its own motivations to influence the boys in this school. Its founder, Thorne Briar, as the first headmaster of this academy, thought to enrich the minds of certain promising young men, using his connections to form agreements among hidden collegiate societies to accept these boys, groomed and taught under Briar, upon graduation. Rumor has it, in order to accelerate these individuals, examination topics are given, answers are dispersed, and the boys will earn top grades so their focus can remain on Briar's hidden, and demonic, tutelage.

There is also a symbol, forged in iron, above a hearth of human skulls—believed to be the heads of ancient, English nobleman robbed from the graves where they rested in peace—but that has yet to be verified—of a raven, spreading its wings within a perfect circle. The slogan, altum volare in tenebris, *means 'fly high in the dark.'*

I now have proof. Thorne Briar is manipulating children of the elite so he may form political and economic history to his preference.

I lean back on a deep, pondering breath. The handwriting is faded, the penmanship rushed in parts, but I turn to the next page, and the next, disappointed to see that the writing has become fewer and farther between, fire damage notwithstanding.

I fear I have been caught.

And, among more indecipherable damage, *Thorne Briar's society is nothing but the manifestation of the narcissistic elite, bored with God, turning to the devil instead to manipulate their greed-inspired destiny.*

There is a secret within the Nobles, one they've lost sight of. From what I've witnessed, it is fast getting out of control, and the women they've used—

—they call themselves the Virtues.

—worse than the Nobles, worse than skulls, or keys, or snakes, or wolves. They have motivations so sinful and blasphemous I can hardly put pen to paper and describe—

. . .

—find their temple—

—should reveal their true selves or I'll be forced to inform the Nobles of their transgressions—

—wanton, wasted individuals—

Then, turn after turn, more blank pages.

A good chunk of papery edges has been destroyed, but after about five paragraphs, the rest of the book is empty.

Now, oh *now*, it's becoming clear why Chase gave me free reign on this "hidden" book within his father's personal library.

The book is a decoy. I'm looking at a frickin' ... wooden *duck* trussed up as the sacred Nobles' rule book for members.

The manual's leather-bound jacket was tempting enough, with Daniel Stone's name embossed under a raven insignia—the *Nobles'* symbol. But the inside? It's just a few pages of the investigative ponderings of a former Briarcliff freshman who decided to make it his mission to break into the Nobles' meeting grounds and record his findings for ... a purpose I'm assuming is similar to my own.

Basically, me as a 1970s boy.

I bite down on my index finger. According to Rose's letter that Piper found, Rose created the Virtues to counteract the uncouth motivations of the Nobles. But according to this Howard Mason, it's not the Nobles that are the problem.

It's the Virtues.

Did Piper know this? Had she read the same journals and letters, coming to the same conclusions as me?

Is this why she died?

I shake my head, backing away from the sooty, crumbling ledger, open to its last written page.

Help me.

The thought of looking up Howard Mason and if he survived Briarcliff is a sobering one. I don't know how many more books I can crack open, letters I can read, fucked up warnings I have to endure, before I become so buried in conspiracies, I lose complete sight of myself.

This book, like the other writings before it, provides me with crumbs, and Chase knew that when he thrust it into my hands. As if Daniel Stone would have his super-secret society rulebook hanging out in plain sight for idiots like me to discover.

He doctored this book into *bait* for idiots like me to discover.

The real one is probably stashed somewhere not even his wife would know about.

This was probably a test to see how far I was willing to go to solve the mystery of the Nobles.

And if I was willing to go as far as Howard.

"What happened to you, Howa—?" I start to whisper, but then I notice a shifting near the closed door.

My eyes dart to the top corner of the room, where the blinking red light of the security camera nestled high in a corner goes dark.

And the shadows start to move.

18

A rustling, hissing sound comes from one corner of the room, but I'm not waiting around for the big reveal.

I hurl my stuff back into my bag, cringing at my handling of Howard Mason's book when I wrap it in the plastic pouch rather than gently tuck it in—

A sharp force hits me in the arm, and I'm sent sprawling before I can secure the book. It goes flying, crunching against the ground, tattered pages drifting out.

My head bounces against the floor, my vision bursting with stars. I push to my hands and try to stand, but a boot to the middle of my back knocks me flat.

Lemony disinfectant fills my nostrils as my face mashes into the floor, but I pry my lips open. "Don't—"

Another shoe kicks me in the mouth, and I cry out, my neck snapping back.

A coppery tang flows across my tongue at the same time a giggle sounds out, girlish and *wrong.*

"Shh!"

"Just get it—"

"—wasting time..."

The whispers swirl, but I don't dare rise again. There's too many of them, whoever they are, and they aren't afraid to get mean.

I keep my eyes stretched wide enough to pick the moving shadows from the stagnant ones, shoes drifting in and out of my periphery, the hem of pale cloaks fluttering around the ankle.

It's them.

My heart scrambles to keep up with the blood rush beneath my skin. "I know who you are!" I cry, and under the influence of such utter realization, I push up, sneering, "*Virtues—*"

Boom.

Another blow across the side of my head, and the sound of glass shattering soon follows.

RUN.

The gut-wrenching, internal warning spears its way to the base of my brain, the spot that's instinctual, ancestral ... reptilian. The part that's telling me to survive and flee.

I scramble onto all fours, then push back on my haunches to sprint past these people—these girls—who were sent to hurt me.

"Hit her harder," comes a whispery growl, but the tone uses the same cadence I heard before. In my classes. In the dining hall.

The certainty that they're here for more than just a prank or a scare burrows to the core of my heart, and I fly forward, my hip banging against a lab desk and my palms smearing across the metal countertops, but I run. I do what I'm supposed to and *flee.*

An amused laugh comes from my left before an arm swings down with another beaker. I deflect it, but not enough. It slices across my cheek before crashing to the floor.

Something else hits me across my stomach, and I curl against the sudden pain before crumpling back to the ground, protecting my bandaged hand as much as I can.

"This is too much," someone whispers. "Stop. Before this gets out of control."

They're all speaking in whispers, as if to disguise their voices, in addition to cloaking their faces, but I know who they are.

The tip of a shoe hits me in the kidney, and I curl on my side with a moan.

"Stop!" the same trembling, hesitant voice says.

"Not until she gets the message." This time, a heavy, rubber-soled foot comes down on my throat. "And since she's so stubborn, I'll make it clear this time."

Sputtering, I grab onto the ankle, as if my sheer panic alone can lift the pressure off my windpipe.

"Piper..." I gasp. "Piper was one of you. I want to know what happened to her. Why are—" I wince at the increase in pressure. "Why are you against that?"

The tallest Cloak leans down, the fabric a shimmering white against the fading moonlight streaking through the windows. "Because you're not doing this for Piper."

"Selfish bitch," another hisses.

"Admit it," the main Cloak—Falyn—says, and though I can't see it through the shadows, I sense her sour smile. "You have some pathetic motivation to study a mystery that doesn't need solving and get into *our* business, read *our* private writings, thinking that by revealing our secrets you'll satisfy your own demons. But that's not how it works, dear possum."

Falyn straightens, waits a few beats, then spits out, "Because *we're* the demons. And regardless of what you discover about us, you won't solve shit. Your mom will still be dead."

I force the tears back, but a few manage to leak out, even as I struggle for breath. Easy, languid footsteps sound out until they stop near the top of my head. Another Cloak looks down, cocking her velvet-lined head, her blue eyes glittering like sapphires.

Addisyn. Somehow, these bitches have decided "virtue" should be part of their names. Despite Rose Briar's best efforts to create a society for good—and deep in my heart, I think her intentions were true—her creation has twisted and curled, tightening around the heart of the Virtues and strangling it until there are no virtuous beats left.

"You've done her no justice," I grind out. "Rose Briar would be ashamed."

Addisyn lets out a tinkling, full-voiced laugh. "You think we care what that ancient, dead bitch has to say? Welcome to our new world, Callie. Now get the fuck out."

She lifts her leg for another blow, but I angle my head at the same time I pivot and twist the ankle pressing against my neck, until its owner screeches and loses her footing, falling alongside me.

"You want in?" Falyn bellows over my head to Addisyn. "Do it, now! Prove you're worthy!"

I bolt upright, scanning the remaining three Cloaks scattered throughout the classroom, one running directly toward me with something metal glinting in her hand. Her hood slips past her hairline, but I have no time for the flutter of truth in my chest when I confirm Addisyn's face. I take stock of the weapon and her manic determination for it to dent my skull. Falyn and I both stand at the same time, and more on instinct than forethought, I turn to Falyn and flip the bottom hem of her cloak well over her head until she's blinded and shove her in Addisyn's path. It's enough for me to gather the distance I need to get to the door.

"*Fuck!*" Addisyn yells, fighting against Falyn's body tripping into her.

It'd be funny, had they not already drawn blood from my face.

A smaller one near the door swipes at my arm as I glide by, but it was a lazy grab, meant to showcase to the others that she tried.

Violet. It has to be her.

I don't want to wait around for Willow's attempt.

Panting, throat swelling, I make it to the door, fling it open, and—

Run into someone whose arms pin mine to my sides.

And they don't let go.

"*Get off me!*" I screech, but it doesn't even sound like me.

I fight against the barricade, but these arms are stronger than mine, the muscles more sculpted, and the torso much broader and flatter.

The perfect canvas to incapacitate a girl against her will.

"*No!*"

My yell is so high-pitched, supernatural and deafening, that I don't hear the voice tumbling out above my head until I stop to gulp in a breath.

"Callie! Hey, Callie! Stop!"

The arms don't loosen their grip, but the less I struggle, the more steadying breaths I can take.

And finally, I process who's speaking.

"Callie, calm *down*."

I swat at the warm hands sliding back to grip my waist, but my fingers get caught on the taut cords of muscle in his forearms, with soft, downy hairs.

My brows scrunch the instant I look up. "Chase?"

"Goddammit, Callie, you scared the shit out of me. What the fuck?" His brown eyes narrow as he lifts a hand to my face. "You're bleeding."

His gaze sweeps over my face and body, taking stock of the stretched collar of my sweatshirt, the burning scratches on my neck, the warm blood on my cheek.

Chase asks, with destructive intent, "Who did this to you?"

I gape at the controlled rage in his expression, his eyes crazed with retribution, as my mind comes back online. "What are *you* doing here? You're suspended."

The wildfire in his gaze tempers slightly. "Suspension ended over the weekend. I have crew this morning and needed to get shit from my locker."

Of course his punishment would coincide with his training schedule. Hell, I'm surprised he was slapped on the wrist at all, considering he assaulted Dr. Luke a few weeks ago and walked away smiling.

Granted, that teacher had an illegal thing for young girls, and we suspected him of murder, but...

"Don't change the subject again," he warns. "Why the fuck are you bleeding?"

I pull out of his hold, and he lets me. I spin to the chem lab, to the door that's conveniently shut, my heart pounding at the same time my brain's assuring me they won't follow me out into the halls, not while Chase is here.

"There was ... I had ... an altercation," I say, still focused on the classroom door.

"At five in the morning? With who?"

There's little point in lying. Especially to him. "The Virtues."

Chase holds his breath, tangible anger exuding off him in heated waves that curl against my back. What is he going to do with that information? Anything? I have the dull sense that he'll keep this news to himself, like he does with all the other mysterious violence that happens to me.

Yet, a cold draft strokes across my cheek as he storms by, headed for the chem lab, his expression so murderous and absurdly angry, it can't be solely because of me.

He throws the door open, and as I come up beside him, we both stare into a messy, deserted classroom.

"They're gone?" My question comes out more confused than factual. How did those girls leave? We've been outside the door the entire time.

I look up at Chase in time to see him bare his teeth, like he wants to chomp this entire lab to shreds, so I round in front, placing shaking hands against his chest to urge him back. "They must've left when they heard you. I think I'm safe now."

"No." His voice is as gravelly as I've ever heard it. "They're showing me you're not."

I stare at him at length before I say, "I was only there because I was reading the book you gave me."

His forehead creases, then he blinks and looks down at me. "You actually read the fuckin' fireball you clawed out of my hearth?"

I raise a brow, though it stings with swelling skin. "I cared enough to pull it out, and it needed special handling. Hence, the chem lab. It was an impulsive decision and no one knew I was here—"

Emma. I told Emma.

Carefully, I school my expression enough that Chase won't sniff anything out, but I can't help thinking, *did she betray me?*

He mirrors my expression. "And did you find the answers you were looking for? Or just draw more trouble to your idiot self?"

"Both." I manage a haughty tone, but inside, I'm trembling.

Chase's shoulders incline on a sigh. His eyes dart to my cheek. "Do you need to get that looked at?"

"It looks worse than it feels." *Lie.* "You gave me Howard Mason's writings knowing exactly what he said in them."

"As a warning. It wasn't meant to be fucking bait for the Virtues." Banked fire breaks through his vision. "Do you think I set you up?"

I ignore the question, because I'm not sure I have the guts to answer it. "And was that your roundabout way of telling me, don't end up like him?"

Instead of answering immediately, Chase gives me a long, silent assessment. The muscles in his jaw go rigid.

I tense under his stare, and though he eyes me like a lion

would an elk, I don't have the same flight or fight response I did in the chem lab. My core aches, empty and hollow, under his gaze. It pulses its need for him, despite my internal incantation that he can't be good. He doesn't have my best interests at heart.

He could be my enemy.

"Howard Mason doesn't exist anymore," Chase says over my unseen, shivering undulation. "Is that enough of a warning for you?"

"The more I'm beaten down," I say, with tremulous conviction, "the more I want answers as to why."

Chase scoffs. "You are so reckless, you're bordering on stupid."

"Is this what happened to your sister?"

That shuts him up. His eyes shoot to mine.

"Did they beat her up, too?"

"Don't do this," he warns.

"No, really, I'd like to know. Was she getting too rebellious as a Virtue? Was Piper? Did their discipline start like this, with surprise beat-downs while their supposed friends wore cloaks meant to signify their gentle nature?"

"Callie." My name turns into a whip under his control.

"I'm starting to see the irony in all this." I laugh with hollowed-out breaths. "You Nobles and Virtues are *nothing* like the names you stand for, are you?"

Chase lifts his head and backs away. "Since you insist you're fine, I'm going to be late to practice."

"You told me your sister lit the fire," I persist. "What did she want destroyed?"

Chase freezes in the middle of the hallway, and his answering tone is gritty and rough. "Ask her yourself. Because I'm starting to think I can't protect you anymore."

I watch him pick up the duffel he must have tossed aside once he saw me running toward him. My fists are clenched and shaking at my sides.

But it's when his echoing steps fade and he turns a corner that I experience real, true fear.

I can't linger, alone in a dimly lit hallway, no matter how stubborn my head says I should be.

After one last look at the chem lab's door, I sprint to the closest exit, my lungs spasming with each haggard breath.

19

*E*mma sits at our kitchenette's high-top counter, her spoon of cereal pausing halfway to her mouth when I burst in.

"Yeesh," she says after a brief once-over. "What happened to you?"

"Nothing you care to know about," I snap, brushing past her.

She slips off her stool and stands. "Hey."

I pause at my bedroom door, throwing my hands up. "What?"

"Need I remind you, I'm the only one with a first aid kit in here, so you might try being nice."

"Nice?" I ask. "*Nice?* You lurk around this apartment pretending you don't give a shit about anything, yet you're so goddamn *nosey*, you know that? Did you tell them I was there? *Did you?*"

Emma jerks back in surprise.

I snarl, "Every *single* person I've come across in this school mopes around with their pissy attitudes and heavy burdens like the whole world revolves around keeping secrets for Briarcliff. But they'll betray good people, *nice* people, for the tiniest entry into a dangerous cult. I'm fucking *sick* of it!"

Emma's brows draw in. "Are we still talking about me here, or have we moved on to my brother?"

I heave out a breath. "The worst part is, the one person who's shown me kindness and that maybe this school won't be so bad if I just enjoy my life and look forward to Winter Formal or Prom—basic, regular, high school yearbook shit—I've ignored. I've shoved Ivy's good intentions aside because I can't control my need to understand you *assholes* better than I understand myself. God, I'm an idiot."

My lips lift in shame, and I whirl into my room, uncaring of Emma's response, if she even has one.

"I didn't tell anyone anything," Emma says through my panting breaths. "You lost the book, didn't you?"

Emma's question causes the air to freeze in my throat.

"If it's any consolation, there wasn't much in there to begin with," she continues.

I slam my palm against my doorframe. "Really? Because my attempt to read it got me attacked."

Emma makes an indecipherable sound in her throat. "That's probably because they didn't know Chase's intentions of giving it to you the way I did."

I stiffen in my doorway.

"It's all about appearances, Callie. You should have figured that out by now."

I hear her dishes clink in the sink, then the door to our apartment opens and closes with Emma's departure. It's only when I lift my head and step all the way into my room that I see the single rose lying across my bed, in pristine, ink-dipped condition.

I unleash a warrior's cry and hurl it against the wall.

On Monday morning at school, I'm told by a student prefect to head directly to the headmaster's office instead of my first class.

Confused but compliant, I step away from my locker and do as I was told.

Paintings of previous alumni leer over my head as I turn into the professors' hall, where all their offices are, trophy and other award cases shining under the lights, recently dusted and polished.

I glare at the hidden raven's crest peeking out from behind a rowing trophy, its deja vu familiarity the sole reason why I started down this secret society's wormhole in the first place.

And how you met Chase.

I flick that thought away when Marron's door comes into view.

There's no time to knock, because the door opens, and I'm greeted with the scowling face of the very person I'm trying *not* to think of.

"What's going on?" I ask, but Chase cups my elbow and drags me in.

I stop the surprise rippling across my face as I take in the other students seated in the office, Marron holding court on the other side of his desk, his frown lines as deep as the crevices on the neighboring cliffs.

Falyn, Willow, Addisyn, Violet, and Tempest are either seated or standing near Marron. Chase takes up position against the far wall, folding his arms so comfortably, I assume that was the pose he took well before I entered into this bear trap.

"Miss Ryan, glad you could join us."

Marron's not glad. He looks about ready to explode.

I scan the room, gauging the temperature, but only Addisyn looks my way, her cheeks wet, eyes red-rimmed, but her expression sly.

"Girls, tell Miss Ryan what you were just finishing telling me," Marron says.

Falyn is only too happy to oblige. "We saw Callie sneaking

into school after hours over the weekend, and, concerned for her reasons for being there, we followed."

Falyn peers over her shoulder at me, batting her lashes with innocence, but I note the cut on her temple, probably from when I tripped her up and caused her to fall on shattered glass.

The thought makes me smile.

"Miss Ryan," Marron barks. "This is a serious accusation being leveled your way, so I suggest you meet it with a modicum of sobriety."

I wipe the smugness off my face.

"She's not part of crew," Willow adds, "and since Falyn and I were on our way to training, we thought it prudent that we follow her."

Marron acknowledges Willow's point. Of course he does, since she's his freaking *daughter*. "Very true, dear. This school, when unfamiliar with its layout, can be rather dangerous, especially in the dark." Marron turns a dry look my way. "It's why we keep the doors locked."

"Yes, sir," Falyn simpers. "Didn't you know, Callie, about the hidden entrances and corridors at Briarcliff? The Briar brothers designed this academy with an eccentric millionaire's flair, I'm afraid."

A shiver crawls along my spine. *That's how they got into the chem lab without me noticing.*

"Now, now," Marron chastises. "Let's not speak of unfounded architectural rumors and get to the point, shall we?"

"Callie vandalized the chem lab."

Addisyn blurts it so abruptly, all heads twist to her.

"I did what now?" I ask.

"We were incredibly disappointed to open the school this morning and find the chemistry room so wholly violated," Marron says, his gaze steady on mine. "And these witnesses have kindly come forward to tell me that it was you that destroyed all the supplies, poured chemicals over the countertops, and good

Lord, drew entirely inappropriate and obscene diagrams on the whiteboard at the front of the class."

I burst forward, my chest threatening to unleash a boisterous laugh at the absurdity of a single girl—me—doing all that to a classroom, for no reason whatsoever. Luckily, my brain wins out. "Are you kidding? Headmaster Marron, they're lying. I did *not*—"

"Is there a reason we're here?"

The placid calm of Tempest's voice eats through my words like the silent work of termites. He quiets the room yet lifts his hand to check his cuticles as if this is all another day in the life of Tempest Callahan.

"Now that you've brought it up," Marron says stiffly, "Yes. Due to the ... tenuous nature of Miss Ryan's relationship with these girls, Willow has assured me that you two were also witnesses to Miss Ryan's unwarranted outburst. Is this true?"

Absurdity gives way to outrage. I stand in the middle of the room, my face hot and my fists clenched to my sides. Even my uniform skirt trembles with the brewing rage inside my body. But, at Marron's words, I force a ribbon of calm over my skin.

There's no way Chase or Tempest would back up these lies. Tempest wasn't even there, and Chase saw me flinging myself out of that room like the gates of hell were in there.

That's not a girl who draws "obscene diagrams" on whiteboards.

But then, oh then, Chase shatters my world. "Yes."

I whip around to face him, my face going numb with blood loss. "*What*? Chase!"

He won't look at me.

"I caught her as she was leaving," he continues. "And she admitted what she did. Tempest heard it, too. Right, T?"

Tempest nods right as a *whoosh* of air leaves my body and shrivels my lungs. I whisper brokenly to Tempest, "You've had my back all week, swearing you were there to protect me, and now you're *lying* for them? Why?" I direct another question to Chase. "Why are you doing this?"

It looks like it pains him, but Chase meets my eye, his jaw grinding. "You need to stop with your delusions, Callie. It's gone too far."

My stomach twists in knots. I feel truly lost, and the words I screamed at Emma last night are the only ones I can find.

...maybe this school won't be so bad if I just enjoy my life and look forward to Winter Formal or Prom—basic, regular, high school year-book shit...

This academy will always be bad, because of the students they enlist, the broken societies they nurture, and the twisted minds they let rule the school.

I face Marron head-on, and say, in the steadiest voice I can conjure, "I was in the chem lab before school hours because I wanted to go through a damaged book I found. I needed the necessary tools." I throw a long stare in Tempest's direction, since he should know. He read it on my laptop, using it to figure out I'd need supplies, and potentially told these bitches to wait until I skipped along the path, after hours, into their waiting clutches.

And I fell for it. Was drawn to his niceties like the lonely, disenchanted girl he knew I was.

Marron shakes his head. "Regardless of your intentions, you broke into a classroom after hours—"

I cut in, "I'll admit that much. But when I was finishing up and cleaning the *small* mess I made, I was attacked."

Marron's brows shoot up. "Excuse me?"

"Look at my face!" I yell, then point to my cheek. "And look at Falyn's! You think we got those wounds separately? She jumped me, and had her friends help. Addisyn tried to knock me uncon-scious a whole shitload of times, and Willow—"

The words are out before I can reel them back in, and Marron's expression darkens with rage. "Listen here, Miss Ryan, it is one thing to defend your actions. It is a complete other aggravation to involve my *daughter* in your concocted story—"

Warning laces his tone. And still, I can't stop. "What makes you think I'm the liar? These girls, your daughter, call themselves Virtues, but—"

Chairs scraping against hardwood halt the flow of my words. First, Addisyn rises, then Falyn, then Willow, using their height as a helpful tactic to stare me down.

"Haven't I been through enough?" Addisyn seethes, her fresh tears becoming dew drops in her eyes. "My sister's dead, my boyfriend's in custody, and now you're accusing me of wanting to *hurt* you?" Addisyn gulps in a dramatic breath. "I'm not violent, but I'm forced to think of it every day. I'm trying to heal, but you want me to suffer!"

"Oh, come *on*," I say.

Falyn speaks before Marron can scold me further. "We're trying, as best we can, to take you at face value and not bring up your past, but you're making that super difficult, Callie."

"Last week you humiliated Addisyn in the new library. And now, what, she passed your initiation by trying to kill me with a Bunsen burner?" I back up on instinct, and when I knock into Chase's back, I recoil. He's staring at a spot past Marron's head, his jaw muscles so tense, they're almost bursting through his skin. Yet he still won't look at me. Tempest eyes it all through his lashes, but he won't lift a finger.

"Listen to her, Daddy. She's clearly disturbed." Willow shifts her gaze to me. "First, you steal a book from Daniel Stone's study. An honored alumnus at this school. Then, you burn it. Thankfully, you second-guessed yourself and saved it from the fire—the whole senior class saw *that* insanity—but instead of returning it to its rightful owner, you invade the Stones' privacy *while* breaking into a classroom you have no permission to be in, and now you're saying we beat you for it? Do you take us for barbarians, or are you just confusing us with your stepfather?"

I suck in a breath, my fist reeling back from my waist to punch her in her too-white veneers, but Chase grabs hold of my hand and bends it against my lower back, my muscles aching and trembling beneath his grip.

No one else has witnessed the exchange, and nothing in Chase's expression gives away his battle over my will, but I wish, with all my might, that I had longer nails so I could cut him as deeply as he's cut me.

"Girls, thank you for your input. Gentlemen, you too. I'd like to speak with Miss Ryan alone."

I must imagine the quick squeeze Chase gives before he releases my hand, because he leaves without a glance or a word, Tempest following behind.

I glare at both of them, but I might as well be staring down river rocks.

Addisyn leads the way for Falyn, Willow, and Violet, but she casts an evil, villainess grin my way, mouthing, *fool me once...*

So, the writings of Howard Mason really were a prop. The Virtues thought I had something else more important. More dangerous.

I ignore Falyn's idiotic malice behind Addisyn, instead directing a heavy-lidded glare at Violet. Violet, who never says *anything* and pretends to be good.

"You're just like them," I hiss in her ear as she passes, and she shrinks against my words.

"Miss Ryan, please sit."

I take Addisyn's vacant seat, as instructed, my continued submissiveness to authority becoming more questionable by the second, but I can't help but believe that adults will look into the facts. Marron will discover the truth through his responsibility and power, and the proper students will be punished.

That's how a headmaster works, right?

Wrong. Willow is his daughter. He more than likely is aware of what crawls under the baseboards of this school.

Marron steeples his hands under his chin. "I've spoken with your parents."

I respond by keeping straight-backed and tight-lipped in the seat across from him.

After a deep sigh, Marron continues, "I had every intention of suspending you for at least two weeks, but your father has made me aware of your past ... issues."

My teeth clench so hard, they ache, but I don't blink away from him.

"He explained, at length, the troubles you've experienced since losing your mother. The paranoid delusions and obsessive-compulsive disorder that drives you, sometimes unreasonably, and has you taking drastic action against your health and well-being unless proper intervention comes in time."

I can't stay silent anymore. "That's ... that's an incredibly clinical way to apply my mom's murder to the rest of my life."

"Don't you understand, dear? What you do has ripple effects."

"I've apologized to my dad." I wring my hands where Marron can't see. "I was wrong, and maybe a bit unstable after she died, but I'm better now. I swear I am."

Marron lifts a brow. "That is where we differ. But I'm not trying to argue with you. What I'm trying to say is, I'm willing to take your mental struggles into account and will assign you a month's detention, assisting with dining hall and grounds clean-up at the end of your classes every day."

What? I'd rather take a week's suspension like Chase. Throwing parties and basically taking a vacation from this gloriously terrible school.

"Headmaster, I—"

"Consider yourself lucky. Your father should be calling you shortly regarding the ways we can make your stay more comfortable here. For everybody involved."

My brows furrow. "I don't understand."

Marron leans back in his seat. "I have a close relationship

with your father's wife, Lynda Meyer. It's due to her conviction that you belong here that I'm amiable to your continued schooling with us. But you are on a short leash, Miss Ryan. I have zero tolerance toward any more acts of aggression coming from you. Keep your head down, pay attention to your studies, and you should get by just fine. Do I make myself clear?"

I stop chewing on my cheek to implore, "No matter how many times I tell you I didn't do it, you're not going to believe me, are you?"

"You're on camera entering school grounds, and I have visuals of you in the chemistry lab, Miss Ryan. Please don't argue with solid evidence."

"But the camera goes black, doesn't it?" I sit straighter in my seat. "All you witness is me doing exactly as I said."

"Reading the book you had no rights to?"

I persist, "Chase lent me—"

"He assures me he did not."

My shoulders slump. *Of course.*

"You don't see me vandalizing anything," I say. "In fact, that camera shows me packing up before it shuts off—"

"Do you recall what I said about ripple effects?" Marron leans forward, folding his arms across his desk. "You're lucky Mr. Stone is not going to his father about the stolen work, though I'm predisposed to do it myself. Continue along this path, Miss Ryan, and I'll be forced to do just that."

"Why are you doing this?" I ask. Pointlessly. Stupidly. "All you have as proof is the bias of a handful of popular kids who are known for their bullying."

Marron goes quiet. As much as I don't want to, I squirm under his study.

"I suggest you leave my office, Miss Ryan, before you say something I cannot dismiss."

More disturbed than I am shaken, I push to my feet, despite

the urge to keep arguing, keep *convincing* this man that he's wrong.

But, the defeatist in me has never strangled my voice harder.

"Attend your last period before lunch," Marron says as I walk stiffly to the door. "After it is completed, report directly to our housekeeper, Moira, and she will give you the supplies needed to clean up that godforsaken mess in the chemistry lab before after-noon classes."

"Yes, sir," I say quietly, before stepping out of his office, and into a punishment I swear, by all I believe in, I will prove I do not deserve.

20

*M*y phone buzzes against the back of my arm as I head to calc, and I realize I'd forgotten to put it in my locker this morning.

I slide my bag to my front and dig into the side pocket, revealing three missed calls, two voicemails, and a slew of text messages from both Dad and Lynda.

One eye scrunches before the rest of my face follows with a cringe, questioning whether I want to deal with this now, or later.

A quick scroll through the messages...

Dad: Call me. Now.

Dad: Though your actions tell me otherwise, if you have any will to keep your social life and phone active, you better pick up your phone, Cal.

. . .

Lynda: Honey, this sounds serious. Call us, please. We're so worried.

Dad: WHAT WERE YOU THINKING??????

... tells me I should bite the bullet.

The school's foyer is wonderfully silent when I leave the West Wing and stop under the chandelier. I glance toward the staircase, and, without another thought, take them up into the Wolf's Den.

The space is deserted, like I'd hoped, and I perch on one of the stools surrounding the high tops toward the back, the stained-glass Briarcliff crest creating broken patterns of rainbow beams across the wood.

I wriggle in my seat until I'm comfortable, and, after a deep breath, call my stepdad.

"Jesus Christ!" he says after half a ring.

I startle, despite the clues telling me they'd be watching his phone like a couple of cats ready to pounce at the phone's slightest vibration, but exhale enough to tentatively say, "Hi."

"What the hell, Cal?"

"It wasn't me."

Dad blows out a breath that rattles my ear drum. "Not a good lead-in, Cal."

Lynda bursts onto the line. "Honey, are you all right?"

A tentative flutter, like a butterfly landing on the base of my heart, tickles my chest at her caring question. "I'm a little beat up, but I'll be okay."

"Beat up?" she asks. "What—"

"Calla Lily Ryan, explain yourself," Dad interrupts. "And do not do it by appealing to my wife's sweet nature. You tell us the truth, and you do it now, or else I'm seriously going to question the logic in putting you back in school. Maybe you should've stayed at the hospital longer."

I hiss in a breath. "Dad—"

"That's what you've lowered me to, honey," he says, but he honestly sounds upset. "I don't want to do it. You understand? I don't *want* to put you in an institution or send you to the city's answer to wayward girls, but this is the line of thinking you've turned me to. Why did you destroy school property?"

I pop my lower lip from my teeth. "First of all, 'destroy' is a very strong word, and I didn't *do* what they're saying I did."

"Marron tells us there's video footage."

"Well, that part's true," I admit, "But it doesn't catch me vandalizing anything. I was there for personal reasons, reading an old book that'd been damaged—"

"Another lie." Dad sighs. "You stole that book from a prominent figure. Cal, I can't tell you how much of a disappointment you've become."

The barb digs and twists at the very spot a butterfly gave me hope only seconds ago. But how can I recover? I can't tell him about the writings of Howard Mason I discovered in the Stone family's library. I can't admit I've been sniffing out Briarcliff's secret society because I think they're involved in Piper's death, even if they weren't the ones that pushed her. And I absolutely *cannot* confess about my sexual relationship with said prominent figure's spawn and my suspicions that both he and his father are responsible for protecting the secrets of the Nobles & Virtues.

Aw, man. Even in my head, this sounds insane.

"Dad, I'm sorry." The apology comes out more shredded than intended. "But everything I'm being accused of came from good intentions. Can you believe that much?"

Static answers me back. I can picture my dad, holding the phone in a shaking hand, him and Lynda leaning over it as my voice comes from the speaker.

My accusation toward him came with good intentions, too. I

wanted to avenge my mother, gain closure, do *something* to stop the demon gnawing on my soul and ripping my heart into its chum.

They'd fought before she died, he and my mom. They were fighting a lot, and during the very last argument, when they thought I wasn't there, I'd heard the slap.

The thump of my mother's back hitting a wall.

The crash of a vase being thrown near her head.

I'm aware of the last part because of her autopsy results. She'd had cuts across her cheekbone from spraying shards matching the pieces of the vase broken at her feet.

I hadn't acted, then. I'd stayed in my room, crumpled into a ball on the other side of my bed, in case Dad decided to unleash his anger on me next.

Because he was mad. So angry, his roars reverberated the walls and shook my lamp on the nightstand.

When I confessed all this to Ahmar on the night she died, his expression darkened, his mouth turned tight and grim, and he arrested my father on sight.

And when my father was released due to insufficient evidence, that demon eating me up inside wore my skin for its own.

"Honey, nothing good comes from retaliation." Lynda's soothing voice comes on the line, brushing against the spindly thorns of those memories. "Whatever happened to make you do this—and Pete, I *know* she didn't do this at random—you report it to a teacher, honey. Or your counselor. Or any responsible adult who can handle the situation appropriately. You understand?"

That's what I did after Mom was murdered, I want to hiss. *And look what happened. I was turned wrong, and my stepdad swore I was too traumatized by loss to see straight. And every single adult responsible for my well-being believed him. Including you.*

"I convinced the headmaster to give you another chance," she continues over the increasing loudness in my head, internal voices that won't shut up, "and I hope you'll take it. We'd also like you to see your guidance counselor weekly, if not every other day. Can you do that for us, honey?"

My mouth opens.

"Do it," Dad says before I can agree. "Or else I'll add behavioral psychiatrist to the list. And I'll make sure they evaluate you for a prescription."

I take a huge breath. Then another. I hope it's enough to stop the quaking of my bones. "Okay. I'll go to the counselor, I'll take the punishment, but I'm not who they say I am."

They're hiding more than I've ever concealed.

I keep that thought to myself, since it will only convince Lynda and Dad of my perceived fragile mental state. Eighteen or not, he can still have me involuntarily committed with this evidence.

"Good," Dad snaps. "You can forget about any parties, too. Halloween is *out*, and the headmaster agrees to keep someone in your dorms to ensure you stay in your room. And if, by Parents' Weekend, you've kept your nose clean, we'll revisit my desire to send you to some serious therapy."

I swallow and attempt to emulate the scolded, contrite, want-to-be-good kid they're determined to hear. "Understood."

"We'll see you in a month, Cal."

"Be safe!" Lynda says before Dad ends the call.

My feet hit the floor with a light thud, and I readjust my backpack with cold, numb fingers. I'm late to calc, and after the talk with Dad and Lynda, it's imperative I wear a squeaky-clean veneer.

I've been exposed to the drugs Dad threatens, and I never want to go back there. Not ever.

I descend the stairs one by one, mentally planning through my growing desperation of how I'm going to keep pursuing the society without setting off more alarm bells.

The Virtues have proven their control and talent for manipulation, but they're so cocky and drunk on the academy's power, they haven't considered who they've come up against. I'm just as skilled as them, if I want to access that buried part of my brain badly enough.

And after this, I do. Oh, I so absolutely *do.*

21

*T*he next couple of weeks inch by with the accompanying snot-trail of a snail.

Halloween night came and went, and I stayed in my room, despite Ivy's How do I know about Riordan's erection? Because after the Halloween dance, Ivy gained access into my dorm, arguing with the college student that she also worked the front desk at Thorne House, and thus, deserved a brothers-in-arms type of trust, and crawled into my bed, delighting me with her summary of hook-ups, fights, and passing outs.

Other than that, the only one other good thing that arose from this time-lapse was the removal of my bandage, revealing a nasty sunburn on my hand rather than an angry, second-degree mottling. The pink-tinged, sensitive skin still needs some doctoring, but as long as I apply ointment and protect it from the sun, I should be all right.

For the remainder of my punishment, I plan to keep my head down (as promised), reporting to my detention and cleaning duties on time and with a closed-lipped smile, despite the injustice inside me demanding I claw at the walls and scream at the top of my lungs.

But I don't, because I've done all that before, and didn't I learn my lesson back then?

Students largely ignore me, and I take enough time to wonder if it's because I remain under Chase's ill-begotten "protection," or if I've just started to smell so bad from picking up garbage, they've all decided I'm not worth the trouble.

The dining hall's become messier than usual, and cleaning up the grounds outside the school is no better. I use the same grasper tool I use in the dining hall, and since it and I have become so close, I've named it Grabby-Hands. We trudge all around campus, sticking everything from fast-food wrappers to used condoms that have somehow been tossed into the hedges.

I don't know why, and I don't want to know.

I've even been designated to empty the trash in the dorms but have been told to only do the girls' rooms.

I suppose Marron has spared me from the truly questionable and haunting items occupying boys' areas.

During class, I sit silently, only answering questions when called upon. It makes me less of a target and much more forgettable, a cloak I'm coming to accept with ease.

Chase goes out of his way to avoid me. On one Wednesday, when I was out near the fountain, clearing off tissues and receipts from Piper's makeshift memorial of flowers and weather-beaten stuffed animals, Chase exited the school, and as he strode down the wheelchair-access ramp and lifted his head, he took one look at me and spun on his heel back inside.

Literally screeched his brakes and did a U-turn.

"Coward!" I'd called after him, but he was no use to me anymore. I didn't give a damn whether he stayed or ran.

At least, my mind didn't care. My heart has other ideas, but I threaten it daily.

Chase lied. He lured me in with a book that turned out to be fairly useless, turned against me without blinking an eye, and sided with the Virtues, basically okaying their attack.

He uses his school powers for evil, and I am so *done* with that bastard.

Instead, my attention turned to Eden, who I've been watching carefully through the veiled lens of boredom as I sit quietly and unobtrusively in the classes we share.

She's the one who told me Piper was a Virtue, meaning she knows more than she's sharing, but I haven't gotten a chance to get her alone.

I plan to change that.

Eden's slippery, though. She's always in some sort of extra-curricular or so intense about her studying, that when I clean up enough to go visit Ivy in the evenings, she actually turns feral if I try so much as to say hello.

But there will come a moment when I corner her. Everyone gets themselves alone at some point during the day, and if I have to back her into a bathroom stall, I will.

Grabby-Hands and I are done for the day, so after swiping sweat-damp hair from my brow, I store him in the janitor's closet and head to the dorms.

Emma might be there, or she might not, but I'm finished pondering over her nightly escapes and where she goes. Ever since Chase showcased his talent for throwing me under the bus, I consider her an untrustworthy accessory.

After keying into our room, I walk into our quiet, deserted central area, peeling off clothes as I go. Emma's door is shut, and I don't bother to call out that I'm home, deciding a hot shower will be a much better greeting than anything I'd receive from Emma.

I spend a lot of time under the spray, enjoying how the water massages my aching shoulders and back, and taking pleasure in washing my hair and scalp. Once I'm confident I smell more like vanilla-orange blossom than day-old pizza, I turn off the faucet and grab the towel.

I'm wiping my face, when my phone dings where I left it by the sink.

The steam I've created in the small bathroom has misted both the mirror and my screen, so I give it a quick wipe before reading the text, continuing to towel off with one hand.

Private Number: You've been accused of something you didn't do.

The towel drops to the floor. I read it again, then reply:

Who is this?

After a few seconds, another message comes through.

It doesn't feel good to be framed, does it? Watch out. They're just warming up. Arresting you for Piper's murder is next.

Goosebumps appear on my forearms, despite the steam.

Me: Whoever you are, you missed the latest. Her sister's boyfriend's been arrested.

Unknown: But did he do it? Or did they?

I worry the inside of my cheek, coaxing my heart into a regular rhythm despite those very words circling my mind every day.

Me: You don't sound too sure either.

Private Number: I have dirt on the Nobles and Virtues, and I'm willing to share it with you.

The phone falls to my side, and I tip my chin up to the ceiling, closing my eyes on a sigh. I'm supposed to be squeaky clean— and not in the literal sense. I shouldn't be dipping into conspiracy tunnels and going off the rails with theories I can't back up. Not now, when my credibility is so shaken. But the temptation is there. No, the *need.*

Maybe I can do this one thing. All I have to do is listen and see what this person has to say. No physical action required, other than being careful.

I go back to my phone.

Me: Meet me in town Saturday morning at the lobster shack.

Private Number: Too exposed. I'll meet you in the public library, at the Briar exhibit in the back.

I suck on my tooth as I stare at the screen. Meeting in the most deserted, low-lit part of a failing library isn't my first choice, but if I scream, Darla will come running. Won't she?

Me: Ok. 9 am sharp.

Private Number: See you then. And keep alert. They're far from done with you.

God. Cryptic as all hell.

I drop my phone in the sink, combing my hair back and studying my face in the mirror. My cheekbones are sharply angled by the new hollows under my cheeks. My eyes, which used to be the same chameleon hazel as my mother's, have dulled to a murky gray. I'm paler than I should be, chewing on multi-vitamins no substitute for food, and my hands resemble blue, veiny claws rather than the soft, long-fingered femininity they once claimed.

A rumbling fear stirs in my belly the more I study my reflection. My inner demon cracks open an eye.

Was that a noise?

I glance at the locked bathroom door, sure I heard the clomp of shoes on the other side.

Emma rarely wears shoes indoors. It's how she creeps up on me so easily.

Another sound, familiar in its clatter, piques my hearing.

Someone's rifling through our fridge.

Visions of my cloaked visitors and the strange roses they leave behind creep alongside my periphery. Nightmares of the Virtues breaking in—Addisyn at the helm—and finishing the job pound against my exposed flesh.

They're far from done with you.

I step back from the door, pick up my towel, and wrap it around my torso. Then, I cautiously unlock and crack open the door.

22

A hunched figure leans into Emma's and my fridge, grunting as he clanks around jars.

I push the door open farther, calmer now that it's clear there's not a hoard of Cloaks ready to descend on my naked, vulnerable form, and pad out into the center of the room.

My gaze narrows.

That butt. I'd recognize that ass anywhere.

"What the hell are you doing with my food?"

My loud question causes him to jump and curse as he nails his head on the top of the fridge.

Chase staggers to his full height and faces me, an open carton clutched in his hands.

He swallows, his glazed stare running over me, then going back to the food. "I'm looking for my sister."

"Well, you're not going to find her inside my pad thai."

Chase grunts, then throws it back in the fridge and slams the door, bottles rattling. "It's bland, anyway."

I lean in for a closer inspection, noticing the red rimming his eyes and how they can't quite focus on a single object. His posture is lopsided, his uniform rumpled, his hair askew.

Yep. He's either drunk or high. Probably both.

My lips go tight. "Haven't you heard the latest? No one's allowed in or out of my dorm room, other than my meandering roommate."

"Mm." Chase pretends to think on the house arrest *he* helped to cause. "My sister's re-acclimating to the academy slowly. I'm allowed in to help her along."

I make a sound of disgust. "You should go back to your dorms, where maybe somebody might be happy to see you."

"Nope. I told you. Looking for Emma."

I glance toward Emma's room but notice her door's ajar and she's nowhere inside.

"Checked there already," Chase says as I turn back to him.

"You won't find her in my room, either. And since I was in the bathroom..." I wait for Chase to finish my sentence. When he doesn't, I sigh. "She's not here, Chase."

"Oh. Damn." Chase leans against the countertop instead of making a move to leave.

When I see where his eyes drift, my grip tightens at the top of my towel.

My nipples, however, have other ideas and demand to be set free, exposed to the air and Chase's sexual survey.

I clear my throat. "Can you leave now?"

Chase angles his head, his attention frozen on my chest. After a moment, he murmurs, "You're gorgeous, you know that?"

Ignoring the traitorous twinge of my heart, I growl, "Fuck off and *go*, Chase."

"I remember what you look like under there." He gives a heavy-lidded blink. "It's singed into my brain, how you curve in all the right places, the way you fit into my hands." His eyes flick up to mine. "Your taste is still on my tongue."

"You don't get to do that," I rasp. "Not after what you've done."

He flinches, and that brief flash of emotion gives me more insight into his thought process than he's ever allowed before.

Chase is ashamed, even though he's made it clear where his loyalty lies. He wants to destroy my time here, or at the very least, ruin it, but I'm starting to think ... is it because he has a personal vendetta, or is there another factor at play?

He doesn't follow up with an excuse, though, and for some reason, that enrages me further.

"Why did you lie to Marron?" I ask him in a stronger voice.

Chase looks up to the ceiling instead of answering, and damn it, I should've expected that. Chase doesn't give answers; he incites more questions.

Yet, he stills as if he's preparing himself for a battering, so I persist. "You *know* I didn't vandalize the chem lab." I suck in a disgusted breath. "If this is some fucked up way of getting back at me for ending what we had, need I remind you, it was *you* who walked out of here after I told you Piper was pregnant. It was *you* who asked me to find out the DNA of the fetus. And it was *you* who gave me Howard Mason's book, pretending like you were trying to protect me when you just wanted to set me up for *them*."

A low rumble sounds from his throat. "There's so much. So much you don't know."

"What have I done to make you want to hurt me?" The question comes out unfiltered, and I wince at the emotional whimper it becomes. "Did you enjoy toying with me? When I fell for your act, when I let you into my bed, were you turned on by the pain you were about to cause?"

In a blink, Chase is centered in my vision, stepping so close that he puts his hands on my waist.

I gasp, losing what little breath was escaping from the thickness of my throat, and look up at him.

This close, I smell the liquor on his breath. The weed.

He's only attracted to me right now because he's lost his sobering armor. That fact is like a bucket of ice water splashing over my head, my shoulders, and my face crumples with the icy realization before I can stop it.

I place my hands against his chest, pushing him back. He doesn't move.

"This isn't you right now," I whisper near his heart. "You can't give me what I want, so I'm not going to give into you."

The barest brush hits the bottom of my chin as he tilts it up. His eyes search mine with bleary melancholy.

At last, he says, "The rules within the academy were written long before you got here. I can't disregard them the way Howard Mason tried and the way you want me to."

"Thorne and Rose Briar created rival societies in this school," I murmur in return. "But what does their twisted past have to do with your relationship with me?"

He strokes a finger down the side of my face, and I turn in to it like the starving, friendless cat that I am. Chase is compromised, yes, but he looks so damn tired, and I wonder if, under his stare, I resemble the same.

"I can't tell you everything but know this..." he says. "I care about you."

I snort, hoping to jar myself back into reality. "But your actions will never show it, will they?"

Chase ensures I meet his eyes, then repeats, "I care about you."

I shove at his pecs. "No, you fucking don't. You *lied* for them. You *helped* them."

He bends close. "Listen to my voice behind my words. I care about you."

My lips slam shut as I search his eyes, the emotion in his tone hitting my ears, but in all the wrong places. It isn't right, what he's communicating. It isn't *fair*.

"So, you lied to protect me? Is that it? You're helping them to protect me?" I push at his shoulders again, but his body doesn't give way to my angry shoves. "My life could be ruined because of your so-called *protection*. I was nearly beaten to a pulp because of it. My dad wants to commit me. Do you know how fucked up that—?"

Chase catches the rest of my question with his lips, the pressure so sizzling, so startling, my body buckles until his grip holds me steady.

We stumble backward, and my head bangs against the wall as his hand cups my cheek and our lips angle to meet each other with a perfect, desperate sear.

My mouth parts to let him in, despite my better judgement's cry to keep him out. I push my chest into his, starving for the friction, aching for him to fill the void he left so wide and echoing when he strode out of here, leaving me in his wake.

Don't think about that, I chide. *Not if you're doing this with him. Take it for what it is. What you want.*

Chase rips the towel from my grip, my naked body molding against his uniform, dampening the school colors with my scent. My hands tangle in his hair when I rise up on my tiptoes, matching his need at the same time he straightens, and I jump so he can catch my thighs around his waist.

He breaks off the kiss. "I care about you," he repeats on a growl. "And it would've been so much worse for you if I hadn't intervened."

I cup his face, my fingers leaving indents in his angular face. "Shut up."

An approving sound comes from his throat as he spins, and it's with the graceful, rower's balance that he carries me into my bedroom and kicks the door shut.

He places me on my bed, but instead of covering me with his body, he takes a long, drawn-out survey, from the top of my head to my toes.

"Chase," I say on a nervous laugh, battling against the need to pull the covers over myself.

"I meant what I said. You're gorgeous."

"You're drunk."

Chase cocks his head. "I'm not so fucked-up that I can't see your beauty."

He unbuttons his collared white shirt, exposing his hairless, carved-in-bronze chest, his six-pack rippling with the movement of his arms.

I try not to gape, because *I'm* not the beautiful one, but I refuse to look away from the visual treat of his muscular, athletic body before he uses its talents.

With a flick of his thumb, his belt's unbuckled and his uniform slacks undone and pooled to the ground. He steps out of his boxers with the same, rapid grace, then puts one knee on the bed as he strokes his straining erection.

And I think, *God, yes. I missed this.*

My core aches for him to fill it, and my starvation must be written all over my face, because he smirks.

With that kind of introduction, I expect him to take me with one thrust, but instead, he moves to settle himself between my legs, but softly strokes my inner thighs. His calloused fingers travel up my stomach, tracing my breasts, leaving shivers along their path, and I'm so lulled by it, so attached to its sweetness, that my heart falls to pieces as his fingers carve their destiny across my naked chest.

Breaths heaving, I internally beg for patience. Noticing my distress, Chase smiles again and dips his fingers down until he's stroking my folds with the same light caress he'd used to trace my body.

I can't meet his quiet seduction with the same amount of grace. It's been so long. Too long. I buck under his hand, twisting and writhing to try to coax his fingers deeper, but he won't comply.

"You're so wet," he rasps out, his focus on his finger, curling it in and out. "So damn ready for me."

"Chase," I moan, so aching and wanton, I have to shut my

eyes and whine into the blackness. If I watch him much longer, I'll explode.

His silky voice hits my ears. "Stroke me."

Chase lifts my hand until I curl my fingers around his shaft. During his worship of me, he hadn't touched his dick, nor did he grind it against me. It throbbed and bounced with the same need he was enticing from me, but now I realize, he was doing it to match my desperation, to draw out our need.

Why?

He groans at the tightening of my grip. I stroke, as he asked, then pump, the tender pinkness of my hand and wrist forgotten as I increase the friction, then, needing moisture, rise up enough to draw the tip of him in my mouth.

Chase sucks in air through his teeth at the contact, tipping over the precipice as he watches my lips encircle his cock.

He grits out, "I need to be inside you."

I release his dick with a *pop*, then ask as I look up at him, "What's stopping you?"

Chase gnashes his teeth, then bends and rifles through my nightstand for a condom. Once he slips it on, he towers over me, pressing my legs apart. But instead of taking me with threatening, animalistic prowess, Chase reins it in, lining himself up with my entrance with trembling, *enraging,* slowness.

"Chase," I beg, but he doesn't acknowledge my pleas.

Inch by tortuous inch, he sinks into my folds, his jaw tight. When his arms come down on either side of me, and I grip his shoulders to bring him closer, I use that momentum to thrust my hips up and wrap my legs around his torso, taking him all the way in.

He buries his face in my neck, groaning, fighting some unseen force. I stroke his hair and whisper in his ear. "You have me. Right now, I'm yours."

Chase lifts his head to kiss me, and it's with such urgent

desire, my teeth cut into my lips, but I don't cry out, though it's dizzying and confusing. I press against him harder.

He thrusts, but not with the same possessiveness as before. He's not demanding ownership. It's more like he's asking permission to go slow, to stretch me to my limits with tender strokes.

When the orgasm builds, I bite down on his neck, my cry of release muffled and tinged with blood.

Chase has his own release, his thrusts deep and quick, before he collapses, his chest falling against mine.

I tangle my fingers in his hair, massaging his scalp, and hope he doesn't move. I like the warmth of him, and his weight has a calming effect, like he's squeezing all the angst from my heart so it can maybe find its lost pieces again.

His head moves. "You okay?"

"Mm-hmm," I say, tracing spirals in his hair.

"I don't ... I don't want to hurt you."

My circles stop.

"It's best for both of us if I stay away from you, but I—you're so damn addictive, with your smell and your taste ... and the darkness you try to hide." He lifts his head. "Like me."

We take a long study of each other, but instead of getting lost in the golden flecks of his eyes, I'm the first to break the silence. "It's okay. I know what this is."

He bows his head, blond locks slipping forward. "You don't. And I hope you never will."

My brows furrow, but Chase lifts off me and bends to get dressed.

I want to plead with him to stay the night, but the futileness of the request prevents my tongue from forming the words.

Why should I ask him for comfort, when I swore to hate him the instant he sided with Falyn and her friends? Or how about when he decided protecting Briarcliff's secret society was more important than exploring the budding relationship between us?

With that in mind, I sit up, gathering the sheets around myself, and watch him dress.

Though I'm liquid and docile with the orgasm he gave me, I'm reminded that the physical is all he's willing to give.

"Emma's probably in the library," he says.

My brows push together. Why would she go to the very place where her life, as she knew it, went up in flames?

"It's where she goes sometimes," he continues. "You may not believe me, but I really was looking for her when I came in, before you and I..."

I nod but don't say anything else. It's not like he'd answer my confusion over Emma's choices.

"And Callie?"

I watch him carefully. "Hmm?"

"I'm sorry." He shrugs on his collared shirt, leaving it unbuttoned. "For what it's worth."

I set my jaw, folding my arms over my knees and waiting a few more minutes, ensuring he's left, before I reach under my pillow and pull out what I'd managed to dig from his pocket in the midst of our foreplay.

I flip it around in my fingers a few times, watching the light play against the laminate, but I don't feel bad for using his sexual weakness for me. Not after what he's done.

After one last glance through my open doorway, I twist and shove his room card into the crack between my mattress and bed frame, then turn over and try to chase dreams instead.

23

*S*aturday morning dawns early and bright—for my side of the dorm room, anyway.

Emma came back late, and I assume is still sleeping behind her closed door as I get ready. It's a relief not to face her the night after my impromptu sex with Chase. Not that she and I are known for sharing secrets, but I'm wary she might notice a change in the air, an electric charge to my step, or anything slightly off that I don't think to hide, sending her twin senses tingling.

I couldn't get much rest after Chase left, my mind alive with our sex and his motives and my plans. Too many possibilities flitted behind my eyes. Not only the risks, but the repercussions would be astounding if I get caught.

They've left me no choice. If Chase can't or won't speak about Piper's involvement with the Virtues, I'll have to dig up the evidence myself.

Just the thought sends shivers along my spine, but I refuse to shake the idea that Piper's murder doesn't stop with Jack, just like it wasn't solved with Dr. Luke. Not only is Jack Addisyn's boyfriend, both Addy and Piper have Virtue connections, a secret society created by Rose Briar that, from what I've seen, prefers unscrupulous activities over wholesome ones.

It begs the question: why did Rose create a rival society to the Nobles? And are they still implementing her wishes, or have they gone rogue, beginning with Piper's downfall?

Ugh. I'm so confused.

And determined, goddamnit.

Before I can get to any of that, however, I have an important meeting which I can't be late for.

Ready just shy of eight o'clock, I throw my tote over my shoulder and head out, taking the stairs instead of the elevator.

I have nothing to hide, so I exit out the front this time, lifting my hand in a wave to the campus officer standing beside our usual college girl and her closed laptop. She's looking more alert than usual these days, and not too happy about it, but permission to study in the public library in town couldn't be denied by Marron—especially considering my *relationships* with other girls in this school who are known to use the school's library.

It's better for everyone involved if I stay away.

The automatic double-doors slide open as I approach the exit. When I hit the sidewalk in hopes of seeing Yael (who I requested ten minutes ago), I almost run into Eden.

"Oh. Hey," I say when I come to a halt a few steps away from her back.

Eden stiffens, then raises her head and shoves her phone into her back pocket. She turns, and I'm hopeful the sound coming out of her lips is a reciprocal, "Hey."

But probably not.

"What are you doing here?" I ask.

Eden shrugs. "Are you saying the only place I belong is Scholarship Row?"

"God. No." I step up beside her. "I've just never seen you hanging out around here."

"I have feet," Eden retorts. "I use them sometimes."

I lift my hands. "Okay. I come in peace."

Eden sighs, going back to staring at Rose House across the drive. "Sorry. It's been a rough morning."

"Already?"

An incoming crosswind causes strands of Eden's black hair to tangle around her nose, and she tucks them behind her ear with an aggravated jerk. "Maybe I'm here waiting for you, to give you a message. How's your treasure hunt going? Have they scared you off yet?"

I cross my arms, mirroring her pose. "Pretty sucky, since most people pretend they don't have tongues when I ask questions. Including you."

Eden purses her lips. "Maybe because I've been you. Before. In ninth grade. I got involved in trying to figure them out and they made me pay for it. I wasn't a chosen one." Eden snorts, continuing her stare-down of Rose House. "So, go ahead and construe my silence as trying to keep you from the same fate."

I huff out a breath. "Another protector? Thanks, but no thanks."

"Don't you get it?" Eden turns to me. "You're not allowed to know about them until they invite you to. Give up, Callie."

"Then why tell me Piper was a Virtue?"

"Because I thought it would make you back off out of fear, not blindly pursue it like a moron."

I roll my eyes but decide to change tactics. "I've figured out most of the players. Falyn, Addisyn, you know, the usual witches of Briarcliff. But what I can't quite confirm ... is Emma a Virtue?"

There might as well have been a car backfiring nearby, with the way Eden startles. But she reconstructs her emotionless mask before I can remark on it. "Why, Callie? Seriously. Why keep doing this to yourself?"

"I'm not going to stop," I tell her in a low voice. "These Virtues? They've messed with the wrong girl."

"They're not even *close* to messing with you. Don't you understand?"

"Then make me." My hands go to my hips. "Because if Emma is a Virtue, then that fire she was trapped in had something to do with them. And her attack. It involved the Virtues, too. Didn't it? That's the level of *messing with* that you're warning me about."

Eden thins her lips but won't break eye contact. I take that as my answer.

"So, the Nobles didn't retaliate?" I ask. "What about Chase? Wouldn't he have done everything in his power to protect his sister?"

Eden takes her time answering. "I suppose it depends on Emma's level of betrayal."

As it sinks in, I whisper, "What?"

"It's a rigorous process to even become a prospect of the Virtues. The hazing is even worse. But betraying the society? Even the Nobles' highest member can't protect you from that kind of downfall."

"Highest member? Who, like their father?"

Eden tucks her hands in her pockets, gesturing to the road. "There's your ride."

I glance in that direction, but by the time I look back, Eden's walking away. "Eden, wait! I—"

She waves at Yael, who gives a cheery salute, but Eden might as well be deaf to my voice.

"Damnit," I mutter as I open the car door. "She's escaped me again."

"Hey there, Callie," Yael greets.

I murmur a hello while buckling my seatbelt, unable to bring my mind in the car with me. It's still under Thorne House's awning, interpreting Eden's explanations.

"What were you and my daughter whispering about?" he asks as he turns from the dorms.

And just like that, my attention dives into the passenger seat. "Eden's your kid?"

"So they tell me," he says with a good-natured laugh, but sobers when he meets my eye in the rearview mirror. "She's had a tough time of it, so if you're getting to know her despite her ... prickly nature, I'm grateful to you."

I respond with a thin smile. "I'm sure the more I get to know her, the more open she'll be."

"I was hoping you'd connect with her," Yael says as we slope through the winding roads of Briarcliff Academy. "I wasn't about to push it. Eden would kill me if I did, but I couldn't lose the hunch that you're dealing with something similar involving the privileged kids on campus."

My gaze darts from the window to my hand, and Yael's fatherly concern.

Yael asks quietly. "Are they bullying you, too?"

I lick my lips in thought. "Not quite. Well, not since Piper, you know..."

"Yes. She was the roughest with my Eden as well. Lord, the shit that brat pulled. Excuse my disrespect of the dead, but she was terrible. Eden's been with these kids since fifth grade, for as long as I've been working as a driver. It's part of the deal. My kids get free room, board, and education so long as I'm employed here. My wife and I thought to remove her many times, but Edie insisted we shouldn't. This is where she can get the best education. The best start. Neither me nor her mom ever went to college, and to think of Edie attending an Ivy League? It was one of the most difficult decisions of my life, wondering whether we should keep her here."

I nod in sad understanding. "Eden's stubborn. I doubt she wanted Piper and her crew to win."

"Hit the nail on the head with that one." Yael turns right on to the forested road heading to Main Street. "But it was ... filthy, what they did to her. She tried so hard to fit in with them, but got garbage tossed at her for her efforts. Her uniform ripped to shreds while she was in a swim meet. Rumors spread about her through social media. One time ... they took a picture of her getting changed in the locker room. Circulated it."

Yael's voice has gone hoarse, his dark-skinned hands clenched around the wheel so hard, his skeleton almost bursts from his skin.

Hearing all this makes me yearn to talk to Eden, to assure her I'm not one of them and I could be there for her as a friend if she wanted me, but ... most of me understands these are nothing but futile words until I gain her trust. And that is so much harder to show than pity.

"Did you speak to the headmaster about all this?" I ask Yael.

"Absolutely. But you can come to your own conclusions on what happened."

I grumble in response. Briarcliff's motto shouldn't be *Rise with Might*, it should be *Money Over Child Welfare*.

Yael and I don't speak for the rest of the trip, but I think hard on his confession. The constant brutality Eden faced probably caused her to pinpoint the source of her suffering: the Virtues. Maybe that's why the bullying escalated, because she knew too much and they had to keep her silent. Especially if, according to her, she tried to become one and failed.

My head falls back against the seat. I want so badly for Eden to confide in me, but is it because I want her to heal, or would I rather satisfy my selfish motive to know more about the Virtues?

No wonder she doesn't trust me.

"We're here," Yael says. His eyes crinkle into a kind smile in the rearview. "Thank you for hearing me out. I hope I haven't..."

I give a reassuring shake of my head. "I won't say anything to anyone or make Eden's life harder. You have my word."

"You're a good kid, you know that?"

I laugh self-consciously as I open the door.

"Knew it the second you stepped off that train, all gangly and sweet."

This time, my smile is true, and I wave as he drives off.

Yael's compliment lightens my steps as I climb up the library stairs. No one has seen me in a good light since my mom, and I hadn't known how much of a hole that perception left until Yael reminded me that, yes, I can be destined for good things.

The library's AC is still at full power when I head inside, and I fold my arms around myself as I nod to Darla. She perks right up, her scarlet-red nails glinting under the light and matching her cat-eye glasses. A paperback sits open at her desk, and I have no doubt the Duchess has been at it again.

I don't slow enough to chat, intent on hurrying to the back and meeting my mystery texter.

Sadly, no one's waiting for me when I get there, but I force myself to gather some patience. Maybe they were held up somewhere. Or, they had to get in line for Yael's services. Who knows?

To pass the time, I linger over the glass cases, installed at waist-level and featuring Thorne Briar's personal items, reading the small placards detailing what they are.

There's his watch, the face cracked and fogged, but the gold touches everlasting. I skim over his ledgers, tap the glass over some leather riding gloves, and cock my head at one of the original bricks from the school's building before coming across the original blueprint of the academy, and—

I halt at the proposed design, somewhat shocked that the Wolf's Den was sketched out from the beginning. Even back then, Thorne had it in his mind to call it a senior lounge, the blue cursive faded with age, but legible.

Wolf's Den. Upperclassmen Privilege Only.

.   .   .

My eyes drift up, to the intricate detail of the map of Briarcliff, the roads painted in a bronze type of acrylic. In one corner, just above the glass displays, is a photo of the Briar family, Rose settled in the middle, between Thorne and Theodore Briar, with Richard and the other wives flanking them. With the help of the placard below the picture, I'm able to put names to faces. They're standing outside Briarcliff Academy, and the brief inscription tells me this was opening day. *September 10, 1920.*

I hold my breath. This photo was taken exactly one year *before* Rose plunged to her death.

Rose is dark-haired, her curls a stark ebony in the black-and-white filter. She wears a pale dress with a hint of a smile on her lips while the men and women surrounding her are straight-backed and grim.

She grins just like Emma did in her family photo, I muse. *Except Emma lost her smile, not her life. Barely.*

"Are you finding these items as interesting as my class lectures, or was I the better story-teller?"

I freeze at the voice, then ever so slowly, turn toward the familiar figure.

Releasing my breath, I whisper, "Dr. Luke."

24

*D*r. Luke is more haggard than I remember, his natural tan highlighting the aging crevices on his face rather than giving him the healthy California glow I'd admired when I first met him.

His chestnut hair is unwashed and flattened against his scalp, his linen button-up wrinkled as much as his slacks, and his eyes are so bloodshot and purple-lined, I doubt he's slept in days. He offers a reassuring smile, but it's stuttered and incomplete—the opposite of the disarming grin he's used on his students.

I back away in response, almost into the glass case. "Should you be talking to me?"

Dr. Luke releases a forced laugh. "Probably not, no. But you're not in any danger—from me. I like my women young, it's true, but I also like them willing."

My stomach curdles at his perverted candidness. This isn't the teacher I remember—the jovial, good-looking professor who gave boys and girls alike heart emojis for eyes.

Then again, he was never the lovable teacher he purported to be.

"What are you doing here?" I ask, my gaze bouncing around the stacks behind him. I calculate the distance to the front desk.

"Still haven't connected the dots, have you?" Dr. Luke shoves his hands in his pockets. "C'mon, Cal, you're smarter than this."

My gut clenches at my stepdad's term for me, but luckily, my breakfast stays down. "You're the one who texted me."

"That's right."

I cock my head, pretending like I'm not frazzled by his appearance. "Why?"

He sighs and steps closer, but when he sees me skitter back, he halts his steps and moves his hands in a calming gesture, like he's approaching a shy horse.

"I noticed your impressive power of deduction this semester," he says. "You chose Rose Briar for your history paper. Notably, you had a theory that almost two hundred years ago, Briarcliff Academy fathered a secret society who knighted themselves the Nobles."

"Which you gave me a C for," I mumble, then internally shake my head. My falling grades shouldn't matter.

Dr. Luke raises his brows. "For reasons I'm sure you can understand."

"You made it seem like I failed," I say. "Because I was using my imagination instead of investigative research."

"You didn't cite any materials after your statements that a society was borne under the Briars."

"Because I *couldn't*," I snap.

"Because you were afraid of revealing your source?"

I shake my head, remembering how Chase had managed to fool me with his father's decoy. "It could've been just another way to screw with me. I was afraid to reference something that could've been faked."

"You're lying."

Dr. Luke takes another step forward, but I don't shrink back this time. I'm in public, of a sort. I'm safe.

"You stumbled on a hidden relic. You found writings that were previously thought lost in a fire," Dr. Luke says, his eyes alighting on mine. "Letters written in Rose Briar's own hand."

I give a sharp inhale. "How do you know that?"

Dr. Luke chuckles, but there's no mirth. "I thought you an astute, if misguided, student. Don't fail me now."

I take a moment to think, and a revelation takes hold. I whisper, "Piper."

"Indeed."

I say, "She's the only other person who could've known the letter still existed. Because she found it first, then hid it."

"On my advice." Dr. Luke lowers his voice, before continuing, "She confided in me. I was the only person she trusted. Not even her sister was a reliable confidant."

I refuse to believe him on sight, but I can't fight the curiosity that slithers into the base of my throat. "Did she tell you what was in them?"

Dr. Luke smiles. "Now, there's the Callie Ryan I was expecting. In my time away, you've found out about the other half of the Nobles, didn't you?"

I raise my chin, refusing to give him the name. Just in case he's baiting me.

The crepe-like skin under his eye twitches, amused at my tactics. "The Virtues," he supplies dryly. "Piper was disenchanted with her role among them. She thought there was some disguised malfeasance going on. Isn't that cute? She searched for a forbidden secret within the secret society."

I shake my head, though his statement nudges for attention. "She wouldn't dare tell you something like that. Societies have strict rules. You were an outsider. She'd get in huge trouble if it were ever found out she confided in you."

Dr. Luke angles his head. "She's dead. So, there's that."

I force my voice to keep working, despite my heart pounding in my ears. "The Virtues killed her?" *I knew it.*

"Not quite." Dr. Luke moves closer, until his body towers over mine. I recoil, but it's like I'm caught under a scope of sunlight, unable to escape.

"This is why I asked to see you," he says. "I know who stole those pages in Piper's diary."

I hiss in air, then respond coolly, "Those pages mean nothing now. Jack's in custody."

"That idiot?" Dr. Luke scoffs. "He couldn't kill a kitten if it bit him in the nuts. He's a fall boy, just like I was, and just like you'll become if you don't start listening to me."

He grabs my arm, and I choke on a squeal, fighting against his hold, but he's relentless. He growls, "I know about the chem lab destruction they're blaming on you. The school arrest they've put you under. They're forming the foundation for your instability, Callie. They *know* about your history. The psychiatric care you required after your mother's death. They have people in play who will break your heart *and* your mind if you let them. They're planning your downfall, and if you'll just hold *still* instead of inching away from me, you will have the chance to heed my warning."

Abruptly, he lets go. I stumble at the shift in balance.

"Or not," he snaps. "Your choice."

I rub the spot he gripped, but don't kick into a run and sprint the hell out of here.

Everything he's saying clangs in my head, along with a tolling of names, over and over.

Piper. Emma. Eden.

They all sparred with the Virtues and lost.

Dr. Luke takes my slumped posture as permission to continue. "They've been using you as their pawn to cover up Piper's murder. A Plan C, if you will—if you'll forgive the coincidence of your name starting with the same letter. Or applaud them for their creativity."

Dr. Luke smiles, and for that brief span of time, he resembles the man I trusted to sit beside me when I was interrogated, because my stepdad and Lynda couldn't be there. I wanted him as my guardian when Ahmar was so far away. This bashful, handsome man, whose grin always communicated it was going to be all right.

Dr. Luke speaks, and what he says saves me from the bittersweet spell.

"They led you to me," he says. "They orchestrated your finding of Piper's diary and the name Mr. S., then largely left it up to your clinical obsession to find out who the nickname belonged to. Your convictions may be wrong, but hell if you don't pursue the destruction of your fellow man with all of your unstable heart."

Dr. Luke chortles, and it slithers down my spine.

"And those missing pages in Piper's diary?" he says. "That was their deliberate concealment of another potential suspect—Jack. She wrote all about her affair with him, how she was going behind her sister's back, how much she *enjoyed* fucking the forbidden fruits of her professor and her sister's boyfriend. And yes, Callie, she wrote about the unexpected pregnancy."

I lean against the glass display, hunching over and placing my hands on my thighs. Most of his speech could be construed as crazy conspiracies or a personal vendetta. But Piper's missing entries? What he says they contain could very well be the truth. Why else tear them out?

"How?" I ask through the curtain of my hair. "How could you know what she wrote?"

"Before you moved in, I was in Piper's room all the time," Dr. Luke says above my head. "I snuck in through the stairs after hours and left before dawn. But when she slept, I'd read her diary. Why not? She was an enigma to me, this girl who reigned terror on her classmates but was a mouse in bed. I felt it was my duty to gain insight into her insecure and wretched mind, in case she ever wanted to use our affair against me."

"That only gives you more motive," I grind out, turning my

head enough to look at him. "She was cheating on you, and when she got knocked up, that must've pissed you off."

"Oh. I was pissed," Dr Luke responds hoarsely. "But don't take me for a fool. We always used protection."

I straighten, taking deep breaths. I was *not* going to be sick.

"I was going to end things, anyway," Dr. Luke continues. "This only made it easier. She called me from that party, upset and drunk, begging me to help her, and I went there to break it up and break up with *her*. She'd gone too far, calling me when her friends were around. Getting pregnant. She'd become a liability. With the way she was carrying on, there was no way she was keeping that baby, but that didn't matter to me anymore. In that moment, she was stupid and pregnant. And when I left her, she was still stupid and pregnant. Because she was *alive*."

He flings callousness the way Falyn flings insults, but I can't duck in time. I'm so appalled. I can't look away from him.

When Chase found out about the baby and that it was potentially his, he was beside himself. He wanted to be there for Piper and was so furious with himself for not seeing it sooner and saving her.

Oh, Piper, I think. *You chose the wrong guy.*

"The baby's Jack's," I say, eyeing Dr. Luke. I have no idea if he's heard the news or how he'll react to it.

He doesn't flinch. "Yes. And who do you think that pissed off the most?"

Dr. Luke crosses his arms, his heavy silence awaiting my answer. He's studying me as if I should know outright, but it takes me a few seconds. Chase is exactly the type to sneak behind the curtains and orchestrate a scene the way he wants it, but I witnessed the raw devastation in his face when I told him Piper was pregnant, and either he is the best undiscovered actor America will never see, or he didn't know.

Then, there's Piper's friends, who would relish the hypocrisy, not end it by hurting Piper and stealing her secrets. They lived off

Piper's rules. Her enemies were their enemies. Her secrets were theirs. It was considered an honor to be part of her group and have her confide in you. Isn't that what Eden said?

The last name I think of, I stumble on. Mostly because it makes too much sense.

I meet Dr. Luke's eyes. "Addisyn."

He nods.

"You're saying Addisyn knew about her boyfriend cheating before Piper died. That she ripped out the pages in Piper's diary."

Dr. Luke straightens, folds his hands behind his back, and levels his shoulders. "No, dear. I'm saying Addisyn killed her sister."

25

Addisyn killed her sister.

The sentence forms a circle in my brain, one end chomping at the other, like a snake eating its own tail, until nothing remains but the husk of Dr. Luke's allegation.

"Think about it, Callie," he says.

The library is suddenly cloying—too hushed, too stale, too warm. My arms itch, and I scrape at them through the denim of my jacket.

"If I didn't work out as a suspect," he continues, "then they had Jack in place as the next one. These people, they *plan*, and human pawns are nothing if not variable. I could've come up with an alibi—which I did. Now, they're directing their efforts at Jack, another innocent man. What if he's next to admit an alibi? Yes, that baby was his, but he didn't kill Piper. I know that, and the society knows that, because I'm positive Addisyn did."

I hold a hand to my head, my fingers digging into my scalp. "How are you so sure?"

"Piper spoke about her sister often, and not on affectionate terms. They hated each other, were always in competition with one another. That need to excel was stoked by their mother, who encouraged their fights and lavished love upon the winner. The loser received the scraps. The chores, the humiliation and disdain, and the worst punishment: complete invisibility. This went on with everything from their academics, to dance, to rowing, to boys."

I level a look at him. "You are not a *boy*."

Dr. Luke concedes my point with what I now know is feigned bashfulness. "All too right. But my point is, Addisyn was always the loser."

"So, what? She killed Piper out of jealousy? Because Piper slept with her boyfriend?"

A shimmer of disappointment runs through me, but I grip it with a firm inner hand. Piper's dead. And if it was her sister, it probably was jealousy. Isn't that the number one reason why people kill? Why should I *ever* be disappointed it's not more complicated than that?

Because you want it to be the society. You want your instincts to be on point. For once.

Dr. Luke clicks his tongue, regaining my attention. "No, Callie. It was jealousy over Piper being a member of the Virtues. Jack's taking her sister as a side-piece merely provided her with an excuse."

I screw my eyes shut, despite my inner devil clawing for attention. *We were right.* "You're wrong. Addisyn's a Virtue. I'm sure of it. She was with the Cloaks who attacked me in the chem lab."

"Uh-huh."

I open my eyes, where Dr. Luke remains straight-backed and focused. On me.

"Continue with that line of thought," he prompts.

"I don't..." I massage the back of my neck, picking up Dr. Luke's facts like breadcrumbs leading me into an oven fire. "Something Falyn said that night. About Addisyn proving herself ... oh, God. Addisyn was *made* a Virtue because she murdered her sister?"

"Ding ding ding! They had to shut her up somehow. Addy was never the brightest, though she tried. Piper won their family competitions more often than not. And when Piper became a Virtue and Addisyn didn't, well ... to say that caused discord would be an understatement."

"And you know all this because Piper told you. Who would've been sworn to secrecy. "

Dr. Luke nods. "If Addisyn read what I did in Piper's diary, *oof.*" Dr. Luke palms his chest. "What a way to find out the one thing you had over your perfect sister—happiness and a steady boyfriend—was nothing but a cruel joke. *And* Piper received a coveted, rare position in the Virtues, which you bet your ass she lorded over her sister, societal oath or not. I'd be fucking furious."

"Weren't you? When you read it for yourself?"

Dr. Luke makes a dismissive gesture with his hand. "Piper and I fucked. We screwed with each other. We trusted each other with forbidden secrets because *we* were forbidden. But don't mistake what I did with her for love. I've made myself clear in that respect: I met with her that night to end things. I'd moved on."

I push off the display. "That baby, if it were yours, and if she had told someone, could've ruined you."

"She wasn't going to keep it, nor would she sully her perfect scholastic reputation over banging a professor who's not even tenured. Did I not just tell you about these Harringtons and their killer drive for success?"

He's running me around in circles. Using hard-hitting, murderous, circular reasoning to make his facts come at me so hard, I'll have trouble sorting through them.

"Addisyn's a bitch, but I don't see her as a killer," I say, keeping my voice level. "You didn't see her at Piper's memorial. Or when she found out her boyfriend was arrested. She was devastated."

"The Virtues are out to protect themselves, not the Harrington family line. Jack was the next viable option, much better than Addisyn herself, who could blow the whistle on the hidden society while in custody. No, instead they made her a member, allowed her access to all their shiny things, groomed her response to her sister's death, and in return, she had to stay quiet. Even during her boyfriend's subsequent arrest."

"But I—"

"Do you think they want police crawling all over the place? Asking questions? Showing up with a warrant for blueprints to all the hidden corridors and rooms in the academy?"

He has a point, but I don't concede it. I narrow my eyes at him. "What are you getting out of this? Why meet me anonymously when you could just go to the police? I doubt you're allowed to be around—"

"Kids?" Dr. Luke flashes a sardonic smile. "You're eighteen now, Callie. And I'm at least two thousand feet from Briarcliff's campus while I await my hearing. Can't I be seeking you out because of the revenge in my heart? Those bitches ruined my life."

I curl my lip at him. "They didn't force you to have sex with a teenager."

He waves me off. "If you want more convincing evidence, read the missing pages for yourself. They're in Addisyn's room."

Bile spreads across my tongue at the thought of how Dr. Luke could know something like that, unless he was lurking around campus, going into her room ... "Addisyn looks almost identical to Piper. If it weren't for the years between them, they'd be twins. Does that turn you on, Dr. Luke?"

His face turns to stone. "Focus on what's important, Callie."

Dr. Luke turns to leave, but I stop him with one more question. "What is the Nobles' role in all this? Why aren't they doing anything to stop the Virtues?"

He turns his head and smiles at me in profile. "Oh. They're helping you, don't worry."

Dr. Luke retreats into one of the stacks, and I race after him, nowhere near finished, but I can't risk calling out his name and drawing Darla's attention. Instead, I hiss, "Dr. Luke!"

"Don't forget about Plan C," he says over his shoulder, but doesn't slow his steps.

He's gone before I make it to the front desk.

A hard exhale billows from my lips as I stare out the library's large windows to Main Street.

"Trouble, honey?" Darla asks.

I fix my jacket and clear my throat in an effort to calm the raging river of blood through my veins. "I'm fine. Thanks, Darla."

"You spent a while at the exhibit back there. Pretty fascinating stuff, isn't it?"

I glance at her, mustering up a smile. It all seemed like standard artifacts to me. But then, perhaps my perception of history has become a little skewed. "Sure is."

"I'm such a sucker for romance." Darla leans her elbows on her desk, a dreamy look in her eye.

I hate being rude, especially to someone so nice, so I prepare myself for a little small talk, despite the bomb going off in my head. "I noticed. What are you reading?"

"Oh, this?" Darla giggles as she lifts her paperback. "*The Duchess and the Brave Butler*. Good stuff, though Rose Briar's affair is so much juicer."

I go still. "I thought it was her husband who had the affairs."

"Oh, no, dear." Darla pulls herself up in her seat. "Well, he was a womanizer, to be sure, but Rose took up with his *brother*."

Now, my brows hitch up. "Say what?"

Darla leans in close, as if confessing a crucial secret. "She took up with Theodore Briar. Rumor has it, they had an illegitimate child together, one she had to give up in secret."

I point toward the stacks, my cheeks going numb. "*None* of that is over there."

"Well, no, dear. It wouldn't be. This is just some local talk I'm giving you, passed down by the generations. Anything pertaining to Theodore and Rose's affair, if it ever existed, would've been destroyed in the school library's fire, unfortunately. That academy holds on tight to their founders, I must say. It's a miracle we've gotten this much to display."

Huh. I cross my arms, gazing toward the exhibit, though it's blocked by columns of books.

Could the Nobles and Virtues be protecting the more scandalous aspects of their founders? It's not too much of a stretch to believe.

Darla chatters on, but the more I ponder on the limited exhibit items, the more it makes sense. It's plausible that not everything would've been stored in the old library, where any student interested in the history could come across it. Especially when choosing a founder to research is a required American History essay.

If they were smart, the societies would store the greatest scandals and the questionable origins of Briarcliff Academy somewhere safe.

Protected.

Private.

Buried, but not destroyed, because these elite societies have too much pride in their roots to set fire to original documents, no matter how damaging they are.

And it's exactly how Piper would've gotten her hands on Rose Briar's letters regarding creating a rival society.

She was looking into the Virtue's origins, because she suspected a wrongness, a poison running within the veins of the Virtues, or the Nobles, or both.

That gives me pause. Was Piper simply a nasty, spoiled twat, or was she smarter than a lot of people gave her credit for, including me?

Damn it. I guess I'm trusting Dr. Luke's words more than I thought.

"Honey? Have I lost ya?"

I blink. "Sorry. I'm a little stressed out."

Darla titters. "And here I am gabbing your ear off about century-old affairs. Go on back to school now. You're welcome back any time."

I send her a genuine smile. "Thank you for your help."

"Gah." Darla waves me off, but her cheeks blossom with color. "I'm just the town gossip."

"You're one of the nicest people here," I say as I head to the doors, and I mean that sincerely.

Darla doesn't stop beaming until I leave her sight.

26

*B*reaking into Addisyn Harrington's dorm room should be easy.

I'll walk right in, because I have access to the girls' dorms through evening trash-emptying on weekdays while everyone is at dinner.

It will be finding the perfect moment that's hard. I'm supervised by the dorm's housekeeper, who keeps an eye on me in the hallway when I enter each room.

Planning isn't my strong suit, but I resolve myself into applying that section of my brain for the rest of the weekend. I'm not responsible for trash clean-up on Saturdays or Sundays. My stepdad and Headmaster Marron both agreed weekends should be reserved for catching up on my studies, not impeding them.

Now that I'm back on school grounds, I feel watchful eyes on the back of my head, tracking me from the windows, guidance counselors and teachers clocking my progress to the dorms.

There's no real reason to believe Marron or even the guidance counselor I'm seeing would be pulling their curtains back and glowering down at the top of my head as I wander by, but with the strict supervision that's been placed on me, I wouldn't be surprised if *someone* was watching me, with their own eyes or through security cameras.

Whether those witnesses are official Briarcliff employees or not remains to be seen.

I can't stop Dr. Luke's revelations from circulating inside my mind. If he's right, if Addy really *is* Piper's killer, and she's being protected, then the purpose of the Virtues is more twisted than I'd originally imagined.

My lips flutter with a sigh, and I dig my thumbs into my backpack's straps as I trek down the hill to Thorne House. Most of the mysteries I've uncovered surround the Virtues, but they weren't created first. There was a reason Rose retaliated—

I halt in the middle of the pathway.

Rose's affair. I can't believe I'm only mulling over Darla's information now. A secret relationship with Thorne's brother? A possible illegitimate child?

Holy jeez, there's a lot to sort through. I've almost become an anchor, detached from its lifeboat and sinking into the depths of the ocean, because of all this.

I screw my eyes shut, giving my head a shake. What did Mom always say? Start fresh with the first point. Simplify it, then attach your theories to facts—not the other way around.

"Okay," I say to the surrounding landscape, the word followed by a hot cloud of air.

It's with my mom's calming voice that I decide to restart with what first grabbed my attention in the first place: The Nobles.

And Chase's key.

With a refreshed bounce, I start walking, turning a small corner around a row of expertly cubed hedges, until Thorne House comes into view.

"Callie! Hey!"

I slow my steps and turn at Ivy's voice.

"I've been trying to catch up to you since I saw you get out of the car," Ivy puffs as she comes up beside me. "You're a speedy devil when you want to be."

I smile an apology. "I have a lot on my mind."

"That must be it," Ivy says. "Because you totally ditched me for lunch."

A little pebble of guilt *plinks* into my belly. "Shit, I'm sorry. I got caught up in the public library, and—"

She waves me off. "It's totally cool. You're here now, but the dining hall's still open. Feel like doing a U-turn and having a late lunch?"

"I want to, I really do," I say with a pained expression, "but ever since I've been tasked with cleaning up the tables during the week, my stomach kind of turns at the thought of hanging out there."

"Right." Ivy mirrors my expression. "Falyn and her witch-bitches have been extra putrid lately, haven't they?"

The vision of cottage cheese poured into coffee, then spilled on tabletops, clots my vision at Ivy's reminder. And gravy mushed into stewed peas. Beef tips mashed into apple juice. The list of gagging textures goes on, especially when I have to mop it up with dishtowels and it slops onto the floor...

How are these girls meant to be so evil, yet so petty?

"Ugh," I say, smacking my lips at the warning saliva bubbling up in my mouth.

"Heck, their hot messes will get anyone's gag-reflex going." Ivy hooks an arm through my elbow, redirecting me back to the school. "Wolf's Den it is. They have some sandwiches up there."

I let her lead me along, since I haven't eaten anything since an early breakfast, and catching up with Ivy would be nice. And normal.

Ivy kicks up a conversation about her crew training, and how intense it is despite it being off-season, and I listen the way a good friend who has no interest in rowing would—with enthused effort—until she mentions a name I've been primed to viscerally react to.

"—until Addy became our stroke."

I swivel my head to look at her. "Addy's a what?"

"She's our stroke," Ivy says on a heavy sigh. "And our new captain. She's a *junior,* and she gets to lead our pace, our team, everything. I'm not one to get upset over these things, but it's really unfair."

"Uh, you can be upset," I say. "You've been wanting to be captain forever."

"I've been working hard for it," Ivy admits. "And no way did I enjoy how the spot opened up—when Piper died—but I thought, this is my chance. I can really show Coach that I have the technique and can lead the rhythm of the boat. I could bring the crew to championships. And now ... well, I'm still the seventh seat."

Ivy has told me boat positions before, and I dig up those memories to better console her. "Seven is still amazing, right? You're still part of the stroke pair. Or stern pair? Whatever it is, you're second in command."

Ivy bobs her head. "Yeah. It's not the same, though, when a girl who's had maybe a semester of training takes your rightful place."

I murmur in agreement but can come up with an answer pretty easily as to why Addisyn got the coveted spot in crew.

The Virtues.

As part of her deal to stay quiet.

I send a guilty look Ivy's way, wishing I could tell her that the whole system is fucked, and no matter how talented she is, that seat will never be hers because of the hidden politics at play. The problem is, would she believe me, or just consider me Callie the Crazy Conspiracist?

I'm afraid of the answer, so instead, I allow part of the truth to come out. "You deserve that spot more than anybody, and it's fucked up Addisyn got it over you. Do you think she's playing a sympathy card?"

"Coach is tough. I'd never think she'd have a bleeding heart under her athletic suit, but anything goes. Addisyn doesn't have the racing stats on the erg to back up her position, but Coach won't hear any arguments about it. She shut us up with a bunch of bull-crap about teams supporting their members."

"Totally screwed up," I agree, squeezing Ivy's arm lightly, but inside, I'm heavy with duty.

Now, more than ever, I have to get into Addisyn's room to see if Dr. Luke was telling the truth. If the Virtues are now guiding Addy's every move.

I open my mouth to impart more genuine sympathy, but a group of guys heading out of Rose House splinters my attention.

Chase.

The hitch in my step is unintentional, but it causes Ivy to pause, too.

"What is it?" she asks, but I'm too distracted by the way the afternoon sun glints across his hair, and how a plain T-shirt hugs his muscles just right as he jingles car keys in his hands and turns to say something to Tempest.

"Uh-oh. Which one?" Ivy murmurs into my ear. "Do you dream of a blond Adonis, or a raven-haired rebel?"

I jerk from my reverie. "What? No. Never."

"My bet's on Chase," Ivy smirks. "You try so hard, girl, but your drool always gives you away."

Ivy pulls me into a casual stroll again, but it's like my chin is attached to string as I continue to follow Chase's moves, how he swings into his BMW and the low purr of the engine vibrates under my shoes the way his voice hummed against my—

Oh, God. Don't go there. He's meant to be the *enemy*, not a relentless sexual fantasy.

That I've made into a reality.

Ivy bursts out with laughter. "Collect yourself, or he's going to notice you."

I blink, then rub my eyes. "I honestly don't know what's wrong with me."

I shouldn't be staring at him like this, desiring him from afar, when I've stolen something from him, and if he ever finds out the way I used him, he'll be...

Unforgiving.

But I can't stop. I don't, until his eyes meet mine, appearing black under the tint of the car's window.

He studies me for an indeterminable length of time, and I him, until Tempest jumps into the passenger seat and says something to Chase.

Does he know what I took?

My stomach coils at the thought. I haven't seen him since last night, and since he's come from his dorm unconcerned and at ease, I'm assuming he found a spare key.

Chase angles his head to his friend, responding, then swings his car out onto the road and roars past us without a second look.

I'm hoping that means he's not the least bit suspicious of me.

Or ... he could be super pissed.

"Dude." Ivy gives my frozen form a playful shove. "Explain."

"I, uh..." am getting *so* bad at keeping my conflicted feelings for Chase in check. Ivy can't know I stole his room key with the intention to search through his personal stuff, so, I go with the most believable. "It's a stupid crush. That's all."

"On the most sought-after guy in school?" Ivy leans into me. "I never thought you to be so basic."

She intends no malice, but I prickle nonetheless. I love her, but Ivy is a gossip whore. I don't know how she'd react if I told her I've been sleeping with him, but even if she didn't intend it, my hook-ups with Chase would be wildfire in this school, and regardless of my cruel intentions, I *like* keeping Chase as mine. It feels good, too good, to share naked, clandestine nights only with him.

"I'll show you mine if you show me Riordan," I say from the corner of my mouth.

Ivy shrieks and shoves at me, as I knew she would, and we both stumble with laughter.

"That was a moment of weakness," she defends. "I'd never get under him, even if I had a ten-foot pole to prop between us…"

"Yeah, right," I say, striding up the hill to the academy with her. "I saw the way you were all googly-eyed at Chase's party, and don't blame Jameson for your bad decisions."

Ivy laughs. "Fine. Maybe whiskey made me weak for *one* night, and I let him touch my boobies."

Now it's my turn to shriek. "You didn't!"

"I did!" she crows.

"Did he record it?"

Ivy snorts. "Maybe he's a little too involved in the goings-on at campus, but can we not at least agree he's a hot voyeur?"

I tip my head and laugh, the heavy load of this morning escaping my body.

In a moment of pure emotion, I throw my arm around her shoulder and pull her close. "You are the absolute best, you know that?"

"Aw." Ivy taps her cheek against mine. "Are you saying we're besties?"

I smile, my lips moving in a way they haven't since fifth grade, when Sylvie pulled me aside, demanding exactly fifty percent of a bestie friendship by offering me a half-heart necklace.

The necklace she was wearing when she OD'd and barely survived.

I don't think on the curse of my friendship when I kiss Ivy's temple, the wind blowing our hair back as we stroll through Briarcliff's pavilion.

All I can think of is my ache for a best friend and the familiar comfort of a kindred soul shining through an open, affectionate face.

Ivy isn't destroyed on the inside like I am. She's sunlight, and I've been starving for it.

So, I look her in the eye with a bright smile, saying, "Fucking right we are."

27

*J*vy and I spend the rest of the afternoon, and late evening, hanging out and catching up on subjects I've woefully fallen behind in.

Nothing pointed out how brutally my priorities had shifted than when I received my quarter-term grades. I listen to Ivy as she helps tutor me in my worst subject (ahem, calculus) and she helps me brainstorm with the ones I'm better at—history, biology, and English. We spend most of our time in a corner of the Wolf's Den, other seniors also using the quiet afternoon to get work done, with the added benefit of constantly refreshed snacks.

When we first arrived, the Wolf's Den floor was awash with sunlight streaming through the stained-glass crest above our heads. Students came and went, our breaks were few and far between, and soon, my worries over Addisyn, the societies, Chase, and Piper's death, slumbered for a while as Ivy focused my thoughts and tested my academic knowledge.

We end up being the last ones in the Den, and Ivy's in the middle of showing me a trick to finding the value of the integral, when I notice the floors beneath our feet have gone dark with shadow.

"Huh," I muse, then check the time. "Omigod, Ivy, it's nearly ten."

Ivy lifts her head, her pencil pausing on my notebook. "Yikes, is it? We missed dinner!"

I slide a glance to the pastry cart, a spot we'd been plundering every time a staff member came up to restock it. "I doubt our stomachs will mind."

Ivy straightens in her seat, lifting both hands into the air and turning them. "Look at me, I'm literally throbbing with caffeine."

I snort, then start packing my books and laptop. "That's our cue to leave."

"For sure," Ivy agrees, and we both clean up our table.

The academy remains well lit, despite the time, with electric wall sconces and the large chandelier in the foyer, but I expect someone from the faculty to come up any second and kick us out, since the school closes at about this time.

With the amount of echoing noise we're causing by shutting our textbooks and shoving them into our bags, we're the last ones in the vicinity.

"Thank you," I say to Ivy when I zip my bag shut. "I really needed this."

Ivy pats my shoulder. "You didn't come here to fail, and I don't want to see it happen."

"I can't believe how much I've let this place affect me," I say as we head to the staircase. "I'm usually so good at making schedules and sticking to routines, but I guess, ever since my mom..."

I can't finish the sentence, and Ivy doesn't make me.

"It's easy to get distracted." Ivy clomps down the stairs behind me. "Outrageously beautiful boys, scandalous teachers, suspicious roommate deaths ... you deserve to be a little distracted, ya know?"

I shrug, facing forward. "Not like this. I've been—something like this has happened before, and I swore I wouldn't do it again."

"Like what?" When I don't answer, Ivy turns so I face her at the bottom of the stairs. "Callie, what's going on?"

I hesitate, then scold myself. With everything Ivy's done for me today, she deserves some honesty. "After my mom died, I kind of ... lost it."

"Well ... that's to be expected."

"No, I ... clinically lost it. My stepdad committed me. And when I was released, I went to every party I could find—college, high school, random, it didn't matter—looking to score. My friend Sylvie was down for it, so I never questioned my safety when we both went. But soon, I was going by myself, drinking by myself, then ... snorting powder by myself."

I carefully watch Ivy for her reaction, but the only emotion she's exuding is furrowed brows of concern.

"The drug-use got bad. I, um, I know now it was because I accused my stepdad of murder and .... I kind of fell apart after that."

Ivy says, "Callie, oh my God. You've never—"

"I blamed him," I blurt. "I'm the one who got him arrested."

Whenever I think of it, the lump of coal is still there, burning its embers at the base of my throat. I don't think the guilt of ruining his life will ever go away. It'll just stay buried in the earth until those rare moments when I dig up the black elements, like now.

I look to Ivy for judgment, then jerk back in surprise at her scoff. "I doubt your word alone sent him to jail, Callie. They must've had other evidence to add weight to what you were saying. You know, I've noticed something about you from the minute I met you."

I ask with hesitation, "What's that?"

"You give everyone else such a free pass in life but wrap your own in chains."

I stare at her. "I don't get it."

Ivy folds her arms. "Do you remember when I ran to your room once I heard Piper was dead? And how Chase waltzed in?"

I grumble at the thought of Chase bursting through the door, his brown eyes blazing with the Earth's core as he stared me down. "Yes."

"And when the detectives came, he pointed at you and said you did it."

I suck on my lower lip as it dawns on me where she's going with this.

"Did they arrest you on sight?" Ivy asks. "Put you in hand-cuffs, send you to jail? No. Because they had other facts in play. A list of other suspects, which, I guess, is growing as we speak. The point *is*, Callie," she says, pushing me by the shoulder when I instinctually hunch over, "is that his word, as strong as it is around this school, still wasn't enough to get you in major trouble." She bops me on the nose, and I wrinkle it in response. "And I'm guessing the same can be said about what happened to your stepdad."

Heart sinking, I shake my head. "I haven't told you everything. There was a fight between him and my mom, which I witnessed, and he slapped her, and I told the police..."

"Yeah. More outside facts proving your word. Like I said."

I frown. "No, I—"

"You're not going to convince me you're a bad person, dude. Not when you're sucking face with Chase in your mind every time he passes by, *despite* what he tried to do to you."

A snort of ashamed laughter escapes my nose.

"Which goes to my point," Ivy says. "Why do you punish yourself so much worse than the people who've wronged *you*?"

Because I was told I was unhinged. Incapable. My opinion drugged and voided.

I peer up at Ivy, who's studying me kindly, and I can't give voice to more truth, not when she's so convinced I'm not that girl.

Maybe she's right, and I don't have to keep recalling the old

Callie, the one who wanted to hurt her stepdad, the kid who wanted to punish and maim and destroy the world that had destroyed her mother.

I say, cracking a small smile, "I liked you better when you were teaching me about studies and not real life."

Ivy playfully punches me in the arm. "I only tell it how I see it. C'mon, let's head back."

"You go ahead," I say. "I want to drop some of this stuff in my locker."

"Want me to come?"

"Nah. I know you have an early morning training tomorrow." I point to three custodians who are leaving the maintenance room with cleaning carts. "I'll stick close to these guys."

Conflict crosses Ivy's face, and I'm sure it's her worry over my well-being battling with her need to go to bed and catch a few hours rest before her 4 AM wake-up call.

"What else could they do to me?" I ask. I don't need to say who. "Send me to more clean-up duty? There's a ton of security now because of Piper *and* my latest 'break in.' I'll be safe. Promise."

Ivy chews on the inside of her cheek, but I don't expect her to argue. Not when I've concealed so much from her, including the Virtues attacking me. All she knows is that it was Falyn and her friends who set me up, and I got the cut on my cheek by accidentally breaking a beaker while I fumbled in the dark to read a damaged book. With her firsthand witnessing of me dousing my hand in flames, how could she question my story?

Considering my track record, I'm deeply reluctant to involve her in my real shit.

And ... I'm *so* afraid to lose her.

After a few more seconds of looking me up and down, Ivy gives in. "All right. You'd better."

"It's five minutes of dropping off my stuff. I'll be fine. See you tomorrow, okay?"

"Yeah," Ivy says, her brows low as she regards me. But she turns on her heel, and I don't look away until I see her duck through a door politely opened by a security guard passing through the foyer, and disappear into the night.

I do feel safer as I trudge down the East Wing to the locker area, as I pass by five other security guards doing their rounds, and even a grumbling Professor Dawson as he locks up his office, telling me to hurry it up before the school closes.

With this much action on a Saturday night, it'd be difficult for even the Virtues to frame me for some other outrageous spoof.

They're forming the foundation for your instability, Callie ... They have people in play who will break your heart and your mind if you let them. They're planning your downfall...

I refuse to let Dr. Luke's words guide me as I turn a corner and find my locker, quickly depositing my things.

All the lights are on. Security and maintenance staff are everywhere. I'm *fine*.

Until I exit the cubicle of lockers, round the corner, and notice that everyone is gone.

he electric sconces lining the hallway flicker until they're dim, then turn off.

"Shit," I mutter, but with a lighter bag, I jog down the rest of the hall until the academy's foyer comes into view.

An additional line of sconces goes black, as well as overhead lights, and in a moment of awareness, I skirt to the edges of the wall, unwilling to be caught running smack in the middle of a darkened corridor.

They're here.

It's a visceral realization, felt along all the hairs on my body, but my mind can't believe it—not when I've seen the amount of guards and the cleaning crew scouring the grounds mere minutes ago.

The Virtues couldn't control them, too, could they?

I itch for Ivy's soothing company, but it's for the best that she's not here. I don't want her involved in this fuckery. Whatever happens to me, I cannot take another good friend down with me.

Approaching footsteps draw my head up, and I crouch beside the nearest awards case, most of my body obscured by trophies, as whoever it is passes the East Wing and strides into the foyer.

After waiting a few minutes, I creep out, hunched over and using the lightest steps I can.

As I near the foyer, I notice more than one silhouette, outlines of tall bodies, broad shoulders, and short hair cast in a hazy glow from the dimmed chandelier hanging above.

Men. These are men. Or schoolboys.

One belts out a masculine laugh, cementing my theory, then stifles it when hushed. The guys ... I'm counting about ten bodies ... all form into a single line, until the one in front turns and motions for them to take the stairs.

At this point, I should expect nothing less than a mysterious line of men in the foyer of the academy after hours, but honestly, this shit never gets old.

Crouching, I curl my fingers over the edge of the corridor, ensuring that only an eye and maybe a sliver of cheekbone show as I peer into the lobby.

The men silently ascend, and no one's talking now. As I watch, my body trembles like a tuning fork. *They're headed into the Wolf's Den.*

For reasons I want to find out.

When the last foot disappears over the top stair, I scuttle forward, ears perked for any additional sounds coming from above. All I catch is the tiniest *beep*, more shuffling, then silence.

I pause under the indoor balcony, head cocked and braced to run, but I don't hear so much as a squeak of rubber soles against marble.

They can't possibly all be standing in the Wolf's Den saying nothing. Are they watching something on a screen? Meditating? *Sleeping?*

I can't bear the mystery of all those guys going upstairs and then doing ... nothing, so I creep to the base of the stairs and bend slightly over the railing to see the opening above.

I scan everything up there I can see, from the front of the balcony to the top of the stairs, and there are no shadows, creaks, or exhales—anything to indicate there are people up there.

My brows crash down. *Wtf?*

Grasping the handrail, I swing to the front of the staircase and tiptoe up, sticking to the shadows, keeping low and quiet, in case I'm inadvertently crashing one of the extra-curricular club's sleep-ins.

But ... I don't think that's what this is. It's much too quiet.

As each step takes me closer, and I can make out outlines of the Wolf's Den furniture, I don't notice any accompanying people draped over the chairs or clustered in any corners.

I'm so busy studying the interior, I don't register that I've moved to stand in the middle of the darkened room until I'm directly centered with the coffee table.

With not one person nearby.

I murmur my shock and put my hands on my hips, spinning in place. I've never witnessed or been told where Thorne Briar designed secret passageways and hidden rooms, but I'm pretty sure I've just discovered one location.

But the question remains: Where the hell did everyone go?

I make my way to the back wall, since the front is a balcony and the two sides are crowded, one with coffee stands and pastry displays, and the other an elevator door beside the staircase leading up.

I start on the left, faced with a half-wall of books, the other half wood paneling. High-top tables and stools take up the middle section, including the table Ivy and I sat at for hours. Were we really gabbing beside a secret entrance the whole time?

The question brings up Chase's party, and how I acted in his father's office—so convinced of a concealed chamber behind those books. Instead, I was shot down with the existence of a panic room, standard protocol for the uber-rich, and left questioning my convictions.

Here, though, there is no panic room. Ten bodies did not

disappear into the back of a senior lounge where no staircase or elevator exists—those are both in the front.

I skim my fingers along the books' spines, but none of them, as I tip and pull at the spines, do anything but puff dust mites in my face.

"Damn it," I curse, tipping my chin up and scanning the top.

What am I missing?

Then, I look down.

The bookshelves take up half the wall. The other half is wood molding, carved in 3D designs often seen in pictures of nineteenth century mansions. Briarcliff decorates with layered rectangles carved vertically, and intricate lace trim in the corners.

I take one step back, studying the wainscoting and trim, but focusing most on the rectangular panels.

Could I ... push one?

Shrugging, I figure I'll have at it, since I haven't come up with any better ideas.

I end up pushing against all ten panels, bending and using all my strength, but none of them move an inch.

I stare up at the ceiling and sigh, thinking, *if only you could see me now, Dad and Headmaster Marron.*

Then I think, perhaps I'm approaching this wrong. Any student could technically push against the panels by freak accident or just plain curiosity.

If I want to know where those guys went, I have to start thinking like a society member, and not simply a student kicking in walls.

So, I start pushing gently on the corners of each panel, starting again from the left. The first four don't budge, but undeterred, I keep trying the others.

It's the ninth one that clicks.

I suck in a sharp breath when the upper right corner presses down, and I'm able to swing open the entire panel.

Omigod omigod omigod.

My heart pounds with the strength of Pegasus wings, and I'm feeling just as high and mythical. *What have I found?*

Fingers shaking now, I pull the panel all the way to the side and peer in, but my nose hits something hard almost immediately.

Cursing, I lean back, and take stock of a small, metal door with an electronic scanner in the center.

"Dang," I mutter, disappointment crashing my new wings down to Earth.

For shits and giggles, I use my room card, but of course, get a low beep and a flashing red light indicating WRONG.

Then ... I remember.

I have Chase's card. I was going to use it to search his room but had put that on the back burner.

His key sits in my bag, hidden in my wallet for safekeeping.

What's the harm in trying it? I've made it this far.

And so, I fish out my wallet from my bag, find Chase's key, and press it against the scanner.

GREEN.

The door unlocks, pushing itself ajar.

"Holy. Shit."

I straighten, glancing around to see if anyone's snuck up on me, but I'm alone, crouched in front of a hidden door that I absolutely *must* explore.

Every fiber making up my brain tells me so.

Fumbling for my phone, I turn on the flashlight and slowly crawl in, my nose instantly assaulted by stale, briny air. The second metal door has opened inward, so I push against it until it hits the wall and I'm all the way inside.

Using the insignificant, white beam of my phone's lens, I spot a small, stone staircase leading *down*, the flattened steps so limited, they're the length of small squares.

Probably a gnome could bounce down just fine, but I'm having issues just picturing sliding, feet and ass first.

Well, I think, *Alice did something similar in Wonderland. Why can't you in Briarcliff?*

With that resolute thought, I slide forward, feet first, until I hit the first step. I stay like that, foot and then butt, for five or so steps before the staircase starts curving, the steps get wider, and the ceiling much, much higher.

Eventually, wall sconces replace my flashlight, which I hastily turn off the closer I get to the bottom ... if there's a ground level.

They're not the electric ones around the academy, though. These are oil-soaked lanterns, lit by a match, and the flames flicker under the light wind of my body as I pass by.

I can't hear much over the pounding of my heart, and my short, adrenaline-fueled breaths, but I put my entire effort into staying silent as I drift down, down, down...

Soon, I hear voices.

And wherever they are, they're no longer being quiet.

29

"... *T*herein, the second Saturday eve marks our monthly chapter meetings, and I implore all of you to listen intently, study your new members, and remark on your acute abilities that brought you here, as one of us, a Noble member."

I inhale through tight lips and press against the side of the staircase, terrified of being discovered but too vindicated to scamper back up.

They exist. They're here.

And, if it hadn't been for Dr. Luke's revelations today, I would've remembered from Howard Mason's findings that the Nobles meet every second Saturday of the school year.

And *this* is their Vault.

I risk another step, and then another, until a corner wall appears. Instead of peering past it, I turn on my phone's camera, using it as a selfie mirror, and angle it so I can see some of the movement on the other side of the wall.

I'm the shakiest cameraman of all time and will never be hired for any sort of production, but I recognize a few familiar faces lined up in a half-circle around ... three? ... cloaked figures who hold blazing torches. The flames crackle in the silence as the members turn to each other and murmur their motto in Latin, *Fly high in the dark*, as a greeting to their neighbor.

I press a trembling thumb to the camera's button, taking a silent picture.

Behind the cloaked figures is an impressive, massive carving in the stone wall of a raven, spreading its wings and fluttering in motion from the large, hanging chandelier, lit with candles. I gasp silently, in awe of this crypt they've built and the boys standing within it.

James.

Riordan.

Tempest.

Chase.

Of course, Chase.

My camera keeps documenting, and I freeze their faces in time as fast as I can. There are others from lower years, whose faces I recognize, but no other seniors that I can tell. And there are ten boys, in total, the three cloaked figures in the middle making it thirteen.

"Our sisterhood," a Cloak says, his voice gravelly and deep, more middle-aged than youthful, "has had a rough beginning this year, and we must be there for them, always. We've agreed to meet in their Temple for our next ritual, to discuss the loss of their member and who should be the replacement in her stead."

Piper. They must be talking about Piper.

I angle the phone so I can see the speaker better.

"While we don't always agree with their motives, we must keep the Virtues close. And Marquises, you must choose your soulmate on that eve, and be bound to them for life, however you choose to do it."

I suck on the inside of my cheek, eyes riveted to my tiny

screen. A soulmate from the Virtues? Does that mean an arranged marriage of some sort?

"Prince Stone, I implore you to think hard on your choice, since your destined soulmate is no longer with us."

I angle the phone to witness Chase's response, but lose my bearing, wasting time trying to find him in the crowd.

"Yes, Father," I hear Chase murmur, and I gasp, this time, not so quietly.

I freeze, my joints cracking from the ice I've injected into my veins to stop myself from moving, but the speaker goes on as if I haven't made a sound.

"To our initiates, I introduce our Marquises, Mr. Callahan, Hughes, Windsor. You three know what to do."

"Yes, sir," they respond in sync, heads bowed.

The speaker removes his hood, as do the other three, and my stare bores into my camera as I clock Daniel Stone, Headmaster Marron, and Professor Dawson as the three caped leaders.

Daniel Stone steps back, Marron and Dawson following suit. He says, his voice booming, "Earls, Viscounts, look upon your higher lords with respect and submission, as they will show you the way. As for our initiates, the Barons, your time has not yet come. This is the last eve you will be seen as applicants, as you have one more ritual to complete. I will leave it to our Marquises to best dispense the choices."

The three Cloaks turn to leave, and I get ready to hightail it out of here, but they don't turn in my direction. They exit stage right, on the other end, at the same time three additional robed figures walk in, this time in thick, velvet, purple robes.

The three purple Cloaks pause at the base of the stone raven, directly under the chandelier, and sweep the robes off their shoulders in synchronized movements.

And ... they're naked.

"Barons," James cries, turning and standing in the middle of

these ladies who've bared themselves to freshmen and sophomores. "You have a choice. Take a woman now or save yourself
for your soulmate. Whatever you choose, it will be documented
in this hour."

Oh my ... oh my *God*.

Are these prostitutes? Escorts? Adults about to sleep with ...
minors?

I can't—I can't be here. I'm too chickenshit to witness this—

A face, veiled in shadow, darts into my vision and snaps my
phone from my hand. His palm covers my mouth before my
surprised cry causes shockwaves into the tomb.

The back of my head cracks against the stone as the body
presses against mine, but the scent—*his* scent—tells me who it is
before I start to struggle.

My body goes slack in his hold.

Chase bends close, half his profile cast in flickering gold from
the sconce above us. His irises are black lacquer. "Go."

He doesn't remove his hand from my mouth until I nod my
assent.

Chase's skin scrapes against my lips as he abruptly lifts his
palm, and I don't linger. I half-stumble, half-crawl up the steps
and don't stop until I fall into the Wolf's Den and hastily close
both doors to that forbidden, twisted Noble crypt.

I race home without looking back, my hair cascading in the wind.

The pathway clears of leaves, driven by the same eastern
breeze, their decaying, papery skin skittering against the paved
walkway as the wind picks them up in handfuls.

I follow the streetlamps until I'm outside Thorne House. I
show my ID, then burst up the stairs. I don't stop moving until I'm
through my apartment door and my back splays against it.

Emma pauses in the center of our kitchenette, holding her

emptied dinner plate above the kitchen sink. She never eats in the dining hall, preferring all her meals alone, and very late at night.

I meet her eye, my chest heaving, then say, "I want in."

Emma arches a brow.

"Whatever you're doing," I continue, exhaling pillows of air between words, "with your late nights in the library—a place you despise—and whispered conversations with your brother, I want to be a part of it."

Emma thins her lips, then goes about washing up her dishes like I'd never asked anything.

"You're trying to take down the Virtues," I say after a gulp. I rest the back of my head against the door, watching her with half-lidded eyes. "Dismantle them. Fuck with them. Whatever you want to call it. I. Want. *In.*"

With her back to me, Emma finishes drying her plate, then perches it on the drying rack. She then pushes off the counter, heading to her room.

"Goodnight," she says over her shoulder, then shuts her door.

I growl, then slap the front door with open palms before pushing off and stomping to my side of the apartment. I only keep the light on long enough to search my furniture for errant roses, be it black or white, but find none.

I rip my comforter off the mattress, then undo my pants and crawl under, burying myself in black as far as the soft cotton will let me.

Dreams blanketed my mind surprisingly quickly, despite what I witnessed this evening, and I clamor through the harmless adventures until sounds on the other side of my door flutter my eyelids, then draw my head up.

My door pushes open, a sliver of yellow light crossing my bed, and then my form, as I sit up and squint against the brightness.

A silhouette comes into the frame. "Emma says you've figured out what she's up to."

Chase. I'd recognize that low, silky sarcasm anywhere.

I skip the preamble. "Yes."

He folds his arms. "You broke into our ritual room today."

I should probably add preamble to this part, but I just swallow. "Yep."

He fishes in his pockets, and something thuds against my bed. I jerk my legs up, in case it slithers.

"Your phone," he barks. Any amusement that was in his tone has long disappeared. "You won't find any photos on it, or video recordings."

I stare down at the black screen, saying nothing.

"What were you going to do with that stuff?" he asks. "Write some piss-poor exposé? Email it to our school newsletter? You forget—we *own* this school. It does what we demand, and if tonight showed you anything, we demand a whole fucking lot."

I raise my eyes to meet his, but Chase's stare is nothing but a glimmer in the darkness. "Who were they? Those women."

He cocks his head. "Exactly what you think they are."

"And that's common? You Nobles bring in escorts for freshmen to sleep with? Do you not understand how *fucked up* that is, *Prince* Stone?"

"I'm more aware than you'll ever be, Callie."

I curl up against my headboard, as if the light he's bringing into my room is poisoned nectar used by royalty to smite their enemies. "I wasn't there to expose you," I say. "I was there to see what the Nobles are. What the point is."

"The point," Chase says, but his echo is filled with venom. "The *point* is exactly what you'd expect. We are an Order that molds boys into men who will end up taking what they want, whether that be in politics, academics, forming corporate empires, influencing the laws, or amassing funds on a global scale. Our rules are the reigning power, and we abide by no other. We influence the president. We provide advice to sheiks. We strategize in wars."

With each statement, I flinch.

"Is this what you wanted?" he bites out. "To finally be a part of an archaic group that still holds as much power as it did in 1920? To watch men use women for sex and gain money for political favors? Are you happy now?"

"N-no," I grind out, his words like razors on my skin. "But my reasons still stand. Piper was involved in this. She was your ... your *soulmate*—"

Chase's hand spears forward. I wince at the violence of his movement, though he's nowhere near me.

"Key," he says.

I shuffle forward on the bed. "Chase, I..."

"*Key*, Callie. Before I really lose my shit."

I bend over the side, picking up my bag where I dropped it. I toss him his keycard. When his fingers close around it, he says, "You're lucky I caught you before you tripped over a goddamn rock and stumbled into our sacred rites. You have no idea, *none*, on how bad that could've been for you."

"Then why'd you let me do it?"

Chase stills.

"You knew I took your key. You were just waiting for me to use it. That's how you knew to keep watch near the stairs for any flicker of movement. It's how you warned me before anyone saw."

Chase shoves the key in his pocket, light and shadow playing across his features with his jerky movements. "You're relentless."

"I'm right."

He growls in frustration. "You left me no choice. I had to gain some control over the situation while giving you what you wanted, hoping you'd stop after seeing what we are."

We. Not they.

At least now, he's telling me the truth. No matter how much it hurts.

I meet his eye again, and he responds with a haggard exhale. "Of course, now you've taken up with my sister on some asinine quest to blow up the Virtues."

"And the Nobles, too, if they're also bastards," I quip.

Chase's features grow darker than shadows, and right when I'm thinking I've over-stepped, Emma comes into view, placing a hand on her brother's shoulder. "Callie's right. Both societies are drunk on power, and people—kids *our* age—are dying. How far back does it go? How many other students had to die to keep their secrets?"

Chase rips from his sister's hold. "It's too dangerous. I told you that before you came here, and I'm repeating it now. And you are *not*, under any circumstances, involving Callie. She's already a target of theirs, and if they ever find out what she's digging up—"

"Um, I'm right here," I say. "No need to discuss me in third person."

Chase doesn't even pretend to look at me. "Haven't you two been through enough? Why be magnets for more bullshit?"

Emma opens her mouth to argue, but I get there first. "Addisyn killed Piper."

It's enough of a verbal boulder that Chase has no choice but to turn to me. Emma, too.

"What?" Emma says, at the same time Chase asks, "How the hell did you come to that conclusion?"

"A source," I begin, and Chase rolls his eyes, muttering how tired he is. My voice is bristly when I continue. "But I planned to back it up by finding the lost pages of Piper's diary. They're in Addisyn's room."

"Let me guess, you took her key, too?" Chase asks.

"No," I snipe, then choose to appeal to Emma, since she and I may have the same goals. "I'm on trash duty on weekdays, and part of that is emptying the bins in every dorm room. I figured I could get a chance then, but it'd be a lot higher if one of you helped."

After a few beats of silence, Emma asks, "What makes you think I care about Piper?"

I shake my head. "You're hearing me wrong. Whatever kind of person Piper was, she was looking into the Virtues, too. But Addisyn killed her before she found out what the society was hiding from their girls. And the Virtues *rewarded* Addisyn for it. They've given her status, improved her grades, gotten her on the rowing team, and she killed one of their own! Come on, guys. You may not be into the whole sororicide angle, but the Virtues assisting in a cover-up of a murder of their member has got to set your teeth on edge."

Emma places her hands on her hips, facing her brother. "She makes a good point."

"Callie makes a lot of points," Chase says on a sigh. "And more often than not, they get her in trouble."

The barb hits exactly where he intended. "That's not fair."

Chase slants his shoulders. "I'm not saying this to hurt you. I want you to stop this, Callie. Finish this year like a normal student, join some clubs, have *fun*. Don't get sucked into our world. It's lethal. Violent. You don't deserve our demons."

"That's where you're wrong," I say, my fingers tangling in my bedspread. "I've been to hell. I know what lurks there, because it was in the bedroom where I found my mom. And I know I broke down—I've paid for that dearly. I accused a man who, while an asshole to my mother, didn't kill her. He just hurt her, then remarried six months later. To a woman he got pregnant."

Emma inhales a pained breath.

"I don't want your pity," I say to her. "Just like you have no time for mine. I made a mistake, and so did he. We're both working to better ourselves because of it. And *this*, exposing a society that recruits children for their own murderous means, *that* is what will heal me. Getting justice. Not playing cheerleader." I look to Chase. "I can't pretend there isn't a hellmouth beneath my feet. The same way Rose Briar couldn't and your sister can't. And you, too." My voice grows softer. "You're here to stop me. Or save me. And I'm sorry giving me access to your society's sexist ritual wasn't enough to get me to scream and run. I've seen things, Chase. I'm not the delicate flower I'm named after. I need you to understand that." I pause. "I need you to help me."

Chase raises his stare from the floor, connecting with mine. As he searches my eyes, I know I've won, but I don't feel our blooming connection this time. Instead, I absorb his tiredness, frustration, and unwillingness to bend entirely to my will.

Emma takes a moment to look between us, her eyes narrowed.

"Not to get in the way of … whatever this is," she drawls, "but you're thinking by giving the police Addy, you'll be meddling with the Virtues' plans enough to expose them."

"Not to mention, exonerating an innocent man." I flick my glance back at Chase. "Jack's the one who got Piper pregnant, but he didn't kill her."

Chase hardens his jaw under my stare, but grinds out, "You already know who most of the Virtues are. You don't need me."

I hesitate, then ask Emma, "Were you a Virtue?"

Emma doesn't look at me when she gives a curt nod.

Chase says to me, "The Virtues are violent and destructive and barely constrained by us at this point. If pointing the cops to Addy brings them to heel, then I'm all for it—but the rest of the Nobles may not be. By protecting the Virtues, we protect ourselves."

"I can't prove what the Virtues did to me," Emma says, at last meeting my eye, "but if I can show they participated in a murder, then that could be a start."

I want to ask her what she's been planning and how she was

about to get her revenge before I offered up Addisyn, but there's no guarantee she'll tell me. We've built no trust, and what's to stop her from resuming her plans if mine fall through and I can't prove Addisyn did anything wrong?

As Chase looks on, watching his sister with protective caution and me with more of a sinister respect, I know he will need more convincing. Those diary pages *have* to be in Addisyn's room, or else this all falls apart and I'll gain nothing.

I stare down at my hands, the open palms as empty as they were when Dr. Luke insisted Piper was killed by her sister out of jealousy.

Am I really believing him? Could I take Emma down this haunted road with me, trusting we won't get lost?

I glance again at Chase, whose features remain inscrutable in the shadows, but the undercurrent of worry is there in his clenched hands and the way his jaw grinds.

"If I can prove Addisyn is involved in Piper's death," I say, both their heads turning to me, "then you'll let me in on your plans for the Virtues. I think it's a fair trade."

Emma's the first to speak. "Show us the goods, and we'll see."

She moves to the door. When she notices Chase doesn't follow, she stops. "You coming?"

"In a minute," he mutters.

Emma sends a long look my way, but her carefully blank features don't tell me what she's thinking. "I'll be in my room."

When Emma steps out, Chase stalks over and shuts my bedroom door. He turns back around, and the face he gives me is ferocious.

"I know I have no excuse," I begin before he can unleash. "But neither do you. You and your sister are planning some kind of coup on your societies while I run around blind. Are you really surprised I stumbled into your lair after being forced to steal your shit? You left me no choice."

Chase stares at me in silence so long, I cross my arms under his scrutiny. But I don't lower my chin.

At last, his voice slips through the air like a black, silk ribbon wrapping itself around my neck.

"If you're going to accuse me, get your facts straight. I'm not out to destroy the Nobles," he says, his features cloaked in darkness. "I want to control them."

30

"*Y*ou ... what?" I sit straighter in bed, my duvet, the only softness in this room, becoming a comforting pillow on my lap.

Chase moves closer until he stands at the foot of the bed. "You saw who guided the ceremony tonight."

That irresistible scent of his, salty, cedar male, drifts its ethereal allure in my direction. To distract myself from his proximity, I bring to mind the three cloaked adults in the ritual room.

"One of them was your father," I say.

Chase nods. "He's the current Noble King, and I'm his legacy."

"Meaning..." I parse through his words. "You're the next leader?"

"Something like that."

"And you want to gain control."

Chase's sharp profile tips to the ceiling. "You just don't see it, do you? How hard I've worked to keep you out of this."

I risk laying a hand on his forearm, the ropes under his skin hard and hot. "You can't keep me away when all I see is secrets and lies." I wait for Chase to lower his head. "If you want me to step back, try telling me the truth so I can understand the danger."

Chase snorts. "You've seen enough to know you're in hot water, Callie. Don't pretend that my telling you more will get you to back off."

I haven't removed my hand, so I give a light squeeze. "Then make me smarter. A part of you knows this can't go on forever. Their power has to bend."

Chase sighs, staring down at my hand. His profile is so dark, he appears in shades of black, the color of doom enveloping his body, as if he's already given himself over to the underworld.

I'm tempted to turn on the light, to highlight his angelic beauty instead of sitting in the dark with his devil, but that would require moving. Disconnecting my touch that keeps him here, with me.

"You're never going to be happy just being normal, are you?"

His question hits hard, and I rub the center of my chest at the phantom pain. "My average life was taken away a year ago. I've never tried to get it back." I squeeze his arm again. "I've seen evil leave its mark, and ... it's hard to explain, but I feel like it's followed me here. And it won't leave me alone until I defeat it."

I'm staring down at my hand on his skin, and jolt at the brush of feeling down my cheek. Raising my eyes, I realize it's him, tracing my profile with a wishful, tentative dance of fingers across my jaw.

"If I tell you what you want to know, will you stop with the sneaking around where you don't belong? The stealing?"

His tone sounds so lost, his touch so forlorn, that I'm desperate for a joke. "Are you saying you didn't enjoy the exchange of sex for a keycard?"

As soon as it's out, I wince at the crassness.

But Chase responds with a lupine smile. "I'll always enjoy sex with you, sweet possum."

I catch my lower lip with my teeth.

"But," he continues, "that was a low fucking blow."

"You ran with it," I retort. "And let me keep your key, so who's using who?"

Chase acknowledges my point, leaning back.

We sit in the quiet, the lateness of the night silencing the rest of the floor. Even Emma doesn't make a sound. I start to think Chase has second-guessed sharing anything else with me, then the shadows shift, skittering back when his voice cuts through the room. "Thorne Briar created the Nobles for competition and manipulation. He didn't understand why grooming for influential positions in government or the global economy started in college. He wanted to mold minds when they were at their most pliable. That way, older members could maintain their dominance and power through the strict regimen they inflicted on young boys, who would have no choice, no aggression, toward their leaders." He pauses. "Not even when that boy turns into a man and is seated in office."

My brows ache with my pensive frown, but my heart feels light with revelation. "Is that why Rose created the Virtues? Because she wanted to protect the kids?"

Chase rubs his jaw. "She wanted to show her husband that children could be guided instead of manipulated, and she chose to prove it by tapping girls who excelled in their classrooms. It was around the time women were granted the right to education beyond homemaking, and she advanced that learning with secret teachings, first at the boathouse, then, once the membership expanded and women came into power, in their own hidden rooms around campus. She died young, but her teachings lived on through the students who loved her and swore to keep the Virtues alive, despite Thorne's multiple attempts to silence them. Some of these women were at the forefront of gaining the right to vote, the Civil Rights movement, LGBTQ rights, key swing votes in the Supreme Court, all because of Rose's determination to thwart her husband's maxim that the only way to win is through terror and destruction."

The implications of what those boys went through—what *Chase* might've gone through—sits heavy between us, and I'm afraid to move and break the spell, conscious of Chase's ability to withhold as much as he tells.

"In the fifties, the Nobles changed under my grandfather's leadership," Chase continues. "He admired what the Virtues accomplished and their quiet dominance in a man-centric world. The Nobles vetted kids in middle school, sure, but the goals were to enlist the clear leaders of the class, in sports, academics, debate, any kid who showed an uncanny talent for domination. But my grandfather ... he wanted to *inspire* them, not corrupt. He wanted our members to go on to do great things for this country, and to use our influence to make a positive difference in the world. He was less about politics and more about mass improvements through power. And with that, came great relationships with the Ivy League Societies, and a brotherhood within the Nobles that hasn't been seen since. Those boys would've given their lives for each other. For my grandfather, too, before he passed on."

"What happened when your grandfather died?" I ask, though the trepidation within me knows the answer.

"My father took over."

Chase punctuates the sentence by sharply cutting off and staring at my closet door across the room.

"And he's rather fond of the Nobles' origins, so he's gone back to the traditional way of tapping initiates."

I swallow, unsure of how far I should take this, so I choose a safer route, away from his personal memories. "And the Virtues?"

"Poisoned." Chase answers without hesitation. "The Nobles use demanding, sometimes vicious, rituals, starting off in middle school but really pushing the boundaries in freshman year, when we're robed. But the Virtues ... they don't bother with the excuse of molding future minds for the good of humanity anymore. They're comfortable with their power, hedonistic, even. They pursue decadence, not control. They feed off popularity, insecurity, beauty, sexual power. So, my dad's done one thing right, I guess. He's tried to gain control of them through the soulmate rite, same as what Thorne tried to do to leash them when he witnessed, firsthand, how women used their accessory status to manipulate the men. And it's what we do now, to ensure the Virtues aren't completely independent, but they keep a lot of their rituals to themselves, as we do to them."

"So, you're allies ... and competitors," I surmise.

"We're a breeding ground for war."

I hug myself, calming the shudders over my heart and the goosebumps over my skin. I'm getting what I wanted, aren't I? Inside access into the Nobles and Virtues, first witness to their brewing destruction.

Chase twists until he faces me on the bed. "If it turns out Addy has nothing to do with Piper's death, I can't help you anymore, do you understand?"

Slowly, I nod. "My credibility will be shot to shit at that point, so yeah, I won't fight you."

Chase takes both my hands, clenching them tight. "I'm not doing this solely to avenge Piper. I'm doing it for you, too. And for me. We're out of control, because now we're killing ourselves and making it look like an accident. As their future king, I can't let this continue."

I pull my hands from his hold, but not to retreat. I cup his face, and he searches my eyes, waiting for my reply. "Thank you," I whisper.

For telling me. For trusting me. For letting me in.

With my entire being, I'm wishing his heart has opened to me, but I don't dare mix up wishes with hopes. Not when the fragile thread that's connecting us could be shredded at any moment.

Chase lingers in his search, his stare grazing across my cheek-bones, my eyes, before landing on my lips.

Threading my fingers at the back of his neck, I lean in.

He meets me halfway, and while our lips meet delicately, our tongues are unscrupulous in their demand.

Chase pushes me back until I'm lying down, and he's pressed on top of me, our kiss becoming so deep, we're lighting a fire in ourselves. Our hands scrape against each other faster, our clothes lifted, then ripped off, our underwear cast aside.

We break apart only to remove everything that barricades us from ecstasy, until we're naked and my legs are spread, my folds wet, and he hasn't even touched me.

Chase anchors my waist, then spins until he's on the bottom and I'm on top of him, and I take delicious control, lining him up until his tip is inside me, and I make slow, lazy circles in complete contradiction to the raging inferno at my core that wants all of him, right now, his thickness the perfect size to fill me whole.

Chase groans, his hips begging where his mouth refuses, attempting to thrust, but I keep lifting away.

I smile in the light of the breaking dawn, acquiring more power over a guy than I've *ever* had, and totally taking advantage.

"Callie..." he grunts, his upper lip curling. "Goddamnit. Fuck me."

My next grin shows my teeth. "Ask me nicely."

Air whistles out of his clenched lips. "Don't make me beg, sweet possum, because my answering torture will be so much longer. I'll take my fill, through your mouth, your pussy, and your ass, while you plead for yours."

My smile doesn't falter. "That's big talk for somebody who isn't allowed to come at the moment."

He growls. "Neither can you."

Damn it. Chase has a point. How much longer can I withhold *both* our orgasms? I'm throbbing, hot with desperation, so swollen and ready for his dick that it's making it easier for him to slip farther in, taking more territory.

I grab my breasts, flicking my hard, piqued nipples to try and redirect the pleasure to myself.

Chase notices, but I'm so deep in my own, desperate escape, that I fail to take his widened eyes as a warning sign.

"Fuck this," he snaps, then rears up at the same time he thrusts in, yanking on my hair to pull my head back and keep me at the perfect angle.

I cry out, but he covers my mouth with his other hand, so each time he pounds, my moans are muffled for just the two of us.

He takes, and takes, fucking so hard there will be bruises on my inner thighs, but I meet each pound by burying him to the hilt and clenching around him so tightly, I feel the pulsing of his cock inside me.

Soon, I'm riding him, and he releases his hold so he can lean back on his forearms. I press on his shoulders for balance, bouncing, circling, our thighs damp with sweat and the scent of lust, building until we're at that perfect, painful precipice of release and desire.

"I'm almost there," I breathe out, my voice hitched and tight. "I'm ... almost ... oh *God*—"

Chase snarls and pulls me against him until we're molded together, our orgasms in tandem, but my release so much louder than his, since he's buried his face in my neck and bitten down.

The sharp indents of his teeth mix with the swirling orgasm that tightens my core and sends my limbs sparkling, and I fall against him, covered in a cloudy haze, the weight of the world lifted far above my shoulders.

Chase trails his fingers up the length of my spine, then cups the back of my neck. He turns his head, murmuring into my ear, "You're going to be the end of me."

I inhale his cologne, and the underlayer of *him* surrounding my naked body like a needed blanket against the chill. My response flows to the back of my lips but won't go any further. I'm afraid, if I say it out loud, it'll be akin to cursing the hearts of our twisted fate.

And so, I mouth it silently into his shoulder, the salted tang of his skin a seal to my terrified vow. *You're my beginning.*

31

*M*onday evening comes too fast, despite Emma and Chase's assurances on Sunday that they had a failsafe plan to give me time to search Addisyn's room. I explained to them my thoughts on timing the emptying of Addisyn's floor to the housekeeper's cigarette break, dropping anything I was doing (and any floor I was on) to sprint up to Addisyn's room and do as thorough a search as I can before Emma, guarding the front, or Chase, watching the side of the building, texts me the moment Moira stubs out her cigarette.

With them involved, my chances of success are that much higher, but their presence doesn't lessen the nerves. I've been so good up until this point, receiving texts from Dad and Ahmar, and phone calls from Lynda, that they're so proud of me for focusing on school and keeping out of trouble.

If they caught word of what I was up to while I pretended to be the perfect daughter...

The guilt is worse than the betrayal I'd cause them.

My patchwork family wants nothing but the best for me— even my stepdad, who I *think* I've come to terms with—and who's making an honest, genuine man out of himself, sobering up and taking care of his pregnant wife. They've been so focused on me, and my excuses have been so tunneled to them, my incoming newborn sister has taken a backseat. And yeah, my efforts at proving a twisted sister relationship with Piper and Addisyn aren't exactly helping with that.

When this is done, I'm resolved to repairing my remaining relationships. Forgiving as much as I can. And ... moving forward without a black cloud of grief, if that's even possible.

It occurs to me just how much I'm putting the solving of Piper's murder into solving *me*.

Monday starts off innocuous enough, with classes and lunch with Ivy and her other friends. Ivy's part of crew, but for reasons I've yet to dig into, she never sits with her rowing team at lunch or even acknowledges them much during the day. I've stopped myself from asking her *why* a million times—because I'm turning a new leaf once I prove Addisyn killed Piper and the Virtues' involvement. An unassuming, non-nosy, bright, fresh, green leaf, that will finish her senior year quietly.

If Ivy doesn't want to sit with the mean girls more than she has to, why should I question it?

Because she's on their team.

I shake off the thought as quickly as it comes. This is *exactly* what I'm worried about—paranoia taking over reality, ruining people who care about me.

I say goodbye to Ivy at the top of the hill, me starting the last week of punishment, and her heading to crew practice at the boathouse before the dinner bell.

I'm glad for their insane training schedule, because it means Addisyn, their new captain, will also be down there for the near future and unlikely to trek back through the forest path and to the dorms for a few hours.

My features are tight as I take the walkway to Thorne House, so immersed in the logistics of our plan and where I need to search in her room first (under the mattress. Like sister, like sister, right?) that I don't count the three figures idling by the dorms until I'm practically on top of them.

"Shit—" I blurt, then come to a stop, screwing up my brows. I'm standing with Chase, Emma, and ... Eden?

"Hey," Eden mumbles under her blanket of black hair. She keeps close to Emma while Chase steps forward, hands spread and prepared to argue their case.

I start to ask, "What's she—?"

"She's Moira's daughter," Chase says. "And has been helping Emma and I with our ... research."

My eyes ping between each and every one of them, before settling on Emma. "She knows? About everything?"

"*She* has been working her ass off since Emma's been gone," Eden snaps. "I know a helluva lot more than you, Callie."

It makes sense, especially since Eden's the one who gave me the Virtues' name in the first place, but, "Why tell me this now? Why not yesterday when we were guzzling caffeine and solidifying plans?"

Emma answers. "Because I wasn't sure if Eden would be all for it. This kind of fast-forwards our motives, and Eden's nothing if not cautious."

Eden arches a brow. "That's Emma's polite way of saying I'm a paranoid freak who hates outside involvement."

My eye twitches. "I'm not so sure it's the more the merrier..."

"I could say the same thing," Eden retorts. "I was here first."

"Ladies," Chase says, coming between us. He shadows me until Emma and Eden recede in my vision, until all I see is the glossy, melted chocolate of his eyes. "Trust me. This makes it easier on us, I swear."

Eden pipes up behind him, "I can keep my mom talking while she sneaks a smoke. Be honest, Callie, you're not a subtle one when it comes to unearthing evidence."

I sigh at her words, but don't break my stare with Chase. He lowers his head, as if his sincerity is better seen close up.

But, little does he know, he had me the instant he stepped into view.

I answer softly, "I trust you."

"Okay." Chase smiles, squeezes my shoulders, and drifts to the side, our covert intimacy crackling between us. "Then let's do this."

We confirm our phone numbers through test texts, and the three of them continue to loiter outside while I go in, drop my stuff off in my room, and get ready for clean-up duty.

Chase made it clear yesterday that he doesn't have practice today, unlike the girls' crew. Knowing that, and that his presence will be outside Thorne House the entire time I attempt the downfall of Briarcliff's newest princess, comes as a comfort as I put all I have, all I've *discovered*, on the line, with only Dr. Luke's word as my back-up.

What other choice is there, though? Jack's unfair arrest? Chase's continued suffering? Addisyn living her life of privilege, bolstered by her newfound involvement with the Virtues, and allowing these societies' continued reign and manipulation of Briarcliff students?

I'm no superhero, but if I can get Piper's lost pages, I can get them all. *That's* what's leading me. Not Dr. Luke.

After dressing accordingly in Briarcliff-issued sweatpants and a PE Dept T-shirt, I throw my hair up and meet Moira on the ground floor. She's outfitted in the staff uniform of maroon slacks and a white polo shirt with the school's crest on the left side.

She greets me with a pleasant smile, and now that I'm given context, I see Eden in that mouth—just a smidge, since Eden rarely stretches her lips as wide as this.

I now understand why, though.

"Hi, Moira," I say as she hands me gloves and a broom.

"Ready for your last week of purgatory?" she asks with a light-hearted tone, the lines around her eyes crinkling.

"So ready," I say, matching her smile.

"I gotta say, I'll miss having the extra hands. You've been a big help, honey."

I fall into step beside her as we start at the nearest room. Moira knocks, waits a minute, then swipes her keycard and motions me inside.

Veering into the kitchen, I pick up the small trash bin and dump it into the larger trash bag Moira holds open.

"I didn't know you and Yael shared a daughter," I say.

Moira laughs. "You're an astute one, aren't you? Usually students don't take the time to understand interpersonal relationships of staff members."

"He and I make a lot of conversation when he drives me into town," I say. "Eden came up. I didn't know she was your daughter, too."

Moira cinches the bag shut. Her smile falls. "She is."

She walks ahead of me to the next room, and I rush to sweep up the debris and shut the door.

"I'm sorry," I say after Moira knocks on the second door. "I didn't mean to offend..."

"I'm protective of her." Moira keeps her attention on the closed door. "And get naturally defensive when a student mentions her. Edie doesn't have many friends, and, I'm sorry, honey, you're a lovely girl, but I doubt she's warmed to you."

"Not even a little," I say honestly. "But we've spoken a few times. And have worked on ... projects ... together. I'm not out to get her. I can promise you that."

Moira visibly relaxes. "I'm glad for it. I don't mean any insult. I *wish* Edie would spend time with a girl like you, but she's a woman of her own."

"I think she's strong," I say as I wander inside and find the next bin.

Moira goes quiet behind me.

"I don't participate in gossip, but I do get sucked in when it's mentioned." I turn to Moira's open bag, tipping the bin. "And Yael mentioned a little. What she's been through..."

Moira meets my eye over the crinkling trash bag. "I don't contribute to gossip, either, but I know what you've been through, too. And how hard it's been for you to talk about. So, maybe we should leave it at that."

The warning's obvious, but I can't stop the inquisitiveness from slipping out. "Have you heard of the Virtues?"

Moira's features go flat. "We're falling behind with all this chatter. Come on, now, out you get."

Properly shamed, I exit the room while Moira leans forward and shuts the door.

I don't push the limit any further, but Moira's frank dismissal of the Virtues does add an additional layer of guilt to what I'm about to do to her, and that her daughter's involved in it. Not through my doing, but that's a dumb excuse. I know for a fact that Eden's involvement this evening is 100% due to my actions.

"I'm sorry," I say to Moira's back, though she can't know just how much I'm sorry for.

"It's all right, honey," she says over her shoulder. "Let's finish you up so you can get to your homework."

We work in silence on the first floor, and when we get to the second, my heartbeat kicks up. Addisyn's room is in the middle, which she shares with another sophomore. When Moira's distracted changing out trash bags, I send Emma a quick text.

Me: Second floor.

Emma acknowledges with a thumb's up emoji, and I stuff my phone in my pants' pocket when Moira steps from the mainte-nance room.

We continue to work in the quiet, but my back is stiffer, my movements jerkier, as adrenaline leaks into my limbs. Moira doesn't seem to notice, but she's not meeting my eye, either.

"The Virtues destroyed my daughter," Moira says, and at first, it doesn't register.

I pause, holding a bin to my chest.

"We didn't know of their existence, not until we started work here when Edie was a baby," Moira continues softly, but she snaps the trash bag open with a loud *pop*. "We mostly tried to ignore the whisperings, because we liked our jobs and loved the benefits and security that came with it. By the time we realized their influence, Edie was already well into researching them. Trying to *be* one, my impulsive child. Back then, she was bright, cheerful, heavily into swimming. But within a month of freshman year, she changed. Became withdrawn, snuck out at night, endured massive bullying at school. They called it hazing, you know." Moira locks eyes with mine. "Testing her limits in a perverted way to see if she was worthy. And that thing is run by *adults*." Moira hisses out a breath. "My daughter's limit was met when her naked body was distributed around school. And instead of my vibrant, dedicated daughter, who loved her swim meets, I have her husk. Don't get me wrong, I will always, *always*, love my girl. But that group of so-called independent, powerful women can burn in hell."

I gulp. "Those pictures, she was a minor. Did you ... did you go to the police?"

Moira rustles the bag for me to come closer to dump the contents of the bin in my hands. I do, and when I step closer, notice her shaking grip.

"Oh, honey, we did," Moira says, the underline of her eyes going wet. "But by the time we reported, the pictures were deleted. There were none we could point to, and Edie refused to corroborate."

"Shit," I murmur, my heart sinking. It made sense that the Virtues' influence stretched to the police department, but to think they forced *Eden* to keep her mouth shut ... I'm sick at what they could've said, or done to her, to keep her quiet.

Pressure hits my chin, and I realize it's Moira, gently tilting my head up.

"If you're thinking of taking up with them, don't," Moira says, her brown eyes piercing mine. "You are much too sweet and already too tortured to ever endure what they'd have in store."

My swallow hits her fingers, and she releases me, blinking.

"Lord, I need a cigarette after this," she mutters. "Are you okay to do a couple of rooms without me?"

I nod, slightly too eagerly, and work to school my features. "Of course."

"All right, then. I trust you, honey. Hang tight."

After handing me her master keycard, Moira takes the closest staircase exit, and I follow her until she disappears. I'm off-balance and nauseous that I could potentially get her fired. She's had three weeks of trusting me to do my job, and on the last few days, right when she's gotten comfortable with me and even imparted motherly advice, I'm about to betray her.

Then don't. Be done with it before Moira ever gets back.

My phone vibrates in my pocket, and I look away from the exit and reach for it.

Eden: I see her. I'll try for ten minutes. Will text if sooner.

Since we're in a group chat, both Chase and Emma acknowledge the text, and I do too. **Going in now,** I type, then drop my cleaning supplies and jog to Addy's room.

I almost key in immediately before my instincts kick in and tell me to knock first. Stepping back, I do just that, my leg jiggling as I wait for any kind of response.

When there's none after thirty seconds, I key inside.

It takes a minute to figure out which bedroom is Addisyn's. I'm usually only a few steps inside before I empty the trash, then leave. Thankfully, the dorm room is in the same layout as my own, but on a slightly smaller scale.

A few seconds into scoping out the pictures tacked to the wall, I realize I have the wrong room, and sprint to the one across the way.

I'm so bad at this, I think, cringing, but don't take the time to admonish myself completely, because there *is* no time.

I fumble with the bedspread and mattress first, lifting it and finding nothing. I then move to the closet, flicking through clothes, feeling across the top and bottom shelves, opening plastic containers.

Running to Addisyn's desk, I pull out drawers, rifling through but not too hard, finding nothing.

Cursing, I stop long enough to send a text:

Ten minutes isn't long enough. Need more time.

I move to the center of Addisyn's room, taking a moment to *think*. Then, deciding to get creative, I look behind the pictures on her wall and, when that doesn't pan out, move to the backs of the standing photo frames on her nightstand.

Right when I start to believe I'm a genius detective and will find the missing pages behind a photo of Addisyn and her sister, I come up blank.

"Damn it!" I hiss, then return the photo to its proper place.

What would Ahmar do in this situation?

Hands on my hips, I scan the bedroom, cataloguing each shelving unit and drawer that I've searched.

He'd go through it all again.

The answer sets off a lightbulb in my head, and I search the same places one more time, like a true detective would. One sweep isn't enough. One set of crime scene photos won't show everything. Look at all items again, find the spots you missed, thoroughly search the ones you think provide no evidence.

I summon as much of Ahmar and Mom's spirit as I can when I resume my search of Addisyn's closet, stepping in as deep as possible, my face buried in her lavender-scented clothing hanging on the bars.

I burrow deeper, and it gets darker, until I'm all the way in the back, feeling the walls. I'm cross sectioning the area in my head, feeling for ... I don't know, a secret drawer, when my foot hits on a loose floorboard.

"No," I breathe out, stunned as I stare down where my foot rests. Did I just hit the motherload?

Gawking never did anyone any good, so I bend down, using my nails to crack open the floorboard all the way, and reach in before I can second-guess what could be greeting me on the other side. A rat's nest?

A crinkling, papery feel hits the pads of my fingers, and I lift out the sheaf of papers, my eyes feeling bulbous as they bug out of my head.

Is this it?

I rush through the racks of clothes and into the light of Addisyn's room, taking a closer look at the torn, handwritten pages.

I'm pretty sure I'm supposed to feel bad for taking Addy's boyfriend away, but all I feel is a win. She thinks she can do better than me, get the hotter guy, make the better grades, be Virtuous, but that will never be, because I won't allow it. There's only one Harrington girl who matters, and that's me.

. . .

Then, on another page:

Fuck. Addy's getting a little crazy. It's not like I love Jack. I just love to fuck him. Same as I enjoy Chase's dick and the taste of Mr. S's cum. I don't differentiate in levels of caring, but Addy's acting like I'm stealing her husband and am about to move into a little Cape-town house by the ocean, living in Briarcliff for the rest of my life.

FUCK. NO.

Why would I want to marry a poor boy who thinks he's bad and is working towards a future as a fry-cook at the lobster shack?

I can do way better, and so can she. Can't Addy understand I'm doing her a favor? Always following me around, wanting to be me, and the one time I do something for her, she acts like I should die for showing her what a loser her boyfriend really is.

That's what she said, dude. "I hope you die for this."

Dramatic, much?

With each word, my cringe gets deeper, my muscles sagging with disgust and disbelief.

"Jesus, Piper, you really were a caustic bitch," I murmur, skimming a few more sentences. "Not that you deserved to die, but—"

"I know, right? A total and utter cunt."

My head snaps up at the unexpected voice, meeting Addisyn's cool, murderous gaze in the doorway.

32

*T*he loose papers crunch in my hands. "Addisyn, I—"

"Don't bother," Addisyn says, wandering farther into her room.

Her tone is calm, her demeanor collected, as she scans her space, pinpointing the sections I hadn't yet cleaned up. The one tell of emotion is the tightness around her eyes, lidding a glare so hard, so lethal, it's only contained by her unbreakable, thick skin.

It's almost as terrifying as if she came storming in, shrieking at me for going through her stuff.

Instead of apologizing for my clear violation, I focus on what I've found—a worse horror. "These pages, they belonged to Piper's diary."

Addisyn's sweeping stare stops on me. "They sure did."

I wait for a more detailed response, but she doesn't move. I add, "And ... you ripped them out."

"Uh-huh."

Okay. Obviously, I'm taking the lead on this, so I go all in. "You killed her, didn't you?"

Addisyn cocks her head, a night owl assessing the mouse skittering below. "What do you think?"

"You were jealous of her," I say, inching toward the door. I have the innate sense that if I reach for my phone or call for help, she'll pounce on me with her talons, turning wild in an instant. If I take small enough steps, maybe she won't notice. "Because Jack slept with her. Because of her easy membership into the Virtues."

She makes a noncommittal sound but won't stop tracking me.

I clear my throat, standing straighter. "I think it's more the latter. The Virtues have a terrible initiation process for those they deem unworthy, don't they?"

Addisyn stiffens. I've ruffled her feathers.

"Compared to those they think deserve the title," I continue. "See, I've been *ankle*-fucking-deep in this shit—my choice, I know—but with what I've heard and read, these societies *really* prefer the older sibling, don't they? The ... help me find the word..." I snap my finger in thought, feeling more than seeing Addisyn's narrowed gaze. "Legacies. That's it. The eldest kid gets immediate entry, don't they? Piper and Chase are some examples. In fact, they tap them when they're *very* young."

"Fuck you," Addisyn hisses.

"Hit a sore spot. Sorry about that." I'm not sorry, and I doubt I look it, either. "But *you*, you had to go through a ton of bullshit before even being considered, despite sharing blood with your sister. What were they doing to you? Did you have naked photos spread around, too? Or, did they torture you so badly, you had to set fire to a building in retaliation?"

"I'm not Eden, nor am I Emma, so stop using them as fucking examples," Addisyn says.

"Those are the few I've discovered, but I bet I can find out more," I say, ignoring the thickening blood in my veins, urging me to *run*. "If you tell me what they did to you, maybe I won't feel so horrified that you killed your own sister to get in."

"They didn't ask me to do that," Addisyn blurts, but clamps her mouth shut when she sees my smile. "*Bitch*."

"They helped you cover it up, though. Maybe even accelerated your entry into membership because of the dastardly thing you did. Hell, with what I know, it probably impressed them."

"You have no fucking idea," Addisyn says, striding forward.

I almost, *almost,* cower at being run up against her fury, but I hold myself still. "What I can't understand is, why did they reward you for killing one of their own? What was Piper doing that was so wrong in their eyes, she had to die? I doubt it was for fucking your boyfriend, though I'm sure that was enough of an impetus for you."

Instead of snarling like I expect, Addisyn's lips pull up in a sneer. "Oh, yeah? Well, what I understand is, they run this school, not you, and you're about to get your ass handed to you without me lifting a finger."

I raise my brows. "What—?"

"Hey, Ems!" Addisyn calls, without looking away from me. "Eden! Come on in!"

At last, my feet move, but they don't stride forward with confidence. No, they fall back. "What the hell are you doing?"

Addisyn steps aside, revealing the bedroom doorway, and Emma and Eden walking through.

My heart plummets, its descent into cavernous darkness accelerated with the thought of Chase.

Don't let him come next. Please.

"What's going on?" I ask, my eyes bouncing between the two of them.

Emma *tsks.* Eden crosses her arms.

"Maybe next time," Emma says sweetly. "Don't fuck my brother behind my back for favors."

My shins hit the back of Addisyn's bed. "Addisyn confessed. She killed Piper! Why are you here? Eden, where's your mom? Why are you two *smiling* at me like that?"

"You bring up a good point, Callie," Emma says, then gestures to Eden. "Get the pages."

With an agility I did *not* brace for, Eden springs forward and snatches Piper's lost pages from my hand.

"Eden, no!" I cry, but it's too late. She's vaulted back to Emma's side, clutching the writings like treasure.

"And that letter of Rose Briar's you found?" Emma says. "Consider that gone, too. Hiding shit in a textbook? C'mon, Callie, at least encrypt the evidence."

I appeal to Eden. To Emma. Addisyn's off to the side, enjoying the show. "You hate the Virtues. You hate Falyn, Willow, Violet, *Addisyn*—all they represent. Why are you helping them? They hurt you. *Scarred* you. Why would you ever...?"

I can't finish the question, because I'm so bewildered. Here are two girls who've experienced first-hand torture from the Virtues, overheard Addisyn's confession, and yet, they're regarding me like *I'm* the one they need to be rid of.

"You tricked me," I whisper.

"Wasn't all that hard," Emma says. "You're so eager to please Chase, all I had to do was dangle his dick in front of you a few times."

"Ew." Eden giggles. "You're talking about your brother's penis."

I stare on, horrified, my mind rushing to catch up with the *wrongness* of this scene. "Where's Chase?"

"God." Emma moans, her eyes drifting to the ceiling. "You're so predictable."

"You led me to believe you were on my side. Got me here, to Addisyn's room. And I found Piper's missing pages. What was it all for?" I ask.

"First off," Emma says. She looks to Addisyn. "Why didn't you set fire to these pages when you stole them? You're as dumb as she is."

"Probably because I'm not the pyro in this room," Addisyn retorts.

Emma grunts in annoyance, but all the movement highlights

are the angry burns down one side of her neck. A scar I thought she got from an attempt to get revenge on the societies after what they did to her.

The fool is me, I guess, because I never asked Emma for the truth. Never took the time to ask her what instigated her attack, to figure out what she did to deserve a beating from the Virtues that unleashed her wrath in the first place.

I just assumed, and that was my downfall.

Maybe all it was, was an initiation gone wrong. And Emma's still trying to get in.

"I can't believe that," I say out loud. "You've suffered so much, Emma. The pain you endured; it can't have brought you to this point."

Emma bares her teeth. "Get whatever halo you have over my head *off*. I'm not a victim. I never was. The only idiot around here is you. And possibly Addy, for leaving crucial evidence in her room. They thank you for tipping us off, by the way."

They. The Virtues.

But I won't give up. "Eden, I've spoken to your mom. Your dad. You're not this person."

"*Ooooh*, you spoke to my parents," Eden sneers. But her eyes drive into mine, asserting another message I can't immediately read. "Unlike yours, mine don't keep me on a leash. The Virtues are everywhere, Callie. They're not about to be stopped by a bitchy sister murdering another bitchy sister."

"Hey," Addisyn says.

"You're protecting Addisyn," I say, so horrifically awed, my voice comes out breathy and unsure.

"You get props for being so determined," Eden continues, then adds with a musical lilt, "but you're done now."

"We're not here to hurt you," Emma adds. "As long as you stop, you can continue at Briarcliff no problem. Focus on school. Find a boyfriend who's *not* my brother. Eat cakes with Ivy and complain about the popular kids."

The mention of Ivy sends shivers rushing down my skin. "If you hurt her—"

Emma laughs. "I'd be more concerned with your own well-being if I were you."

"Can I show her?" Addisyn asks Emma, suddenly gleeful. "Can we add some confetti to our grand exit?"

Emma pauses, then considers the papers in Eden's hands. "I suppose it can't hurt." Emma turns to me. "Happy belated birthday, Callie."

Emma nods at Eden, who shuffles through the diary entries until she finds what she's looking for, then shoves a single piece of paper in my direction.

I automatically grab it, my mouth hanging open as the three of them move to the door.

"Read it. You'll be sorry you ever found Piper's thoughts," Addisyn says to me. "Then get the fuck out of my room."

"Consider this your final warning," Emma says. "And that's coming from the top."

Eden also looks back, an apologetic look crossing her features before they re-harden until she's almost unrecognizable. "You got this far. It's time to turn back."

"And remember," Addisyn adds. "I'm the good sister. You can thank me later."

When they shut the apartment door, and I'm left in the quiet, my knees buckle until I'm seated at the edge of Addisyn's bed, Piper's single diary entry crumpled in my fist.

What the hell just happened? Their wounds bamboozled me. Emma and Eden's emotional stories enraptured and softened until I was nothing but putty to be molded by their hands.

And Chase?

My heart ruptures at the thought.

Slowly, I smooth out Piper's words. The only evidence I have left.

. . .

Just got off the phone with Mom. I can't believe it. Can't FUCKING believe it. That bitch's spawn is coming here? To my turf?

Mom thinks it's some kind of play. That the bitch is sending her kid here to get money from us, to show us who's really running the show, but that's not it. I've met Bitch Jr., and she says her mom's dead.

I choke.

All this time, the bitch hasn't asked for a dime of child support—well, before she stopped breathing. She must've pissed someone else off real good to get that kind of payback. Did she fuck someone else's dad, too? How many dudes did she sleep with? I doubt her husband even knows. I believe Mom when she says the affair has gone on for decades. What I can't believe is that this pathetic, puppy-eyed bitch, who's drooling after Chase like he's some kind of dog bone, is my half-sister.

I already have one idiot bloodline to deal with. And now I have two? No fair. I'm the only one who deserves to be Virtuous.

33

J'm numb.

Stuck in the cold, even though I'm seated indoors, in a warm room with calming floral smells.

I'm going to be sick.

I launch off Addisyn's bed and reach the toilet just in time, heaving the contents of my lunch. I'm never going to make it to dinner, and at this point, I don't want to.

I want nothing to do with these people. This school.

Coughing, I stand, wiping my mouth with the back of my sleeve and scraping back my hair. I hold the crumpled piece of paper over the toilet before I flush, aiming to mix vomit with vomit, but my fingers can't seem to let go.

On a garbled cry of frustration, I shove it into my pocket and fly out of Addisyn's room.

I run into Moira in the hallway.

"Honey? Goodness, are you all right?"

Moira comes up to me and holds both my arms, peering at my face, but I can't have her touch me. I can't be near such warmth, when she's fostered such coldness and doesn't even know it.

"I can't be here," I mumble, unable to look her in the eye.

"I'm so sorry," Moira says, clucking her tongue at some inner argument with herself. "Yael texted there was an emergency at the house, and I drove over there in a panic, thinking someone was hurt, and no one was there. I called him, and he said he never texted me anything. I called Edie and she said the same thing. I must be going insane, because I have the text right here."

Your daughter stole her dad's phone, probably while he was idling near the school, waiting for a student to ping for a ride.

But I say none of it, because I've seen the heartbreak on this woman's face when talking about her daughter, and I don't want to be the one to add to it.

"I don't feel well," I say. "I think I should lie down."

Moira presses the back of her hand against my forehead. "You feel a little piqued, honey. I think that's a good idea. I won't tell the headmaster. As far as he knows, you completed your punishment today."

I nod, undeserving of Moira's kindness, but too cowardly to push it away.

Instead, I escape up the stairwell as quickly as I can, leaving her confused, muttering self behind.

"Shit, there you are."

I halt so abruptly the staircase door hits me in the back when I reach my floor. "Chase."

He comes within inches of me, holding my shoulders. "Where've you been? I've been texting my ass off, trying to locate you three blind mice, but I haven't received fuck all from any of you. I thought you were caught."

I shake my head, but it does nothing to dissipate the bonfire in my soul. "Where were *you*?"

Chase jerks back. "Me? Coach called. Said the girls' Coach needed help with practice today since their stroke was out sick. I texted you about it."

The girls' stroke being Addisyn, who was busy fucking up not only my enrollment at Briarcliff, but my entire *life* as I knew it.

I set my jaw. "Addisyn wasn't sick."

"No shit. I saw her on my way up here."

"Were Emma and Eden walking with her?"

"What? No." Chase's brows slam together in disgust. "That's the last place I'd find them."

"That's what I thought, too."

Chase side-eyes me. "Callie, what's going on?"

"Did you know?"

"Did I know what?"

Bile erodes my throat. "Did you know I was set up? Did you know your sister was playing for the Virtues all this time? Did you *know* Piper and Addisyn could be my half-*sisters*?"

The last sentence comes out as a howl, but that's what I am. Off-kilter, marooned, groundless and without wings.

Genuine confusion crosses his face, but I don't fall for it. I *can't* fall for it. He says, "What the fuck?"

My voice goes raw, even through taut lips. "We're done."

"What? Callie, hold on—"

"*LET GO OF ME!*"

Chase releases his hold on my arm, then raises his hands in surrender. He says, with softness that breaks me, "Please."

"No." The denial rips from my throat, and I push past him before the pleading in his eyes swallows me whole. "I'm not doing this anymore. I hate what they've done to me, but most of all, I hate what *you've* let yourself become under their rule."

The rare, open vulnerability in Chase's face fades with my words, my accusation like a blast of ice in his face, but I can't seem to stop.

"You're the worst one," I hiss. "You're a coward, because you know what they represent, and you do it, anyway."

Chase says, with the sharpened steel of a blade, "The day you truly figure out my motives will be a day you regret, because you are so, *so* wrong."

I glare at him, communicating my hurt, my pain, my poisoned past and dismal future in that single glance.

"You're right," he says, his eyes tracing my face before landing on mine. His expression carefully controlled. "Maybe you are half-Harrington. You certainly have the kind of hate they covet."

My lower lip trembles with hesitation, but Chase turns on his heel before I can respond.

He disappears down the stairs, and when he's a safe distance away, I let myself crumble. I fold into a ball, bury my face in my knees, and let out a keening wail, mourning for the person I thought I was, and the mother I thought I knew.

34

*B*riarcliff Academy loves its cruel irony, because they've labeled the weekend before Thanksgiving, Family Day.

Or, what the students call the Turkey Trot, a weekend of day-drinking between lake houses that happens the very moment the families leave.

And so, while everyone scrambles around, trying on Thanksgiving-themed costumes and discussing the best selfie angle, I sit at my desk, flipping my pen in my fingers and scowling into the air.

"Scary," Ivy muses as she perches on my bed. "You should definitely dress as a scary turkey, or hey, just wear the face you have on now. Freshmen will scatter at the sight of you."

"Funny," I say, giving her the once-over. "Are you going to wear that when your parents come?"

Ivy grabs the front of her costume and flaps it idly. "Probably not, since my dad would lock me in a basement for the rest of my life."

She's dressed as a sexy turkey—since that's a thing—which in her mind, means a sexy fawn Halloween costume with red, brown, and white feathers glued to her suede-clad, minidress ass. A homemade feathered headpiece and white-glitter eye-shadow completes the look. Ivy's dressed so delicious and cute, I'm thinking on her trip back to her dorms, she's hoping Riordan notices her efforts.

Riordan Hughes, who is a confirmed Noble member. I'm watching Ivy's budding relationship carefully but won't say anything. Ivy's the one who gave me the name of the Nobles way back in the beginning—surely, she's cautious around them.

And if she isn't ... well, I wish I had proof to show her, but everything, and I mean *everything*, has been deleted off my phone and my cloud. Piper's diary. Rose's letters. Howard Mason's musings.

Thank you, oh so much, Chase Fucking Stone.

A week has passed since that terrible evening of discoveries, where it feels as though I gained two friends, then lost them that same day. I avoid Chase at all costs, but he doesn't seek me out, either. The thought that he's content to keep his distance doesn't sit well, because the part of me that's still alive and owns a heart-beat wants him to fight, to convince me, of his innocence.

But he does none of those things.

I haven't called Dad to verify Piper's writings, or told Ivy, or confessed to Ahmar. It's like a cancer that sits inside me now, spreading and growing at an alarming rate, but the worst part is, I don't know if talking to any of them will help me shrink this brewing hate.

My mom's dead, and with her went all her secrets. She'd told me she didn't know who my father was—that he was just a one-night-stand who never knew she became pregnant—which was probably a lie.

All my life, I wished for my biological father, but now that I know who he might be, I want to go back to the faceless dad who never knew I existed.

"I should go," Ivy says as she stands, smoothing her mini

dress. "And remove this gorgeous atrocity before my parents get here. Are you going to be okay?"

The question comes out tentative, since I've been so distant these past few days, unable to confess, but unable to cover it up well, either. "I'll be fine," I say, pointing at the door with my pen. "Go. I'll see you at the picnic."

"God, I hope my parents don't come in costume," Ivy moans as she leaves my room. "How mortifying would that be?"

"Plan on it," I say helpfully. "Because if I were your mom, that's exactly what I'd do."

Ivy scowls at my answer but breaks into a grin and waves before leaving.

Left to my own devices, I try to work on some schoolwork, but come up empty. I push to my feet and head to the kitchenette instead, scooping some old Halloween chocolate I'd ordered online, but conscious of putting myself out in the open for Emma to see.

My fears are unfounded, because Emma hasn't been around this week. Or if she has, she's done it while I was sleeping, and I do *not* want to think on that possibility too hard. More likely, she's staying at her family's lake house instead of the dorms, an arrangement I'm all too happy to abide by.

I haven't seen much of Eden, either, though I constantly picture them scheming like witches, steepling their hands over a steaming cauldron in the forest as they cackle. Their betrayal is a punch to the gut every time I think about it, but I can't let their stabs to my heart hold true. They were never my friends to begin with. We came together with what I thought was a single goal—to take down Addisyn, then the Virtues—and when that goal failed, I should be glad I walked away unscathed. On the outside, at least.

Instead, I was a tool for their devices. A means to score evidence Addisyn was keeping to herself and didn't tell the Virtues.

I wonder if Addisyn will be punished for hiding pieces of Piper's diary or applauded for it.

It's difficult to know what, or who, to believe.

It shouldn't matter. I'm done.

With the noose of Piper's last words wrapping around my neck, I don't want to think about the Virtues anymore.

A light knock on my door distracts my thoughts, and I pad over to it while dabbing the corners of my mouth with my sleeve.

A light, feminine voice yells, "Surprise!" when I open the door, and my traumatized self almost ducks and covers at the sound.

"Lynda!" I say tremulously, stepping aside to let her and my dad in.

I take note of their matching Thanksgiving shirts under their open winter coats, Lynda's saying, "Momma's Cooking a Turkey" over her bump, and my dad's reading, "I Put the Turkey in the Oven."

"Nice outfits," I say, a smile playing at the corners of my lips while internally mortified.

"We know we were supposed to meet you at the lunch picnic, but Lynda couldn't resist coming up here and surprising you," Dad says.

"It looks exactly the same." Lynda rubs her baby bump in awe as she turns in a slow circle.

"You went here?" I ask.

Lynda turns her head to mine. "Well, sure, honey. How'd you think I snuck you in?"

She smiles and chucks under my chin before wandering around and peeping in first Emma's, then my room. "Where's your roommate?"

"Oh, she's uh, at her family's lake house," I say, at the same time my dad widens his eyes at his wife to shush.

I guess they still think my dead ex-roommate is a sensitive topic. *Oh,* if only they knew.

"How about we go find a good table, huh?" my dad says with forced cheer, trotting after his wife and gently steering her to the front door.

"Great idea," I say, and follow them out.

I'm in Briarcliff sweats and a T-shirt, but I'm not feeling up for dress-up, and Dad and Lynda haven't even noticed. Perhaps they think I'm waiting for tonight to go balls-out and get into turkey spirit now that my punishment's lifted, when really, all I'm going to do is crawl into bed and pray my dreams don't involve my dead mom.

After grabbing my coat, we take our time walking from Thorne House to the academy, mostly because Lynda waddles more than she strides. She thwarted Dad's multiple attempts to bring the car around with a crazed look in her eye—*I will walk, damn it, Pete. This baby's taken enough of my body. Do not take my feet*—so the three of us wander, side-by-side, pointing out pretty pieces of landscaping and gorgeous masonry and stonework around the property.

The small talk is slowly strangling me to death. I can't stand beside my dad without asking the question that's been buzzing in my ears and building its hornet's nest in my throat. "Dad?"

Dad glances down at me. "Hmm?"

"Did Mom ever cheat on you with my biological father?"

Lynda's feet scrape against the concrete. Her hand flutters to her stomach. "Oh, Jesus."

My stepdad pales at the question but launches into action when Lynda looks like she's about to keel over. "Honey? What is it? The baby? Contractions?"

"No." Lynda lifts her hand. "Golly, no. Callie surprised the shit outta me is all."

I raise my brows.

Dad goes to Lynda, anyway, holding a tentative hand against her stomach and wrapping his other arm around Lynda's waist. "It, uh, maybe now's not the time, Cal."

Lynda's lips thin. She doesn't budge when Dad nudges her forward. "Peter. She's asked you a question."

"I..." Dad sighs, digging his fingers into his thinning hair.

"I guess that's answer enough," I say, my stomach turning to stone.

"Cal. Hun. Look at me."

Dad's surprisingly hard tone draws my head up. "It has nothing to do with you. Do you understand me? Your mother loved you. *I* love you."

"But how can you?" My face crumples, and I hate how my vision smears with tears. "After all I've done? After what *Mom* did?"

"Honey." Dad releases Lynda and stumbles up to me, bending until he's in view. His hands clamp around my arms, shaking gentle sense into me. "Meredith didn't deserve to die, and you don't deserve to live a life without a mother and father. She was a flawed human being, and when I found out about the affair, I didn't handle—" He stops, emotion clogging his throat. "I didn't deal with it the way I should've. I lashed out at her, and I terrified you."

"Oh my God." His meaning turns my face numb and cold. "Is that the fight I overheard? You found out about the affair?"

"Callie, baby." Dad holds my cheeks. "Yes. I found out she was seeing this man for years, well before me and well after meeting me. But *you* were right. I'm going to repeat that: You did the right thing. I should've been a suspect, and I should've been held and questioned. And it's because of that arrest that the police found out there was another guy. You did a good thing. Okay?"

"I attacked you," I say, meeting his eye with trembling lips. "When you came home, I tried to hurt you. Badly."

"You weren't yourself, Cal. Your mom's death hit you so, so hard, and I didn't understand it at time. I thought you had no idea. I was floored when you accused me, but I'll never hate you for it."

"But I turned on you." I step out of his hold, and his face falls at the distance. "I became the worst daughter in the world. Partying, drugs, ignoring curfew, screaming at you, cussing at you, wanting you to *die* instead of my mom, and you...?"

"I said I loved you, Callie. That kind of vow means I'll be there for you even at your worst."

"No." I clutch at my temples, unable to mix this version of Pete Spencer with the one that's been in my head the whole time. "You hit my mom."

"I did. And I pay for it every damned day."

Lynda comes up beside him, her cheeks streaming tears, but she takes his hand.

"You put me in the psych ward," I rasp.

"I did. It was either that or lose you, Callie. The court was coming for me, saying I wasn't fit to be a father to you, and I ... you'd lost control. I didn't know how..." Dad stops, the thickened emotion in his voice making it difficult to continue, but he blinks and forges on, his voice in tatters. "I had no idea how to move us out of our rotten existence. All I knew is that I didn't want to lose you as well as your mother. You had a home with me. I'm sorry— I'm so sorry I didn't say that to you every day, but even when you were in the hospital, you had a home. I wasn't going to give you up, and I promised myself to be a better man, a better *father*, than the one I was turning into."

"Dad..." I say.

"Callie," Lynda whispers, her lower lip shaking. She opens her arms. "Come here. Please. This doesn't change one bit of your position in our family, okay? You're this baby's sister. Her beautiful, admirable *sister*."

She means to draw me closer, but instead, I'm drifting away. My voice takes on a raw edge. "I could be someone else's sister. Was this man, this guy Mom kept seeing, my father?"

Dad shakes his head forlornly. "I don't know that, honey."

"Do you know who he is?"

Again, he shakes his head. "The night you overheard ... she refused to tell me his name. I was hoping, after I admitted it while in police custody, Ahmar could track him down."

My voice cracks into shards. "Ahmar *knew*?"

"Callie."

My name is sent out into the air with such sharp, ragged undertones, that I draw back. But my dad won't let me. He envelopes me into his arms, hugging me so tight I can only take small breaths.

"You're my daughter," he whispers into my ear. "And I'm sorry. I'm sorry. I'm sorry."

His laments repeat into my skin, dampen my hair, and he doesn't let go. He keeps holding on until I wrap my hands around him, until I'm sobbing, too, and for the first time in over a year, I'm hugging the man who stepped into the role as my father nine years ago.

"I didn't show you before," he says. "You were suffering, and I wasn't doing enough to help you. I know that now. And I will fight for you always." I've never heard him cry before, and it's wrenching. "You belong here, with us. I don't want our wretched past to define our relationship. I want this baby to see you as a sister, and Lynda to see you as a daughter, and for you to see us as a family. Could you do that? Can we try?"

His tone comes in broken waves, and with each crest, I'm pummeled, sobbing harder at his words. My fingers claw into his back as I pull him closer, and added, fragrant pressure against my side tells me Lynda's joined the hug, too.

"I can try," I whisper, so low I doubt they'll hear.

I am so, so tired of being alone, and my baser instinct recognizes this as a pivotal turning point—if I deny them, then from now on, I'll be orphaned by choice.

One day, I'll have to forgive my mom for what she did, and although I know it won't come soon or be easy, I'm certain it will happen. Because she was my mother.

If I can't give my stepdad the same consideration, what does that make me?

I'll tell you: it makes me someone who can't keep love.

"Oh, sweetie." Dad kisses my wet temple while Lynda dampens the other side of my head.

They heard me.

Something bumps against my side, and I pull away enough to look down, because all our arms are around our shoulders. "What was that?"

Lynda laughs, then rests a hand on her belly. "That's Blair saying hello. Do you want to feel it again?"

My eyes stretch wide.

Lynda's lips pull into a shimmering smile. "She's not an alien. Well, I'd argue she's more of a parasite, but go on. Put your hand right here."

I hesitantly lift my hand, pressing it right over turkey baby's red cartoon heart.

Another *bop* against the middle of my palm. And another.

"Holy crap," I say.

"Callie, meet your baby sister. She's going to annoy the crap out of you," Lynda says.

I grin up at her, my joy filled with snot and tears, but tangible.

Lynda kisses my cheek, then says to both me and Dad, "Enough blubbering. We're going to miss the turkey roast, and you do *not* want to know me if I don't get my daily meat intake."

We fall back in line and walk close for the rest of the way to the academy.

For the first time since losing Mom, I can't help but think, maybe this cross-stitched family heart doesn't have to feel so knotted anymore.

❦

The picnic area put together around the wolf fountain behind the school is packed with students, parents, guardians, professors, and all kinds of standing heat lamps, and I manage to score us a recently vacated picnic bench while Dad goes and fills our plates.

"Take a seat," I say to Lynda while gathering dirty paper plates and cups. "I'm just gonna toss these."

Lynda doesn't argue, choosing to plop onto the bench with a prolonged groan.

I meander through the crowd, passing the makeshift stage near the wolf-barf fountain where the Music Club has set up their rock band. They're going for the family-friendly vibe and playing soft rock.

The clotted crowds of people choosing to stand rather than sit cause me to zig and zag to the closest trash can, and I let out a squeak of sound when I'm on top of Chase's table before I can safely retreat.

Every single pair of eyes looks up at me. The stone in my stomach gains more cinder-blocks the longer I'm frozen in place.

Chase is the closest, and his face changes when he notices me, an inscrutable pain flashing through his features before he glances away. Emma stares hard with her implacable aim, while Daniel Stone and his estranged first wife, Chase and Emma's mother, look on curiously.

Sadly, they've also decided to sit with the Harringtons.

Those cinder-blocks become body weights sinking me to the bottom of the ocean.

I can't look at Mr. Harrington, at the same time I do, but I cut my gaze away before any emotion flickers across my face. I'm surprised at the lack of feeling when I meet his eye for one meager second. I'm not shocked at the numbness, because it's already been an emotionally draining day, but in that short time, his features were seared into my mind—burnished hair shot with gray, blue-green eyes, tanned skin and the faint lines of a crow's feet smile around his eyes, which I'm sure would crinkle further if he actually moved his lips.

I see him. I note our similarities. Our vast differences.

And I feel ... nothing.

My skirted gaze lands on Addisyn, who gives me a benign smile, fluttering her fingers in a mocking wave, and Mrs. Harrington, soon-to-be Mrs. Stone, a platinum blonde with dark skin, sits regally at the end, squinting as she tries to place me.

Addisyn purrs, "Mom, *Dad*, I'd like you to meet Briarcliff's newest student, Calla Lily Ryan. Mr. Stone, Miss Loughrey, have you met her?"

Chase's dad murmurs something and shakes his head, but doesn't take his eyes off me. And if Ice Queens were real, I would've been petrified into a statue from Mrs. Harrington's gaze alone.

Mr. Harrington—my possible *father*—clears his throat. "I ... I don't believe we have."

"Perhaps ... Calla Lily, is it? ... should be seated with her own family," Mrs. Harrington says, while her eyes politely communicate *fuck the hell off.*

The barest brush tickles my waist, and I glance down to see Chase's hand retreating to his lap, but it couldn't possibly have been him offering reassurance. He's ignored me for days and will probably resume pretending I don't exist once I leave the table.

I'm not sure what kind of warped family arrangement I've stumbled into, but I'm more than happy to prevent this confrontation from happening right on the heels of my healing session with my stepdad.

"It was nice ... to meet you," I force out, refusing to include Mr. Harrington. "I'm just gonna—"

"Addisyn Harrington?"

The rough voice of authority catches my attention, and I blink at the ensuing scene, unsure if it's real.

Detective Haskins leads the way through the mingling picnic-goers, with three cops coming up behind him, the crowd parting with whispers and gasps as he stops at the table.

Annoyance flashes across Addisyn's face before she turns. "Yeah?"

"What's this about?" Mr. Harrington asks.

Mrs. Harrington rises at the same time her ex-husband does, and though she's a head smaller, her very essence fizzles out any authority Mr. Harrington tries to gather.

She can fell a man with her stare, and she directs all that power at Detective Haskins. "State your position immediately, Detective, because I've already called our lawyers."

"Happy to." Haskins positively beams, immune to Mrs. Harrington's intimidation. "Addisyn Harrington, you're under arrest for suspicion of first-degree murder of Piper Harrington..."

Whispers turn to shouts. Gasps turn to screams.

Someone claps.

"*What*?" Addisyn shrieks, but doesn't move. Haskins decides to help her by pulling her hands behind her back.

"Get your *hands* off my daughter, you deplorable man!" Mrs. Harrington bellows, flipping her jacket lapels back as she strides around the table to get to her remaining daughter. Her face is so frozen in fury, it trembles.

Haskins replies, without looking up, "Don't you come near me, ma'am, or else I'll cuff you, too."

Mrs. Harrington turns redder than Ivy's feathered turkey ass. "How *dare* you—"

"Sabine," Mr. Harrington says, grabbing his former wife's arm. "Perhaps you should let the man do his job. We'll call our lawyers, and—"

"You pathetic, miserable turd!" she hisses at her husband. "Your daughter is being arrested, and your other daughter is *dead*. *DO SOMETHING!*"

Mr. Harrington fumbles in his jacket for his phone, but Daniel Stone beats him to it.

"I'm Addisyn's lawyer. Show me the papers," he bellows, his hand darting out.

Haskins gestures to the officers behind him, who hands Mr. Stone the warrant.

In an attempt to take in more than the central scuffle, I glance first at Chase, who seems just as bemused as me, then at Emma, catching her eye in a way that tells me she's been watching me this entire time.

She smiles.

I clear my throat of the slime that crawls to its base, mouthing, *What the fuck?*

But she shakes her head. Now isn't the time.

I, however, can't close my mouth. Was I just bamboozled by her *again*?

"Callie," Chase says, and I jolt at his sudden presence at my side. "We need to leave. Before this gets out of hand."

"I'm just standing here," I say. "What could possibly happen to me—"

And as if I asked for it, Mrs. Harrington lands her steely gaze on me. "*You.*"

"Now, Sabine..." Mr. Harrington says, throwing a hand between us.

I frown at my supposed, maybe father, at his utter weakness in this situation. Yes, humans are flawed, and yes, his youngest daughter is a kin-killer, but shouldn't he be handling this with a bit more rage right now? Instead he's ... oh, man. The word hits me between the eyes.

He's unsurprised. By any of this.

"We're leaving. *Now*," Chase commands, then drags me back.

We're through the crowd and near the edges before I comprehend my hand in his, our fingers entwined. "Chase..."

He tears from my hold, his warmth retreating as fast as if I doused his flames with lake water. "Go be with your family."

I gape at him. "You can't *possibly* expect me to—Did you know about this? What your sister planned? How did the police know to arrest Addisyn? Why have they made it so public?"

Chase lets out a frustrated sigh but doesn't push me back into the crowd. "I read a piece of the warrant as my dad held it. They have the diary pages, Callie."

I hesitate, but persist. "Are they enough? Is the arrest going to stick? Or is it more of a Dr. Luke situation where she'll be released by fancy lawyers, like your *dad*—"

Chase levels me with a look. "There's a confession tape, too. Now *go*. Before Sabine Harrington loses her shit on you and your secret's out."

My secret. Right. I'm a possible Harrington heir.

Ugh, the thought disgusts me.

Yet, I can't leave. "Confession tape?"

Chase gives me a sidelong glance. "Think about it, sweet possum."

And I do. Addisyn said a lot of culpable shit to me when we were in her room ... and Emma and Eden were standing right outside.

"One of them recorded it," I murmur.

Perhaps, they aren't the savage and heartless lizards I thought they were. But they sure are experts at mind-fuckery.

"Since when was I put on a need-to-know basis?" I demand.

Chase's features go tight, as if he's stopping himself from saying something he'll regret.

I force my thoughts inward rather than argue with him, aware of my penchant for saying and doing things I'm later ashamed to admit.

What Emma and Eden did to me might've been fake, but the words I'd spewed at Chase afterward? Those were real.

"I'm sorry," I whisper, but his only acknowledgment is to put a light hand on my back and gently push me into the gathering crowd.

35

The rest of the Family Day picnic is a complete wash, Headmaster Marron having to intervene and do a long speech in an attempt to distract from the public scandal involving one of his flourishing, most promising students.

Again.

The gathering parted ways, Lynda murmuring a long, sad goodbye to her untouched turkey platter as we exited the quad and they took me back to my room.

"Let me say, scenes like that did *not* happen when I was in attendance," Lynda says as we amble with the rest of the families down the pathway. Then, her eyes widen with conspiracy. "But what a *rush* that was."

"You must be happy with this, Cal," Dad says to me. "Your roommate's case is finally solved. I know I'm glad to hear it. I was worried about who could be wandering campus, meaning harm."

"Yeah," I say, though I put no conviction behind my statement.

"Do you want to come home, honey?"

Lynda's question hitches my steps, the genuine warmth behind it flipping my stomach.

"You've more than proven yourself," Lynda continues gently. "You've worked hard to show us your willingness to change. But if you're not happy here, you can come with us. Right now. If you want to."

Dad shares an affectionate, admiring look with Lynda, then squeezes my shoulder. "Lynda's right. I may have sent you away ... in haste. Perhaps it'll be easier to mend fences with us all together."

I want to say yes.

It's tempting, so incredibly easy, to leave this fucked-up school with its dangerous societies, fixed grades, and chauvinistic games far behind.

But, coming home would mean facing my mother's treachery. Forgiving my stepdad whole-heartedly. And I genuinely don't know if I'm ready for that.

Besides ... Ivy ... and Chase.

Relationships I'm not ready to release.

"I think I'd like to stay," I say.

"Are you sure?" Dad's caterpillar brows come crashing down. "Because it doesn't seem like you're comfortable here."

I can't deny the observation, so I work on a deal. "I'll stay until Christmas. Come home for Thanksgiving. And we can talk on both of those holidays. I'd like to take my time making such a big decision in my life, you know? I want to make sure I'm doing the right thing, by staying or leaving."

The skin around Lynda's eyes creases with a smile. She notices my prolonged stare, but doesn't take it the way I mean it to come across: *you're beautiful when you smile. I hope my dad deserves you.* "Lord," she says, rubbing one corner of her eye. "I miss my damn Botox."

I snort, and Dad catches me by the shoulder and pulls me to his side. "Deal. We'll reevaluate then, but any time you change your mind, you call us. It's not just you that'll turn over a new leaf at this point. I will, too. And it starts with working on my patience and ... *trying* ... to trust your judgment."

I nod, focusing on his willingness to work with me and not against me, and we part ways outside Thorne House, Lynda squeezing me tight, and the baby kicking me in the gut. Dad's hug is more tentative, but it holds more promise of a fatherly touch than it has in years.

"See ya next weekend, Cal," he says, studying me softly before taking his wife's hand and heading down the drive.

I wait until I can't see them anymore, then enter my dorm with a sort of melancholy cheer. Overjoyed that Addisyn got what was coming to her, happy that my relationship with my stepdad is on the mend, but heavy with Chase's and my argument, the societies' continued rule, and Dr. Luke's strange visit that lead to a crucial clue. Basically—I'm torn over all the unrest Briarcliff protects.

Was choosing to stay the right thing to do?

I step into my room with hunched shoulders, ready to pack it in instead of locate a turkey costume. I'll have to text Ivy, but other than that, I can quietly slip under the covers and...

A folded note on top of my laptop catches my attention.

Curious, I open it, recognizing Chase's handwriting.

Going old school for this, sweet possum, but I feel it's warranted. So, here's a letter instead of a text.

We have a lot to figure out.

Meet me at the boathouse at sunset? I'll be the guy with a fucking turkey painted on his chest.

Oh, and the only dude at the end of the dock.

. . .

A wistful smile crosses my lips before I can scold it into a frown. Checking the clock, I calculate about an hour's worth of time to get ready before meeting him.

Because yes, I'm meeting him, and while he has some explaining to do with regards to my phone and all my missing evidence, no, I will not be listening to him in day-old sweats and unwashed hair.

I shower, shave, blow-dry, and make-up until I'm satisfied. There's no time to put together a costume, so I put on leather pants and an artfully destroyed $60 white T-shirt, both "seasonal" and gifted by Lynda, figuring I'll be creative and say I was attacked by a turkey.

The forested pathway to the boathouse is silent as I descend, most students attending off-campus parties or dorm room pre-games, the Turkey Trot in full swing and the drunken recapping of Addisyn's arrest at full tilt. The rare few who would find themselves on this path will probably be here to hook-up, so I clomp as fast and quietly as I can through the trees, hopeful not to see anyone's bared full moon.

I reach the clearing, the golden hour of the sun hitting the placid lake like molten metal, the ripples of the lake glittering with the shards of sunlit diamonds.

I'm early, so I'm not concerned when I don't see any figure waiting for me at the end of the dock.

Moving to the boat house's side door, I creak it open, glad it's unlocked, and head to one of the boat bays opening up into the lake, figuring I'll enjoy the view before Chase and I grow serious, and maybe, have a true discussion for once, with equal give and take.

A girl can hope.

There's no figure, but something—an object—catches my eye at the end of the dock. Tentatively, I make my way over, thinking maybe Chase has left me something in his stead. I cringe as I throw my hands out for balance, the quiet laps of water under the dock more threatening than calming.

Chase is lucky I like him so much. He's the only person who's managed to get me to walk to the end of this floating piece of driftwood more than once.

I stay well in the middle, my boots making clomping, hollow sounds, punctuated only by the lonesome calls of birds not yet asleep in their nests.

Once I'm close enough to make out the object through the fast-setting sun, I notice the white rose laid out at the end, a fluttering note attached to it.

My immediate reaction is to sneer. I hate this form of communication—these damn roses—but if it's here, then someone knew I was coming and wants me to read it before I see Chase.

These secret admirer gifts have never harmed me before, so I walk forward until the end of the stem brushes the tip of my boot.

The same breeze lifts my hair as I bend down to pick up the exquisitely bloomed flower and read the note, attached to the stem with a black ribbon.

Unfolding the expensive, thick paper, I read the simple embossed sentence, then blink and read it again.

You're in.

Huh?

I glance up, staring at the forest on the other side of the lake, like it can provide me with answers.

A howl rises up behind me, but it can't be a wolf. Or a bear, because it sounds too human.

I put a name to the cry, and it rips from my throat. *"Chase!"*

I move—

Until two hands slam into my back and push me into the lake.

You're in.
**The Virtues respectfully ask that you meet them in FIEND, the
final book in the Briarcliff Society Series.**
<u>**TAKE ME THERE.**</u>

A NOTE FROM KETLEY

Thank you so much for reading VIRTUE! Callie and Chase's story just keeps getting better in my head, and I can't wait for you to read the final installment, FIEND, out soon!

If you have the time, I'd love for you to leave a review on your preferred platform, or tag me on social media to let me know your thoughts. Those golden little stars are what drive me to keep writing.

The final book, FIEND, is up for preorder! <u>TAKE ME THERE.</u>

You can also join my new readers' group, <u>Ketley's Crew</u>, on Facebook! I'd love to meet you!

If you'd like to read more of my books, check out the next page.

xoxo, Ket.

ALSO BY KETLEY ALLISON

Players to Lovers

Trusting You

Daring You

Craving You

Playing You

Rockers to Lovers

Sing to Me

Strum Me

Sync with Me (Coming Soon)

Corrupt Empire Duet

Underground Prince

Jaded Princess

Vows Duet

To Have and to Hold

From This Day Forward

Briarcliff Secret Society

Rival

Virtue

Fiend (Coming January 2021)

ABOUT THE AUTHOR

Ketley Allison has always been a romantic at heart. That passion ignited when she realized she could put her dreams into words and her heart into characters. Ketley was born in Canada, moved to Australia, then to California, and finally to New York City to attend law school, but most of that time was spent in coffee shops thinking about her next book.

Her other passions include wine, coffee, Big Macs, her cat, and her husband, possibly in that order.

facebook.com/ketleyallison
instagram.com/ketleyallison
bookbub.com/authors/ketleyallison
amazon.com/author/ketleyallison
goodreads.com/ketleyallison
pinterest.com/ketleyallison